HARLEQUIN
Celebrates i

*Two decades of bringing you the very best
in romance reading.*

*To recognize this important milestone,
we've invited six very
special authors—whose names you're sure to recognize—
to tell us how they feel about Superromance.
Each title this month has a letter
from one of these authors.*

In 1992 Karen Young—whose foreword
appears in this book—helped celebrate an earlier
milestone in Superromance history. Her book,
The Silence of Midnight, was the 500th Superromance
published and won the RITA Award for
Long Contemporary the following year. In her letter
prefacing this book, Karen writes, "...Superromance,
with its eclectic lineup each month, will not disappoint.
I'm proud to be an author in this line."

Matt's Family by Lynnette Kent has a
well-earned place in Superromance's
"eclectic lineup," and offers readers a complex and
compelling story of family dynamics.
It's the second of a two-book series—
THE BRENNAN BROTHERS—in which the relationship
between two brothers is stretched to the limit
by their feelings for one woman and their
commitment to family and children.

Dear Reader,

I live near one of the largest army posts in the U.S.—Fort Bragg, North Carolina, home of the 82nd Airborne Division and the Special Operations Forces. My daughters attend school with kids who are here one year and gone the next...to Germany, to Japan, to Kentucky or Kansas or North Dakota. Our community is enhanced by the many talented people who come into the area for just a year or two and yet donate their time and energy to local causes. We always miss them when they get orders to move, and always hope that maybe one day they'll come back.

As the wife of a career navy officer, I understand the commitment demonstrated by men and women in the armed forces, as well as the devotion required from their families. Military service is not an easy job, but it is an honorable and invaluable one.

The hero of *Matt's Family*, Major Matt Brennan, comes from a long line of military men, and he is worthy of his heritage. He's given five years of his life—and those of his wife and their daughter—to the service of his country. Can he consider his duty done?

More important, can Matt find a way to bond with a little girl he didn't know he had? And can he convince his wife that their marriage isn't merely duty, but the heart and soul of his very life?

I hope you enjoy Matt and Kristin's story, the second of THE BRENNAN BROTHERS books. I love getting letters from readers—please feel free to write me c/o P.O. Box 1795, Fayetteville, NC 28314.

All the best,

Lynnette Kent

FOREWORD BY KAREN YOUNG

Matt's Family

Lynnette Kent

HARLEQUIN®

TORONTO · NEW YORK · LONDON
AMSTERDAM · PARIS · SYDNEY · HAMBURG
STOCKHOLM · ATHENS · TOKYO · MILAN · MADRID
PRAGUE · WARSAW · BUDAPEST · AUCKLAND

ISBN 0-373-70938-2

MATT'S FAMILY

FOREWORD BY KAREN YOUNG

Many thoughts come to mind when I consider my experience as a Superromance author. First and foremost is my delight in having the editorial freedom to write the kind of books that appeal to me. I have never underestimated the discernment and sophistication of Superromance readers. Consequently, I have come up with a few plots that featured some pretty strong elements, but they were stories that I felt touched the lives of the women who were reading them. Maybe a sister was married to an abusive husband, or a reader knew of a child who fell through the cracks in our foster care system. Maybe someone's heart had been broken by an unfaithful husband. I've created characters who wrestled with those life crises—and more—and my editors at Superromance were always completely supportive in allowing me that creative freedom.

Also, as a Superromance author, I seem to need the additional length to fully develop a story once I've come up with an idea for a book. I have written shorter contemporary books, but I never really hit my stride as a writer until I had a larger "palette," so to speak, to paint a picture with emotional depth as well as a strong plot. Superromance afforded me that opportunity.

Finally, I believe the women who comprise our audience of readers are far more sophisticated today than when the romance novel first appeared on the scene. Superromance recognized that growth on the part of our readership early on and it was reflected in the quality of the books offered each month. So, whether your taste as a reader runs to a plot that makes you laugh or one that makes you cry or one that makes you think or one that deftly manages to do all of the above, Superromance with its eclectic lineup each month will not disappoint.

I'm proud to be an author in this line.

To the military wives I've known, and those I haven't:
Whatever it took, you always held things
together somehow.

And to Mary Bacon,
the wife and mother of military men:
You've served your country and your children
with honor and love.
Thank you.

PROLOGUE

Christmas Day, 1996

MATT BRENNAN PARKED on the curb in front of the small, neat house and sat for a minute, trying to relax.

He was finally home. Myrtle Beach, South Carolina, U.S.A. Five years late, true. But at least he'd made it. Two of the soldiers captured with him on that covert mission in Africa would never see home again.

And inside this robin's-egg-blue house was the reason Matt had come back. Sweet brown eyes and an easy laugh. Smooth, tanned skin, sun-streaked hair, gentle hands. A woman willing to listen, to share, to face life beside him wherever it led.

"Kristin."

Her name had brought light to five years of darkness. Saying it aloud now built up a fierce need inside him. He'd waited so long. But he didn't have to wait another minute.

Opening the car door, he stepped onto the pavement, once again aware of the unfamiliar sensation of shoes after spending half a decade in a tropical prison, barefoot. A soft, damp breeze blew across his face, and he closed his eyes for a second to appreciate the moisture. His life had been dry for so long.

No more. Grinning like a fool, with his heart pounding

in his chest, Matt crossed the spiky grass to the front door of the house. Kristin didn't know he was coming—none of his family knew, yet, that he was alive. The Army could keep secrets very well, when it wanted to.

His finger shook as he pressed the doorbell button. He closed his fists at his sides as he waited, braced against the wild excitement that kept stealing his breath. After so long…

The door opened. Looking over her shoulder, laughing at something behind her, Kristin didn't see him for a second. In the time it took her to face him, his world shattered.

She held a baby in the bend of her arm, a little girl in a pink gown with a wisp of silver hair caught up in a pink bow.

If he could have moved, Matt would have left before a word was said. But he was frozen in place. And so the woman he loved—Kristin, his fiancée—turned to see him standing at her door.

Her brown eyes went round, and her lips parted on a gasp. The color left her cheeks in a rush. Staring at him, she didn't appear to notice when the baby in her arms pulled at a strand of her bright gold hair.

"Matt?" No sound filled in the word. "Oh my God." This time he heard her whisper. "Matt?"

Joy flashed in her face, bright as fireworks. And just as fleeting. Shock, dismay, even fear, followed immediately.

He cleared his throat. "Hi, Kris."

The patter of bare feet on tile filled the paralyzed silence. A child peeked around Kristin's waist, another tow-haired little girl, several years older than the baby.

"Mommy, who's that?"

Kristin's left hand dropped to rest on the girl's head. In the pale winter light, Matt caught the flash of a ring on her third finger.

"This is…" Her voice died again.

"Kristin?" A man's voice called from the back of the house. "Who's ringing the doorbell at 8:00 a.m. on Christmas morn—"

The skin on the back of his neck crawled as Matt recognized the voice. He dragged his gaze away from Kristin's horrified face as his brother stepped up behind her. "Hey, Luke. Merry Christmas."

Luke's hand—also wearing a wedding ring—closed over Kristin's shoulder. "Matt?" Welcome shone in his gray eyes, in his wide smile. And then faded away.

Matt tried for a grin. "That's right. Uh…surprise?"

His younger brother didn't laugh at the feeble joke. Luke glanced at Kristin, instead, and at the baby she held. He looked down at the older girl for a long moment. And then raised his eyes to Matt's. His next comment went straight to the heart of the matter. "Dear God, Matt. We're in a hell of a mess now!"

CHAPTER ONE

May, 2000

MATT WOKE UP as his wife of almost a year slipped out of bed and left their room. He squinted at the clock. Two-thirty, later than usual. She was often out of bed by midnight or one.

Staring up at the ceiling, he listened to Kristin move through the house. Minutes passed, then half an hour. The microwave beeped—she'd made herself some tea. A faint glow at the doorway indicated she'd switched on a lamp.

So here they were again, him lying in the dark, waiting, while she sat in the kitchen downstairs, thinking. About what?

Did she think about the same things he did? Did she wonder how their life could be so good...yet so wrong? How two people could live together and, at the same time, be so far apart?

He rolled to his side, facing the door. He'd made love with Kris just a few hours ago. Tonight, as always, she'd given him more pleasure than any man had a right to know. She gave him everything, including her own satisfaction. Her whispers, her sighs, the shudders that ran through her body as he touched and kissed and moved— every reaction conveyed Kristin's delight in what he did.

But she never asked, dammit. Never demanded. Never

abandoned herself, selfish—even helpless—in her need for him. After nearly a year together, sex seemed almost like a contest to see who could please whom the most. A quid pro quo kind of experience—neither of them relaxed enough to simply take.

Matt knew he never felt really at ease—because he never knew what Kris was thinking anymore. Was she afraid to tell him what she wanted because she thought he would resent the implication that he'd failed? Or was sex something she did because she saw it as her responsibility?

Was the whole marriage simply a matter of responsibility? A debt to be paid?

He closed his eyes at the painful grip of that thought. The idea that Kris had married him because she owed him hurt too much to consider.

In the hallway, her footsteps padded lightly toward their door. She eased back into bed, barely disturbing the mattress or the covers. If he wanted, Matt could pretend he hadn't known she was gone.

That wasn't what he wanted to do. He wanted to take her again—make love to his wife until she was so crazy she couldn't think. Love her until she forgot about loving him back, until she just accepted everything he had to give, until she came apart in his arms and cried out his name. Then he'd know for sure she trusted him, needed him. Wanted him.

But when he finally turned over, he heard her soft, even breaths. She'd fallen asleep. He could wake her, and she would welcome him. Duty, or desire? Matt had no way to know. He wasn't even sure he wanted to find out.

And so he just laid his hand lightly on the blanket covering her hip, and forced himself back to sleep.

"THAT'S PRETTY, Mommy!"

"Thanks, Jenny." Kristin patted her younger daughter's blond head and stepped back from the counter to survey the results of her morning's work—a three-layer chocolate cake, iced with butter-cream frosting and decorated with an American flag. "I think so, too."

The real question was whether her mother-in-law would agree. For the first time in eight years, Matt's mother had allowed Kristin to contribute to the family's Memorial Day picnic menu. A bowl of potato salad waited in the refrigerator, as picture perfect as she could make it. Her cake looked professional, if she did say so herself. Surely even Mrs. Brennan would be pleased.

Running footsteps sounded in the family room. Eight-year-old Erin dashed into the kitchen, sun-streaked hair flying. Her perpetual shadow trotted close behind. Buster—a dog of mixed ancestry—was nearly as tall as Erin when he stood on his hind legs, and weighed more. He followed her as far as he was allowed and slept at her feet every night, a long-haired, black-and-white bodyguard.

"Hey, Jenny, look what I found under my bed!" Erin waved a purple stuffed toy.

"That's mine." Jenny climbed off the stool at the counter. "Give me my dragon back."

"I found it, I get to keep it." Erin held the dragon above her head.

Jenny jumped, but couldn't reach. "Mommy, tell her to give me my dragon that Daddy got for me!"

Kristin picked up the cake and held it protectively. "Erin, give Jenny her dragon. You've got one of your own." As she pivoted toward the other side of the kitchen, a warm, furry form wrapped itself between her ankles.

"Buster!" She shuffled her feet, trying to step free. The dog gave a loud yelp as her bare heel came down on his paw. Kristin jumped, shifted her weight...and lost control of the cake. With a slurp, the plate tilted inward, pressing the American flag into the front of her shirt.

Jenny gasped. "Mommy, you hurt Buster!" She broke into tears.

Kristin stood frozen, eyes closed in horror, hands holding the plate against her chest.

Jenny cried louder, working up to a real tantrum. Kristin finally jerked herself into motion and eased the cake back onto the plate. "Hush, Jenny, love. Let's look at Buster's paw, okay?" She set the plate on the counter, then knelt in front of the dog, who immediately licked at her shirt. "Which paw did I get, Buster? This one?" He wagged his black-and-white plume of a tail as she checked all four feet. "He's fine, Jenny. Don't worry."

Erin stared at her from the end of the counter. "Mommy, you've got icing all over you!"

Kristin sighed. "I know." The top of the cake looked like a bomb crater. So much for her perfect Memorial Day dessert.

She was whipping icing and wiping tears out of her eyes when Matt came through the door. "Hey, Kris— whoa! Did a hurricane blow through?"

Kristin glanced at his immaculate uniform, around the wrecked kitchen, at the ruined cake and her filthy shirt, and blinked back more tears.

"I had a problem with the cake, that's all."

He frowned. "I thought you were making potato salad."

"I did." She added more sugar to the bowl. "I said I'd bring dessert, too."

"That doesn't leave much for anybody else to cook."

She shook her head. "Of course it does. Sarah and Luke are bringing a green salad and baked beans. Your mother and dad are supplying the hamburgers—"

Matt raised his hands in surrender, laughing. "Okay, okay. I just meant you shouldn't work so hard." He skimmed a dollop of icing off her neck and sucked it off his finger. "Mmm. You taste wonderful." The kiss he placed under her ear sent a sweet shiver down her spine. "Are the girls ready?"

"Not yet. I'll be finished in a few minutes."

"I'll get them dressed." He headed for the stairs. Kristin thought about calling him back—the girls weren't exactly cooperating today. But they liked going to their grandparents' house. Maybe they wouldn't put up a fuss. If they did, Matt could handle it. Right?

Thirty minutes later, with a smooth, plain coat of icing on the cake, Kristin hurried down the hallway to the bedrooms. She peeked into Jenny's and found it empty. But the outfit she'd ironed earlier this morning—the one Matt's mother had given them—still lay on the bed. What was Jenny wearing?

Erin's nice clothes lay crumpled on the floor of her room. She picked them up. "Girls? Matt? Where are you?"

"We're in the bathroom, Kris." His voice sounded tired.

She pushed open the door of the big yellow bathroom. Matt sat on the floor with his elbows propped on his bent knees, a spray bottle in one hand, a comb in the other.

Facing him stood Erin and Jenny, wrapped in their towels, both with wet, tangled hair.

"What's going on? Why aren't you dressed?"

Matt ran a hand over his head, then simply looked at the girls. Erin stuck out her lower lip. "It hurts when he combs my hair."

Kristin sighed. "Erin, you say it hurts when *I* comb your hair. We're as gentle as we can be. Your hair has to be combed. Did you use the untangler spray?"

Saying nothing, Matt held up the bottle.

She took it from him. "Okay, I'll spray it again. I'll do your hair, Erin, and Matt can do Jenny's. We only have a few minutes to get ready."

But Jenny backed up against the vanity. "My hair hurts, too. And he got soap in my eyes."

Jenny always complained of soap in her eyes when Matt was in charge of bath time. This wasn't a real grievance. This was mutiny, plain and simple.

And the grimness in Matt's face, a despair he was trying his best to hide, testified to the mutiny's effect.

Kristin fought down a surge of irritation. "Well, we could stay home and let you both sit in your rooms with tangled hair. But that would disappoint Grandmom and Granddad, who are looking forward to seeing you." She held out her hand to Matt.

He slapped the comb onto her palm. Getting neatly to his feet, he stepped by her to the door. "I'll change clothes," he said quietly. And was gone.

"I'll comb hair." Kristin turned Erin around with a firm hand. "And I don't want to hear any complaints from either of you. We're going to be late, as it is."

And they were. By the time they got the girls settled

in the car and fought beach traffic, they were a long, tense, forty minutes late.

Wishing the afternoon were already over, Matt parked the van in his parents' driveway and released the door lock. As if they'd been freed from jail, Erin and Jenny ran through the grass and around the back of the house to the deck on the beach.

When he opened Kristin's door, she took a deep breath and slid carefully to the ground, cradling the covered cake. Then she looked up at him somberly. "I'm sorry about the girls."

His resentment melted. He smiled a little and set his hand along the angle of her jaw, stroking his thumb across her smooth cheek. "I'll be okay."

Eyes closed, she pressed her head into his palm for a second, then stepped away. "We'd better get inside."

"If you say so." Matt followed her toward the kitchen door, carrying the potato salad and appreciating the chance to watch Kristin from the back. Bright sunlight did great things for her soft tan and shiny hair. Her dark-blue sleeveless shirt showed off her arms, while white shorts and sandals left a nice length of her legs in view. The first time he'd seen her, he'd known she was the prettiest, sexiest girl he would ever meet. More than ten years later, he'd never encountered another woman who could make him change his mind.

His mother looked up in surprise as they stepped through the kitchen door. "I wondered what had happened to you. It's after four-thirty." She brushed at her silver bangs with a fingertip and stared at Kristin expectantly.

Matt stepped forward to run interference. He bent slightly to kiss Elena Brennan's cheek. "Sorry, Mom.

Sometimes the girls need more time than we think they will. How are you?''

''Well, thank you.'' She took the bowl of potato salad out of his hands and placed it precisely on the counter. ''Your father is on the deck with Luke and Sarah.''

Kristin came closer. ''Where shall I put the cake?''

Elena arched her eyebrows. ''Oh, I didn't think you'd have time to make dessert. Let's put yours over here beside mine.''

Kristin squeezed her eyes closed as she relinquished the plate. Matt didn't see a problem with the nice, smooth icing…until his mother set Kristin's cake next to her own berry-laden version. Suddenly, the white cake looked a little drab.

He put a hand on Kristin's shoulder. ''Anything else we can do, Mom?''

His mother smoothed her red slacks over her still-slim hips. ''No, dear. I believe everything is just about ready. Why don't you start the grill?''

''Sure.'' He moved Kristin ahead of him. ''Don't worry about it,'' he whispered in her ear as he opened the door onto the deck.

Looking back over her shoulder, she gave him a rigid smile. ''Worry about what?''

Matt stared at her back as she walked outside. As difficult as his mother could be, Kris would never admit to being upset. That she couldn't share something so obvious, so basically harmless, indicated a significant lack of trust.

Or was Kris hiding something so terrible she couldn't share *anything* with him, in case the worst slipped out? What the hell would ''the worst'' be?

''Well, Matt, it's about time you showed up.'' Across

the deck, his father sat beneath an umbrella, filling his pipe. "Your mother's been wondering."

"Getting two little girls ready for a party doesn't always go smoothly, Dad." He reached out to shake the Colonel's hand as Kristin sat down on the glider nearby.

"Isn't that the truth?" The man sitting in the chair to the Colonel's left set down his drink.

Matt turned to face his brother's wide grin. "Yeah— I'm always amazed at how long it takes." They shook hands amiably enough, then Matt looked to Luke's right and smiled at his new sister-in-law. "Hey, Sarah. How are you?"

"Wonderful." Her clear, sunny expression reminded him of Kristin...back in the old days. "When I called this morning, your wife said you'd gone to work. It's a holiday, remember?"

He eased down on the glider beside Kris and put his arm along the back, behind her shoulders. "Just paperwork. I get a lot done with nobody else there."

The Colonel snorted as he lit his pipe. "It's about time you gave up this recruiting nonsense, isn't it? Get back to the real Army?"

"I'm still thinking things over, Dad." Matt relaxed his clenched fist. "It's a big decision now that I've got a family."

"I'd imagine your commanding officer is wondering what you're waiting for." His father wouldn't let go of his point.

"I haven't heard anything from him." Matt tapped Kristin on the shoulder. "Where'd the girls go?"

"They're playing in the sand at the bottom of the steps," she said, without meeting his eyes.

Luke sat forward in his chair. "Do I have time to take them for a walk before we eat?"

Matt pulled in a deep breath against the resistance he couldn't extinguish. "Since I haven't started the grill yet, I'd say you've got about twenty minutes."

"That'll be great." Luke and Sarah crossed the deck arm in arm and descended the steps. "Hey, munchkins." His words blew back on the wind from the sea. "Want to walk down by the waves?"

"Sure, Daddy!" Erin loved the ocean.

"Can you carry me, Daddy?" And Jenny loved her father.

The voices faded as the foursome approached the water. Matt sat still, waiting for feeling and function to come back to his brain.

After the bath fiasco this afternoon, he should know what to expect. As far as Erin and Jenny knew, Luke *was* their father. The hard part for them was understanding what had changed, why their mother had divorced him and married another man.

The hard part for Matt was being that other man.

SUDDENLY UNABLE to sit still, Kristin got up and walked to the deck railing to stare out toward the ocean. Usually the sound of the waves and the warmth of the sun made life seem simpler, easier to manage.

Not today. Not with Matt closed off from her by a wall of hurt and misunderstanding. Not when she just kept making mistakes, each one more destructive than the last. Like getting pregnant nine years ago without being married. Then getting married to Luke because her baby's father—Matt—was dead. And, finally, divorcing Luke and marrying Matt.

Out by the water, Luke and Sarah chased the girls. Jenny squealed as Luke caught her around the waist and lifted her high in the air. They made quite a picture—the handsome black-haired man and his precious silver-blond daughter.

Erin outran Sarah, then kept on running, just for the sheer joy of moving. She loved being outside, like her father. And she moved with the same easy stride, the same long-legged grace Kristin had always adored in Matt. Erin would be tall one day, with Matt's blue eyes and his serious, considering stare. Luke was tall, too—cops had to be a certain height—but his eyes were a laughing gray and his body more compact than his brother's.

When would Erin notice the differences? When would she ask to be told the truth?

"Is the grill ready, Matt?" Mrs. Brennan stepped out onto the deck.

"Yes, ma'am. Whenever you are."

"Where are the girls?"

"On the beach with Luke and Sarah."

Even from across the deck, Mrs. Brennan's sigh indicated impatience. "Why does he always take them away just when we're ready to eat?"

Matt didn't answer. Kristin glanced at his back, which was all she could see, then turned again to the ocean and her own thoughts. Almost two years ago, before he'd even asked her to marry him, she'd made Matt a promise. One day, as soon as possible, Erin would be told that she was Matt's daughter, as Jenny was Luke's.

Every time Kristin thought about explaining, though, she felt physically sick. The revelations wouldn't stop with Erin. Matt's parents—and her own—would have to be told. When Erin was born, Kristin had let them all assume she was Luke's daughter. Now everyone would be privy to the mistakes she had made, the poor judgment she'd used. Could she ever look anybody in the face again?

Especially her daughter?

Out on the beach, Erin stopped her cartwheels and waved. Kristin waved back, then motioned for them to come in. Mrs. Brennan would be waiting.

Matt was waiting, too. He never said a word, but Kristin could see the question in his eyes. *When?* he wanted to know. *When can I tell her she's mine?*

She turned to watch her husband as he stood at the grill, flipping burgers and hot dogs. His straight back, his square shoulders filling out his blue knit shirt, were as much a part of him as his military haircut and his natural air of command.

But she could read the tension in his body. Luke's relationship with the girls tortured Matt. Erin and Jenny were comfortable around Luke, sure of themselves and him. They spoke the same shorthand language, as people who lived—and loved—together often did. Erin and Jenny and Luke had been a family.

Until Kristin tore them apart.

BEFORE MRS. BRENNAN could get really upset, Luke brought the girls back. They rushed up the steps and across the deck toward the house. Erin stopped in the doorway. "Come on, Mommy. Let's eat!"

Kristin joined the rest of the family in the kitchen. The air-conditioning raised goose bumps on her skin. She rubbed her arms, trying to get warm.

"Memorial Day is important." Seated at the kitchen

table with an arm around each granddaughter, Colonel Brennan started his annual remembrance speech. "Americans should take time to remember the men who have died serving their country."

"And women," Sarah said quietly. Kristin would never have been confident enough to make that comment, but Luke's wife possessed a special brand of courage.

With a glance at his daughter-in-law, the Colonel cleared his throat. "For five years our family celebrated this day thinking we had lost someone we loved in the cause of freedom."

Kristin fought back a shudder. For five years she'd thought Matt *was* dead, because the Army said so. She'd made herself a life during that time. A different one than she'd hoped for, true. But her daughters had been happy, and safe. Luke was a good man and a great dad.

The Colonel continued his comments. "Now we celebrate in thankfulness at having him returned to us."

Then Matt came back. And everything changed.

Beside her, he shifted his weight. Kristin glanced up at his face and saw that his cheeks had reddened. His embarrassment was endearing, and she smiled at him, linking her elbow through his. He pressed her arm closer into his side.

"Daddy Matt was gone for five years?" Erin counted on her fingers. "He left before Jenny was born?"

Tension struck the room like a lightning bolt. Across the counter, Luke gave a quick smile and a small shrug, which left the answer up to Kristin. "That's true, Erin," she said. "Even—even before you were born." Was that the right thing to say?

"Mommy, did you know Daddy Matt before I was born?"

"Of course, love. I knew…all the Brennans then, and for a long time before." Matt had gone still as a stone beside her.

"But—" Erin stopped and seemed to reconsider her question.

"I'm hungry," Jenny announced with a five-year-old's directness.

"Of course, Jennifer, dear." Mrs. Brennan placed a smooth, pale hand on Jenny's shoulder. "Let your grandfather say grace, and I'll make you a plate."

During the prayer, Matt's stiffness subsided. He didn't draw away from Kristin, but he didn't press her close again, either. Had she disappointed him? Should she have told the whole story right then, to everyone?

What, in God's name, could she say?

With dinner finished and cleaned up—a task for which Mrs. Brennan refused to accept any help—the adults sat on the deck finishing coffee while the girls splashed in the pool. Matt seemed preoccupied—Kristin could guess with what.

After a pause, Luke sat forward and braced his elbows on his knees. "Sarah and I wanted to run something by you, Kristin." He glanced at his brother. "And Matt. We're spending a couple of weeks in the mountains in June and we'd like the girls to come with us. What do you think?"

Kristin couldn't think at all, for a moment, couldn't decide what her reaction should be.

"You'll be back for our annual Independence Day party, of course," Mrs. Brennan stated firmly. It was not a question.

Luke flashed his mother a grin. "Definitely."

"We're renting a condo with two bedrooms and a

kitchen," Sarah said, putting a hand on Kristin's arm. "They'll have lots of room."

Kristin's doubts had nothing to do with the accommodations. Before she could quite grasp her reasons, Matt stirred.

"I think it sounds great," he said. "They'll have a good time."

Luke sat back in his chair. Obviously, he hadn't missed the hint of reluctance in Matt's comment. Just as obviously, he'd decided to ignore it. "Okay, then. We'll be away the last two weeks of June—I'll wait a while to tell them or they won't sleep between now and then."

"Good idea." Matt stood up and held out his cup. "Anybody else want a refill?" Everyone shook their heads. He looked at Luke's wife. "Sarah, you sure you don't want some coffee?"

She smiled—more brightly than the question called for, Kristin thought. "No, thanks. I'm cutting out caffeine."

Kristin watched Sarah and Luke smile at each other in the soft light of sunset. "Um...do you two have something else you want to mention?" she asked.

Luke's grin widened. Sarah looked over. "It's that obvious?"

Kristin smiled back, though her insides felt as if she'd taken the first hill on a roller coaster. "Now that I think about it, yes."

The Colonel drew on his pipe. "What's obvious? What's going on?"

"A minor detail, Dad. We're having a baby."

"Congratulations, son." Colonel Brennan got up to shake Luke's hand and give Sarah a hug. "Maybe we'll get us a boy this time."

"Another little girl would be wonderful," Matt's mother said firmly, still seated in her chair. "When are you due, Sarah?"

"Around the first of December."

Elena Brennan sighed softly. "A Christmas baby. How lovely."

Babies were lovely at any time of year, Kristin thought. But she couldn't help worrying about Erin and Jenny. What would a new baby do to the precarious balance they were reaching for, after a divorce and two new marriages?

Especially if she rocked their world at the same time with the announcement that Matt was Erin's father?

Matt had stepped over to shake his brother's hand. He bent to give Sarah a kiss on the cheek. "Let's hope, boy or girl, the baby gets your looks, not his." He nodded sideways at Luke.

"Thanks, bro."

"Anytime."

Kristin knew she had to say something. "I'm so happy for you both. You'll love having a baby. Who's your doctor?"

The question led them into a discussion of symptoms and signs and preparations. The men dropped out—Luke went into the pool to play with the girls while Matt and the Colonel talked basketball. Mrs. Brennan unbent— babies had an amazing way of softening her up. The Brennans had lost a daughter, before Luke was born. Kristin tried to remember that tragedy when her mother-in-law became a challenge.

Like now. Mrs. Brennan broke into a short silence. After a moment, she said, "You know, Kristin, you and Matt have been married longer than Sarah and Luke.

Don't you think it's about time we heard the same good news from you?''

"Maybe not just yet, Mom." Answering his mother, Matt felt Kristin's stare as she turned in her seat to face him. "My career is kinda up in the air—if I take a transfer back to Special Forces, we may need to move. Two little girls is plenty family for us." He cleared his throat. "For now."

"But surely, Matt—"

"So you *are* thinking about going back in. I knew it!" His father pounded the arm of his chair at the same time, drowning out his wife's argument. "Good man!"

Kristin didn't say a word. Matt felt her gaze leave him, felt her withdrawal like a drop in air temperature. He should have kept his mouth shut. Hadn't he learned long ago to let his mother assume whatever she wanted, just to avoid the hassle of a discussion?

But he couldn't imagine a baby in their house, especially after today. Erin and Jenny hadn't come close to accepting him as their dad. How would they feel about having another child—especially *his* child—in the family?

Late that evening, as he made the drive home from his parents' house with the girls asleep in the back seat and Kristin silent beside him, Matt laughed at himself.

Family—us?

Not by a long shot.

CHAPTER TWO

LUKE AND SARAH had the girls over for dinner on the Wednesday before their trip and broke the news about the mountain vacation. Erin and Jenny came home that night dancing on the air.

"We get to go to the mountains!" Erin gave Buster a hug and then flopped down on the floor beside him, her chin on her hands and her legs bouncing off the floor in alternate arcs. "Isn't that neat, Mommy?"

"An' Daddy says there's a castle we can see." Jenny had climbed into her mother's lap. "We get to see a real castle."

"It sounds just wonderful." Kristin smiled but Matt didn't think the effort quite worked. He could see the sadness behind her eyes. "I know you'll have a lovely time."

"You could come, too, Mommy." Erin cast a guilty glance in Matt's direction. "I mean you and Daddy Matt. We could all go to the mountains."

Matt set his jaw, waiting for Kristin's response. When she didn't seem to have one, he figured he'd better say something. "I think you and Jenny will have fun with your...with Luke and Sarah by yourselves. We'll stay home, and then the four of us can take a trip later. Two vacations in one summer. How does that sound?"

Jenny stared at him with her mother's serious brown

gaze and sucked her thumb. Erin shrugged. "Okay.
Maybe we can go back to the mountains. Daddy says
you can see for forever in some places, and in some
places the clouds are so close to the ground you can't see
anything. That's why they're called the Smokey Mountains. Can we get a book from the library on mountains,
Mommy? I want to know all about 'em before we get
there."

Erin was still talking about mountains when Kristin
herded the girls up to bed. Matt dropped his head back
against the chair and stared at the ceiling, keeping his
mind a careful blank until Kristin returned.

"Did they go to sleep?"

She sighed and dropped onto the couch. "Jenny did.
Erin's still reading. She found that book about North Carolina Indian tribes that Luke gave her and is learning all
about the Cherokee Nation."

"Oh." In the silence that fell between them, he argued
with himself about mentioning—again—the possibility of
telling Erin the truth. Nothing major had changed in their
lives to warrant a new request. Kris would never agree
to break the news just before the girls left for a vacation
with Luke. Why say anything at all?

Because…because the awkwardness and the dishon-
esty of the situation were tearing him up, dammit. He
couldn't keep quiet. "You know, I've been wondering if
this summer would be a good time to explain…
things…to Erin."

Kristin stared at him. "Now? Before they go away?"
She shook her head. "I don't think—"

He held up a hand. "No, not right now. But afterward,
we could go somewhere, like I said—a theme park, or

maybe Stone Mountain—and talk about it while we're there. Neutral territory, and all that.''

"But—'' Kristin didn't know what to say. The suggestion made sense…and it terrified her. "I'm not sure Erin is…is ready.''

"Just how will you know when she's ready?'' Matt's voice was dangerously even.

She gripped her hands together in her lap. "Well, when she's more accepting. When she counts less on Luke.''

"And how's that going to happen when she spends two weeks with him in the mountains?''

"You liked the idea!'' The words exploded before she thought them through. "You said yes before I could even decide.''

He shrugged and looked away. "I figured you'd agree.''

"I'm not sure whether I would have or not. But you didn't give me a choice.''

"However it happened, there's no going back. So let's plan what to do about the rest.''

Kristin pressed her fingertips to her pounding temples. "I don't think I can do that right now. Why don't we just get through the next couple of weeks, get them back home, and then figure it out?''

"That's what we've been doing for the last two years—postponing the inevitable, waiting for the 'right' moment. Or…'' He looked over, his eyes suddenly those of someone Kristin wasn't sure she knew. "Maybe you've changed your mind about ever telling her.''

The last thing she wanted was for Matt to know that she'd considered that option seriously. "N…no. I think it's the right thing to do. I just want to be sure that the timing is…right.''

Gathering all her courage, Kristin met her husband's stare. Right away, she saw that he recognized her hesitation, interpreted it correctly. His face held disappointment and anger and a deep, deep hurt.

But he was a grown man—a soldier, in fact—who was used to dealing with difficult situations. Erin was still a little girl who needed care, understanding…protection. Whose view of the world would be forever changed when she finally knew the truth.

''Well.'' Hands pushing against his knees, Matt got to his feet. ''I won't argue with a mother's instinct. You know Erin better than I do, so I guess you're right.'' The tone wasn't sarcastic, but the words stung. ''I think I'll head on up to bed. Are you ready?''

She was exhausted, yet too keyed up to sleep. ''I think I'll watch TV for a little while. You go ahead.''

Matt lifted his chin, as if to take a punch. An instant longer he stood still, gazing at a horizon beyond the walls of the room.

Then with his quick, long stride, he crossed to the couch. Bending, he kissed her on the forehead and briefly, on the lips. ''Okay. I'll see you later, then.''

''G'night.'' She wanted to add, ''I love you.''

But somehow she didn't think she'd be believed.

''Is IT REALLY wise to let Erin and Jenny go so far away?''

Kristin looked up from folding little-girl underwear. ''They'll love the mountains.''

Her mother picked up a pair of socks and rolled them together. ''But—''

"Just tell me what's on your mind, Mom. Where do you see a problem?"

"It seems strange to take a vacation apart from your children. Especially when they're so young."

"That's what happens in divorce." She set a neat pile of laundry in the basket, then shrugged. "Strange arrangements have to be made."

"I wish—"

Kristin simply waited.

"I wish this had all turned out differently for you."

Didn't they all? "How?"

"If Matt had never gone away—"

"He's in the Army, Mom. That was his job, and still is."

"Well, maybe he needs another job. At least he could stay out of the Special Forces." Her mother folded the last nightgown. "A man owes his wife and family consideration in matters like this. I imagine if you spoke to him—"

"But I'm not going to, Mom." She held her temper with an effort. "I married Matt knowing he was Army, knowing he was Special Forces. That's a commitment I made. It wouldn't be fair to ask him to change now."

A worry line deepened between her mother's eyebrows. "But if something happens…how will you manage?"

Kristin put her arms around the other woman's shoulders and squeezed. So much had already happened. "I survived five years thinking Matt was dead, and I survived him coming back. I survived ending a marriage. I know the risks of Matt's job, but I'm not going to ask him to give up the career he loves. We'll deal with whatever comes up."

Irene Jennings sniffed, and returned the hug. "I just want you to be happy." She stepped back and smiled. "Shall I make some coffee?"

"That sounds good. I'll take these upstairs. Be right back."

But in Erin's room, Kristin sat down on the bed and put her face in her hands. Her brave words aside, she wasn't at all sure what would happen next in her marriage, or how to face it.

And the one person who could help—her husband—was the last person she could ask.

ELENA BRENNAN TRACED the edge of the photograph with her finger. Matthew and Luke grinned at her from the paper, posed on the very rim of Arizona's Grand Canyon. At twelve, Matthew had been tall for his age, gangly in the way adolescent boys are, passionately interested in the canyon and its history. He'd always been a serious, responsible child. With his father gone so much of the time on Army assignments, she'd depended on Matt as more than just a little boy. He had never let her down.

A hand came to rest on her shoulder. Elena jumped slightly, and looked up to find her husband standing behind her. "Didn't mean to startle you, m'dear. What have you got there?" He sat down at the table.

She turned the album toward him. "I was dusting inside the cabinet in the family room and came across these pictures of our different vacations. We took this one at the Grand Canyon."

William nodded. "I remember. We lost Luke our second day there and were lucky to find him before he started down into the canyon with a group of climbers."

He chuckled. "That boy could find adventure wherever he went."

"Scaring us all to death in the process." Elena didn't share William's fondness for Luke's exploits. She'd worried too much, having to handle such an unpredictable boy on her own. She'd often needed Matt's help to keep his brother from getting completely out of hand.

"What else is in this album?" William flipped through the pages. "The skiing vacation in Utah...the beach trip...the tour of Washington. We did have some good times when the boys were young, didn't we?"

"Of course. You made sure we took a special family trip every year." She leaned over to kiss his cheek. "I knew many Army wives whose husbands made no apologies for missing family times. I always felt lucky." She got up from the table. "Shall I get dinner?"

"Whenever you're ready." He sat at the table, browsing through the photograph album as she prepared their meal. Only as she set their plates on the table did William speak again. "I'm worried about Matt. He's taking too long on this decision to get back into Special Forces."

"I expect Kristin is behind that delay. I seriously doubt she supports the idea."

"You think she would prevent him from returning to his unit?"

"I think she could make it very difficult for him to do so."

"What can we do to help him get back on track?" As William set down his fork, his face reflected his troubled thoughts.

She reached for his hand. "Perhaps you should talk to Matt alone. Without Kristin listening, you might make some progress."

William nodded. "I'll do that. I bet the boy'll stop looking so beaten once he's back in the real Army."

Elena wondered, as they finished eating, how a change in Matt's career would affect his marriage. She'd never thought Kristin truly appropriate as an Army wife, and she had hoped Matt would realize that in time. But then he had gone missing and Kristin had taken up with Luke, which confirmed all of Elena's opinions.

The divorce and remarriage, after Matt's return, had been such a mess, and so embarrassing, that she'd supported him in his plans, just to have things settled.

Now Kristin would have to realize her responsibilities. If she didn't...

That young woman might find herself even further outside Army life than she expected! And as long as the little girls stayed with Matt, Elena wouldn't whisper the first word of protest.

EARLY SUMMER was a busy time for recruiters—or what passed for busy, anyway. High-school graduates who didn't plan on college suddenly realized they needed some means of support, and the military looked like a sure bet. Matt counseled and interviewed and helped with application forms, did the paperwork, and kept his files neat. The easy routine had been a godsend in the months after he came back from Africa.

Now it just dragged him down.

When the bell on the door jingled, he braced himself for another round of question and answer. But as he stepped out of his office, he saw his father standing at the front desk.

They shook hands. "Planning to reenlist, Dad?"

"Don't I wish." The Colonel shook his head. "Life outside the Army never feels right."

"Come on back." Matt led the way and waved his dad into a chair. "Coffee? Soda?"

"No, thanks. Your mother and I just finished lunch."

"What's Mom up to? She's always got some project going."

"Planning the Fourth of July party. As soon as Memorial Day passes, she starts on that one. How are my granddaughters?"

"A little bit crazy. Since Luke told them about the trip to the mountains, they've been bouncing off the walls."

"They're a lively pair." William Brennan's hawkish gray eyes softened. "Enough spirit for several more children."

"That's for sure." Matt closed the book he'd been reading and set it to the side.

His father leaned forward. "If you've got time to read, son, you need another job. What's the book?"

"That new account of the battle at Gettysburg."

"You've already got it?" He extended his hand and Matt passed him the book.

"Yes, sir. The guy's done his homework, and he's got a way with words. He almost puts you on the front line."

The Colonel looked up. "Which is where you should be."

"Don't start, Dad."

"It's time you got back to the job. You owe your country the use of your mind and your strength."

"I've given the Army most of my life since I was sixteen years old and joined Junior ROTC. That's nearly twenty years." He tried not to sound defensive.

"Some men give their entire life. You can't ask for a greater honor."

"I understand that perspective. But this is a different age from Gettysburg, or World War II, or even Vietnam. Maybe the country needs more than just…more than soldiers."

"Like what?"

"Well…" *Think, Brennan.* "Teachers? Government leaders? People to see what the future holds and prepare our kids to handle the challenge?"

"There are plenty of men out there who can teach, make plans. Your combination of skills is what makes the Army work."

This conversation was destined to go in circles. Matt leaned back in his chair. "I understand, Dad. I'm giving the whole issue a lot of thought. Anything else I can do for you today?" An abrupt change of subject.

But effective. His father drew out his pipe and clamped it between his teeth, avoiding Matt's eyes. "I got to wondering last night what you and Kristin planned to do for your first anniversary celebration."

"We haven't talked about that. I was thinking dinner and that new Broadway show out at the theater. Why?"

His dad actually looked a little embarrassed. "I just…a little fatherly advice here… Why don't you and Kristin take some time off? Get away, just the two of you, while the girls are in the mountains with Luke and Sarah?"

Matt stared at the man across the desk. "What brought this up?"

"Nothing, really." The Colonel shrugged. "Well, except it occurred to me that Kristin's had a rough time these last few years. She might feel…better…if she has you to herself for a while."

Matt realized he should have thought of this one without help. Maybe that was part of the problem—maybe he'd been taking Kristin for granted. "You're absolutely right—we should make our own getaway. Where would be a good place to go?"

His father held up his hands. "I'm not meddling any further. You take it from here."

"I will." They both got to their feet, and Matt put out his hand again. "Thanks for thinking about us."

"My pleasure. Kristin will make a good Special Forces wife."

Laughing, Matt pulled back the glass door panel for his dad to step through. "Give Mom my love."

The Colonel settled into his beige Cadillac. "Sure thing."

Matt turned back inside. The office seemed small all at once, and the air smelled stale. He felt as if he'd been cooped up inside forever. How long had it been since he'd slept out under the stars? Maybe he and Kris should go camping...

No. Kris worked hard enough at home—she ought to get a chance to simply relax. But they lived in a beach town, with the ocean just a mile away from their house, so a beach trip wouldn't mean much. He didn't like the idea of following Luke to the mountains—sure, there were lots of mountains, but did he have to imitate his little brother right down the line?

So where?

His eye fell on the Gettysburg book and he sat forward to pick it up. Ever since grade school, he'd been fascinated by all aspects of the Civil War. And he'd long promised himself a chance to visit some of the places forever marked by that violent conflict.

Why not now?

A couple of hours of planning later, Matt whistled as he closed up the office. What a great idea this was. He could hardly wait to tell Kris!

ON THE FRIDAY EVENING before the girls were set to leave, Matt caught Kristin's hand as she got up to start clearing the table after dinner. "I've got a surprise for you."

As she sat down, her heart bumped hard against her ribs. "A surprise?"

"Yeah." From beside his chair, he brought out a big manila envelope. "You and I are going to take a little trip. An anniversary trip." He pulled out a sheaf of shiny brochures. "See what you think."

Fredericksburg. Arlington. Manassas. Antietam. Gettysburg. "Battlefields?" Kristin stared at him blankly over the tableful of dishes. "You want to visit battlefields?"

He nodded, his blue eyes bright. "And other historic places around them. I've lined up some great bed-and-breakfast inns for us to stay in on the way. We can cruise country roads, soak up the fresh air and space, stop when we feel like it, do whatever we want to. How does that sound?"

"You're planning to bring the girls?" She couldn't picture Erin or Jenny at their ages being interested in an old war.

"Nope. Just you and me this time. While they're in the mountains."

"Oh." She swung from one kind of dread to another. "Just us."

"No beds to make, no dishes, no meals to cook, no

laundry. Ten days with nothing to do but relax, kick back, enjoy.''

''That…that sounds really nice. But it sounds kind of expensive, too. Can we afford a long trip like that?'' Could they afford that much time alone? What would they talk about? Would they discover there was nothing between them anymore but…but duty?

''No problem. Our savings account is pretty fat. I think we can spare the cash.''

She was running out of excuses. ''Can you get off work so soon?''

''My leave has already been approved.'' His grin disappeared. He searched her face, his eyes wary. ''You don't like the idea, Kris? We can do something else if you want. Or we can stay home.''

''Oh, Matt. No.'' Now her heart cramped with guilt. She took his hand with both of hers. ''It's a beautiful idea. I love that part of the country, and it'll be great to get away from the beach crowds for a while. I'm just…this happened so fast.''

''That's because it's a surprise.'' He drew her hand to his mouth and kissed her knuckles as Erin and Jenny and Buster tumbled into the kitchen.

''A surprise? What surprise?'' Erin grabbed at her half-finished glass of milk. ''For me?''

''For me?'' Jenny asked, climbing into Kristin's lap.

Buster sat on his haunches and stared expectantly.

Kristin drew her hand back and managed a laugh. ''No, for me. Matt and I are…taking a trip just like the two of you.''

''You're coming to the mountains, too, Mommy?'' Erin nodded. ''That'll be cool.''

''No, love. We're going to visit some historic places

in Virginia and Maryland. You'll still get time with just your dad and Sarah.''

Jenny tugged on Kristin's shirt collar. ''Where's that? Can I go?''

Matt drew a paper out of the brochure stack and unfolded a map. ''I can show you, Miss Jenny. See, this is the mountains, where you'll be. And this green line over here...'' He traced a route north from Myrtle Beach through Washington, D.C., and beyond. ''That's where your mom and I will be driving.''

Jenny stared, her thumb inching toward her pouting mouth. ''Is it very far?''

Erin stood, hands on her hips, studying the map. ''What's at the places with circles?''

Kristin pulled Jenny in closer. ''Battlefields, historic houses, um...museums.''

''That doesn't sound like much fun.'' Erin frowned.

''Maybe not when you're almost eight.'' Matt refolded the map. ''I like history, though. And these places were really important during the War Between the States.''

Facts always caught Erin's attention. ''What's that?''

''A time when our country was divided into two parts, and the northern part fought a war against the southern part.''

''Why?''

Kristin smiled at Jenny. ''Want to help me clean up while they talk?'' As Matt explained the Civil War to Erin, Jenny brought the dishes to the sink and Kristin stacked them in the dishwasher. Both exercises were finished about the same time.

''Can we go to the beach?'' Erin asked.

Kristin nodded. ''Sure, it's early. Go get your swimsuits on.'' She gave a sigh of relief. The girls had adjusted to the idea of their trip without nearly the resistance she'd expected. Now, if she could only adjust to hers!

SUNDAY MORNING arrived soon enough and went by so fast that Luke and Sarah were at the door before Kristin realized the time had arrived.

"Daddy!" Erin—followed by Buster, as usual—ran through the hall and into Luke's arms. "I'm all packed. Let's go!"

He laughed and gave her a hug. "I'm ready if you are. Where's Jen?"

Jenny came toward them, pulling a wagon loaded with stuffed animals. "These go with me, Daddy." She extended the handle. "Don't drop them."

The four adults gazed at each other, trying not to laugh. Then Luke squatted down to Jenny's level. "You really need all these animals, Jenny Penny?"

She nodded silently, clutching her very favorite bear to her chest.

Luke looked into her eyes and nodded. "Okay, then. I don't think we've got room for the wagon, but we'll get these critters in somehow."

"Would you like some coffee before you go? Tea?" Kristin tried not to sound desperate, though she was.

Luke smiled at her. "You know, I think we should just get on the road. That'll be easiest."

She blinked back tears as they all walked out to the car. Maybe she could change her mind…it wasn't too late…

But Matt's arm was firm around her waist, giving her the strength she lacked. She could do this. For the girls' sake, she had to.

"Okay, Erin, Jenny. It's time for you to head off on your adventure. Give me a hug." She caught Erin from the back, kissed her cheeks and the top of her head. "Be good for your dad and Sarah. Help out, okay?"

"Okay."

She allowed herself to pick Jenny up. "Say hello to Smokey the Bear for me, love."

Jenny's eyes widened. "I can see Smokey the Bear?"

"He lives in the mountains. You just might."

"Oh, boy!"

And then the girls were strapped in, with Buster sitting between them. Kristin hugged Sarah, and Luke shook hands with Matt. The brand-new van backed out of the driveway, with all four occupants waving wildly as they drove away.

Kristin smiled and waved as long as the blue van was in sight. When it disappeared, she took one deep breath in the emptiness they'd left behind. Then she turned, buried her face in Matt's chest and began to sob.

CHAPTER THREE

Sunday

Dear Diary

Mommy gave me this book to remember things I do and places I go. What do I write?

Today Jenny and me went with Daddy and Sarah to go to the mountains. We rode forever. Jenny fell asleep. I brought lots of books to read. Daddy and Sarah played some of my tapes and we sang songs. Sarah sings pretty good. Daddy doesnt but he makes up funny words for the songs.

Jenny woke up for supper. We had pizza.

It was almost dark when we got here so I dont know what mountains look like. Its cold and smells like trees. We have a little house like where Sarah lived before she married Daddy. A kondimium. Me and Jenny have a bedroom with two beds. She cried at bedtime coz Mommys not here.

I didnt cry. I know this is just vakashun. We will get to go home. Mommy sent us off with Luke and Sarah so she an Daddy Matt could go away all alone. I keep tellin Jenny we have to get used to things this way. My frend Trina never sees her dad much. At least we can see Daddy sumtimes. An we have Mommy all the time.

Only Mommy isnt happy now. She doesnt laugh

much. Maybe she will be happy when she gets back from her trip.

Im tired of writin. My eyes hurt. By.

Your friend
Erin Elena Brennan

"READY, KRIS?" Matt called up the stairs Wednesday morning.

"Almost. I have a few more things to pack." Kristin waited with her eyes closed, praying Matt wouldn't come to find her sitting on their bed, paralyzed with fear. She breathed a sigh of relief when his footsteps receded toward the family room.

Vacation. Who knew the word could be so terrifying? The prospect of ten days alone with her husband should have been the fulfillment of a dream. Instead, she wasn't sure she'd even survive the next hour. Her heart kept threatening to jump out of her chest.

She drew another deep breath and stood up. This trip would happen whether she was ready or not. Best to be ready. A few more shirts, a couple of pairs of jeans, a sweater...oh, and her makeup bag, in the bathroom.

Kristin fetched the bag, but stopped on the threshold of the bedroom. The pouch was too light. Turning back, she set the bag down on the counter and checked the contents. What had she missed?

Oops. Birth control supplies. This was the first time she and Matt had ever been completely alone. Chances were good they'd be spending time together in bed.

She smiled a little as she took the small pouch out of the drawer and added it to the bag. Thinking about making love with Matt eased her butterflies. Things worked between them, then. His smooth shoulders under her palms and his mouth taking hers… Kristin had no problem anticipating those hours in the dark.

But she had a real problem figuring out what to do with the rest of their day. Talk? About what? Battlefields? War? It was, after all, Matt's job.

She recalled her mother's advice—talk him into changing careers. Even if she could bring herself to ask for that sacrifice, she doubted Matt would agree. He'd worked long and hard to get assigned to a Special Forces unit. Instead, maybe they'd discuss when he would go back to regular duty, volunteering for the chance to get himself killed. Or just locked up in a foreign jail for five years, like last time…

"Kris? Kris!"

She jumped and whirled to see Matt standing in the doorway to the bathroom. "I'm sorry. Did you want me?"

He grinned and gave her a sexy wink. "Well, yeah…but I'll wait. Erin's on the phone." He held out the receiver.

"Oh!" Kristin put the handset to her ear. "Erin, love? How are you?"

"Good. Mommy, I got some moccasins!"

"Wow! Are they comfortable?"

"Yes. They're red. Jenny got tan ones."

"Lucky girls. How's Jenny?"

"She's okay. She keeps getting into my bed, though."

"Why?"

"She says she's afraid 'cause you aren't here."

Kristin blinked back tears. "Poor Jenny. Can I talk to her?"

"Um, sure." The phone changed hands.

"Mommy?"

"Hello, sweetheart." She bit back the urge to comfort and console—that would only give Luke and Sarah more problems. "I hear you have new shoes."

"Uh-huh."

"I bet the mountains are pretty."

"The roads are all twisty."

Kristin laughed. "I remember that from when I was a little girl. What's your favorite thing you've done?"

A long silence. "Can I come home?" Tears thickened the small voice.

"Jenny, love, why would you want to do that?"

The mumbled reply wasn't clear, but Kristin got the message.

"Your daddy is so happy to have you and Erin there, Jenny. He and Sarah would be sad if you left. You know that, don't you?"

Jenny's reply was a small sniff. "Yes."

"That's my girl. You're going to have a great time." She put as much conviction as she could muster into her voice, though she felt precious little. "I love you, sweetheart. Now, let me say goodbye to your sister."

Erin came back to the phone. "Mommy, when are we coming home?"

"You've got so much to do, I guess it will be a while yet. Your dad's got some great ideas. The time's going to fly. And then we'll all be together again."

This time Erin sighed. "I guess so. I love you, Mommy."

Kristin's eyes burned. "I love you, too. Sleep tight."

"Bye."

"Bye, Erin." She clicked the button to end the call and stood for a moment leaning against the wall, her eyes closed with her fingers. After just three days, she wasn't sure she could bear this any longer. Maybe she and Matt should go get the girls, bring them along on the trip to Virginia. The drive from here to Banner Elk in the mountains was about eight hours…

"I got your suitcase. Are you ready?" Matt stood in the bathroom doorway again. "Everything okay with Erin and Jenny?"

"Yes, I think so." Kristin straightened up and eased past him into the bedroom. "They miss…us…a little bit."

"Yeah, I imagine." Only the slightest edge to his voice betrayed that he knew the truth. "And we miss them."

She nodded.

He put a hand on her shoulder. "Do you want to go get them?"

Her eyes filled up again. Matt gave so much, to the girls and to her. She couldn't ask him to give up this trip.

Taking a deep breath, she managed a smile. "No. They'll be okay. Luke and Sarah will see that they enjoy themselves. And we've got some battlefields to visit, right?"

His blue eyes searched her face. Kristin hoped she'd hidden her worries well.

"Yeah, we do," he said. Leaning forward, he pressed a kiss to her forehead, dropped a light one on her nose and brushed her lips with his. He started to draw away, but his arms came around her hard and tight and he found her mouth again, in a kiss that started at a fast burn and only got hotter.

Then on a shuddering breath, Matt straightened up. "There," he whispered. He cleared his throat. "That'll give us something to look forward to at the end of the drive.''

His hand slipped to hold hers and lead her out of the bedroom. Comforted, aroused and suddenly eager, Kristin followed him without a backward glance.

As the first hour of their vacation passed, Matt discovered the flaw in his plans.

He and Kristin weren't used to talking anymore.

Of course, they actually talked every day. About the girls, about the day's schedule, about what Erin had done and who Jenny had played with. They talked about his parents, and hers. About furniture to buy and car repairs, checking accounts and insurance premiums. All the plain "stuff" that made up normal life.

But take those things away, and what was there to say?

Judging by the last sixty minutes of driving... Nothing.

Matt glanced across the car. She seemed calm enough, her excellent legs easily crossed, her shoulders relaxed, face turned to catch the scenery speeding by the side window. A movement in her lap caught his eye. Her hands were clasped loosely. But one thumb tapped an anxious tattoo on the other.

Okay. Kris was nervous about this, too. What could they talk about?

He said the first thing that came to his head. "I got a surprise phone call the other day."

"Who was it?" Obviously willing to break the silence, she shifted in the seat to face him, curling her legs up underneath her.

"Lee Holt—he was stationed with me up at Fort Bragg."

"Where is he stationed now?"

Matt suddenly had second thoughts about where this conversation would lead. "Uh…he's been out of the Army for about three years."

"Oh, really? Did he stay the full twenty before retirement?"

Matt cursed his own stupidity in ever bringing up the subject. "No, as a matter of fact. He was a couple of years behind me." The next question was predictable and unavoidable.

"Why did he get out so early?"

"After…Africa…he didn't have the heart, he said, to stay in."

"He was in Africa with you?" The sudden chill in the air had nothing to do with the air conditioner.

"Yeah."

"For all five years?"

"Uh…no. He was there for about two and a half years, I think."

"He came home before you did?" Kristin dragged in a painful breath. "And he didn't tell us you were alive?"

"He couldn't do that, Kris. Our mission was classified."

Kristin stared at her husband. *Oh, God.* She and Luke had still been sleeping apart at that point. If she'd thought for one moment that Matt would come home…

Jenny would never have been born.

She covered her face with her hands. "I can't believe anyone could have been so heartless."

"He had a responsibility to the Army. And he was under strict orders to keep quiet."

She dropped her hands and looked over at Matt's grim profile. "Could *you* do that? Would you have done that to some other wife?"

His knuckles whitened as he gripped the wheel. ''Kris, I can't—''

''*Are* you doing it…right now? Is there someone still left over there, someone whose parents or wife or children believe he's dead?''

Matt didn't answer. Kristin turned to stare out the side window again. There was some logic here, she supposed, from a military point of view. Too bad the military had long since stopped being human.

Perhaps her husband had, as well. ''You've never said very much about what happened to you over there.''

She turned her head to watch him. For a minute, she didn't think he would reply. Then he cleared his throat. ''There's not much to say.''

''Or not much you *can* say?''

''That's part of it. But outside of what's classified, there's not much to tell. Each day was about the same as all the others.'' His resistance vibrated like an electric field between them.

''Did you have books?''

''No.''

''TV?''

''No.''

''What did you eat?''

Matt slapped the steering wheel with the heel of his hand and muttered an ugly word. ''Look…I've worked hard every damn day of the last four years forgetting the details you're asking for. Remembering takes me back. I don't want to go there again. Can we just drop it, please?''

He could have hit her, and she would have felt better. Her grievance quickly became guilt. ''I'm sorry,'' Kristin whispered. "So sorry." She covered her eyes with her hand to hide the tears.

"Aw, Kris…" They rode in silence for a long time, until at last Matt cleared his throat. "What do you feel like having for lunch? Where's a good place to eat in Wilmington?"

Kristin sat up straight. If he made an effort, so would she. "I don't know. Let's see what we find when we get there."

Their mood gradually eased as they ate fresh shrimp and coleslaw and hush puppies at a table overlooking the Cape Fear River. Then Matt talked Kristin into dessert. "At least split a piece with me. Would that be so bad?" He knew her weakness against the temptation of chocolate.

Kristin sighed. "Yes, it would. But I can't resist." She raised her head and looked at him across the table. "You fiend, you."

But her brown eyes laughed at him. Matt felt a weight lift from his shoulders, just knowing he'd made her laugh. Especially after the way he'd blown it this morning in the car.

He'd just have to work harder in the future to keep the conversation away from minefields like Africa…Luke… Erin… Too bad the inn in Fredericksburg where they were going to stay the night was still seven hours away.

A mere seven hours of intimate, meaningful discussion but no controversy?

Mission Impossible. Matt pulled in a deep, doubtful breath and concentrated on his share of dessert.

FREDERICKSBURG TURNED OUT to be even farther than seven hours—a bridge on the main road had been washed out by flooding. The detour markers led straight into the dark Virginia wilderness and then vanished, without showing the way out again.

"We must have missed another sign," Matt muttered at about 10:00 p.m. as they sat parked at a roadside picnic area in the middle of nowhere. He studied the map. "I don't see state road 3407 anywhere on here."

Kristin rubbed her eyes with her fingers. She'd been driving for the last three hours while Matt navigated.

"Let's call the B&B," she said. "Maybe they can help."

But the owners of the inn confessed to being transplanted Yankees, still learning the country themselves. They promised a bed would be ready whatever time the Brennans showed up.

He clicked off the cellular phone, dropped his head back and yawned. "Man, I'm tired."

"Me, too." Kristin leaned her temple against the window. "We can rest for a little while, can't we?"

Matt stared at her awkward position for a few seconds. Then he climbed out of the van and in again—onto the back seat. "Sounds great to me. Turn off the light and come here. We can stretch out and be warm." He grinned and held out his arms.

Kristin's smile was all the answer he needed. By the time she crawled into the back, he had stretched out on his side, his head pillowed on the armrest. With a sigh, she lay down in his arms, resting her cheek on his shoulder. He let his other arm curve across the dip in her waist just made for that purpose. "Better?"

"Mmm." She wiggled a bit, slipped her knee between his and, finally, relaxed. "Wonderful."

He pressed a kiss on the top of her head, catching the sweet berry scent of her shampoo. "Me, too."

But minutes passed, and sleep didn't come. Somewhere in the woods a whippoorwill called. An owl hooted, answered by a different one. Crickets and bullfrogs scratched and croaked.

Kristin lay with her eyes closed, listening to Matt's even breathing and the beat of her own heart…a beat that became quick and unsteady as she soaked up her husband's scent, his nearness, his sheer magnetism.

In another few seconds, she knew he was awake. The very air around them was like a force pressing on her skin, making breathing difficult.

Matt put a finger under her chin and lifted her face. As she closed her eyes, his breath brushed her temple and her cheek. When his lips finally settled over hers, Kristin surrendered completely to the firmness of his mouth, the graze of his teeth on her lower lip, the sweet pressure of his tongue against hers.

"We haven't made out in a car in a long time," he whispered when they broke for breath. "Feels good." He rubbed his knuckles gently along her spine under her shirt. "You feel good."

His touch created an unbearable ache. Kristin shifted even closer. "You make me crazy," she murmured against the base of his throat.

"I hope so." Somehow he unfastened her bra—Matt had always been good with his hands. He covered her breast with his palm. "I'm trying."

She pulled his shirttail out of his shorts and smoothed her hands over his back, across his ribs and chest. "Let's see if I can do the same for you."

"Oh, yeah," he groaned. "Whatever you say."

Heated minutes followed, while the soft sounds they made pleasing each other filled the van. Matt's shirt disappeared, and her shorts. Smiling, quivering, Kristin remembered that this wasn't the old days. They were married now. They didn't have to stop.

Or did they?

Drenched with reality, her mind cleared. Birth control. They needed to use birth control. "Matt," she whispered against the soft, short hair on the top of his head. "Matt, wait."

"Hmm?" He raised his head and looked at her, his blue eyes heavy with desire. "Waiting is fast becoming a non-option, lady." His sweet smile as he came in for another kiss robbed the statement of any demand.

"Matt. We need to stop for a minute." She closed her hands on his shoulders and pushed. "I need to…get ready."

He blinked. "Oh. Yeah." Sitting up, he ran a hand over his face. "Sure."

Flushed with embarrassment, Kristin made her way to the second-row seat and leaned over the back to reach her suitcase. She snapped open the latch and lifted the lid. And stared.

Her makeup bag wasn't there, on top, where she'd put it. How could it have gotten moved? Or did it just sift down through the clothes? Heart pounding, she felt her way through the entire case. She found her hair dryer, her curling iron, her clothes iron and her three extra pairs of shoes. But no makeup bag.

Kristin crossed her arms on the back of the seat and buried her face in them.

"What?" Matt put a hand on her back. "Kris, what's wrong?"

"My makeup bag," she whispered without lifting her head. "I left it at home."

"And?"

"And my diaphragm was inside."

"That means—"

"Yes, it does." She turned around and sat facing him, pulling her shirt down over her hips. "We don't have any protection. We can't do...this...anymore."

CHAPTER FOUR

MATT SWALLOWED HARD. "Kris, we're married. We can take the risk." His body begged him not to debate the issue very long.

With her face hidden in her hands, she shook her head. The gold of her hair picked up a glint of moonlight.

His skin was beginning to chill. "Why not?"

"This...isn't a...good time for a baby."

The truth didn't soothe his frustration or his temper. "Just when will be a good time?"

"I—"

"What exactly is it we're waiting for?" His voice was too loud in the dark, and out of his control. "Can you give me a hint about how to recognize when we get there?"

Kristin looked up, her eyes round and dark. "I'm sorry," she whispered. "I didn't mean to."

Matt muttered a rude word. He found his shirt on the floor and shrugged it on, then eased back onto the seat beside his wife.

"Don't apologize. It's not your fault I'm a jerk." Slipping an arm around her shoulders, he turned her to sit next to him, then tipped her face up with a finger under her chin. "I just wanted you so much. For a minute there, I wasn't thinking with my brain."

The corners of her mouth tilted into a small smile. He

breathed a sigh of relief. "You should put a pair of jeans on. It's getting chilly." He resolutely closed his eyes during the process. His system was still revved way too high to resist temptation.

"Done." Kristin sat down again. "I guess we could start driving, try to find our way to Fredericksburg."

Matt yawned and slouched down in the seat. "I vote we just get some sleep and wait for daybreak. Okay with you?"

She snuggled under his arm and rested her head on his chest. "That's fine. I could probably sleep until noon." She rubbed her eyes with her free hand, then set it lightly on his belly. In another minute, Kristin was asleep.

Matt dropped his head back and stared up at the ceiling of the van. He'd almost lost his temper—about sex, of all things. It wasn't as if they hadn't made love last night, or wouldn't get another chance.

But... A small voice in his head insisted on being heard. *But what would be the problem with having another baby? What is she afraid of?*

He closed his eyes. Did Kris worry that he'd disappear again, leaving her with *three* children to care for on her own?

Or maybe the insomnia, the distraction, the sadness, was a hint that Kristin wasn't sure *she* would stay.

No way should they create a child, only to get a divorce. Their lives were messy enough already.

A divorce. This was the first time he'd let the word into his mind. Did Kris want one?

Do I? he asked himself.

Kristin cuddled a little closer, and he tightened his arm. God, no. He didn't want a divorce. This woman was all he'd thought about for five years. Every day he'd imagined her at home, at the grocery store, on the beach. He'd woven elaborate stories about Kristin's days…and her nights. With him.

Reality had been different. The Kristin he came back to was not the one he left, and she wasn't the woman of his fantasies. Four years later, he was still coping with the changes.

But Matt knew he wouldn't—couldn't—give her up.

KRISTIN AWOKE the next morning with Matt's kiss on her mouth. "Happy first anniversary, wife of mine."

She smiled and stretched, without opening her eyes. "Mmm. Are we having breakfast in bed?"

He chuckled. "Sure. Just as soon as we see a fast-food drive-through."

She raised one eyelid to look at him. "That means getting up, doesn't it?"

"I don't know about you, but I'm ready for a walk in the woods."

"Oh." She felt her face flush. "Me, too."

"And then," he said as they climbed stiffly out of the van, "we can work on finding breakfast *and* Fredericksburg."

They reached their first important battlefield stop around 10 a.m. In the rain.

Matt stared up through the windshield at the heavy gray sky. "This is not what I planned. Is anything on this trip going to go right?"

Kristin didn't have an answer, especially since she was the reason things hadn't worked out last night. What a dumb move—forgetting her birth control. Even dumber, remembering at the wrong time and putting them both through the frustration of backing off.

And Matt was right. They could have taken the risk. The "worst" that might happen would be a baby. With Erin and Jenny getting so grown-up and independent, Kristin ached for another tiny person to hold. And how wonderful it would be to introduce Matt to the joys of babyhood. He'd missed more than half of Erin's childhood.

"I really would like to walk around," he said. "But you don't have to come. I won't take too long."

She glanced at dripping trees and sodden grass, thought about sitting alone in the car with just her fears to keep her company, then unbuckled her seat belt. "I think I'll walk, too. What's a little rain?"

His grin warmed her inside. "Nothing at all. Let's go!"

They left the van near the visitors' center, got maps and brochures and started walking.

Matt obviously didn't need to read the brochures. "This is the bloodiest land in the country. More than a hundred thousand men died here during four major battles of the Civil War."

Kristin gazed at him through the steady drizzle while he recalled for her the details of the war. His eyes had a faraway look, as if he'd stepped back in time to witness the very scene he described. She'd never known he had such passion for military history. They'd never had a chance to talk about it.

They'd never talked about a lot of things.

Ending his account, he stood silent for a moment, then glanced at her sideways with an embarrassed grin. "You should stop me when I get carried away. I could talk about this stuff forever."

"No, it's okay." Kristin put her hand on his arm. "I

don't think I paid enough attention in history class. Tell me more.''

Matt closed her fingers inside his. ''Woman, you're in trouble now.''

The rain stopped before lunch, though the day remained cloudy and damp. Matt refused to talk about the war after they ate. He insisted that Kristin explore each of the unique shops in the town's central historic district instead, an offer she was quite willing to accept. They got back into the car late in the afternoon with presents for the girls and a pair of antique silver candlesticks for their dining-room table to mark their first year together.

As the engine turned over, Kristin eased off her sneakers and rubbed her tired feet. ''Where to now?''

Matt just smiled. ''That's an anniversary surprise. You'll find out.'' Nothing she said convinced him to explain further. But in just under two hours, he stopped the van at the curb of a wide thoroughfare in downtown Washington, D.C.

''The Willard Hotel,'' Kristin read on the front of the imposing building. ''Wow.''

''When I planned the trip, I thought we deserved at least one night of real class. Considering last night spent in the car, I'm sure of it!''

The next sixty minutes flew by in a whirl of activity. Kristin showered, fixed her hair and changed into the nice dress Matt had told her to bring. At eight o'clock, he escorted her into the marbled and gilded dining room of the Willard Hotel. They ate an elaborate meal on starched tablecloths and bone china place settings, shared a wonderful bottle of champagne in cut-crystal flutes, and indulged in the lightest possible conversation. Tonight, no controversy would be allowed.

The room spun pleasantly around Kristin's head as they left their table. "I'm glad we don't have to drive a car to get home."

"Just the elevator." Matt steered her down the hallway. "I think I can handle that."

The lights in their room were dim and the bed turned down, with chocolates resting on the pillows. Kristin slipped off her high-heeled shoes. "This is really wonderful, Matt. I've never stayed anywhere so elegant. Thank you."

"My pleasure." He switched on the radio, and soft music floated into the room. "Would you like to dance?"

Kristin simply held out her arms.

At some point during the dreamy dance, Matt eased the zipper of her dress down and slipped his hand over the skin of her shoulder blades. A little while later she pushed off his jacket and loosened his tie. Soon his shirt was gone. The light dusting of hair on his chest tickled her cheek. Kristin pressed a kiss on his warm skin, heard and felt his sharp intake of breath. Arms wrapped around his waist, hands flat on his back, she pressed more kisses over his firm pecs, the muscled arch of his ribs. When he drew her close again, she could feel his arousal pressing against her belly. A dark shudder swept through her and she lifted her face to his.

Matt accepted the invitation with a kiss that claimed everything she wanted to give. In another moment they were tumbling onto the bed.

As he drew her dress away, Kristin surfaced briefly. "Do we have to stop this time?"

Matt grinned and reached over her to open the drawer in the bedside chest. She heard a metallic rustle as he dropped something on the top. "Only when we collapse,'' he promised. Then he came back to her and swept them both away.

ＥＡＲＬＹ ＴＨＥ ＮＥＸＴ ＡＦＴＥＲＮＯＯＮ, Kristin leaned back against the broad trunk of a tree at the top of one of Arlington National Cemetery's rolling hills. She was grateful for the shade—without cloud cover, the summer sun burned fiercely. "The only people buried here are soldiers?''

"And some family members, plus military nurses from the Spanish–American War to the present.'' Matt stood with his feet planted wide and his hands in the pockets of his shorts, gazing toward the elegant facade of the Lee mansion, once home to the Confederate general himself.

"War costs so much.'' Kristin murmured, taking in the panorama of rolling green hills striped with row after row of small white stones.

Matt came over to lean on the same tree. "Yeah, but sometimes it's necessary.''

His words stirred her temper. "I would expect you to think so. You're trained to believe in war.''

He rounded the trunk to stare at her, his eyebrows high with surprise. "I believe in protecting this country and the people who live here.''

"And how did your trip to Africa provide anyone in the U.S. with protection?'' She shocked herself with the question, especially after yesterday's confrontation.

Matt's expression turned grim. He'd warned her to leave the subject of Africa alone. Maybe she should respect his privacy.

But those five years had changed them both so completely.... Kristin couldn't just ignore what had happened. She wanted to *know*. "What did you actually accomplish?"

He opened his mouth and started to shake his head. She held up her hand. "I know you can't give me specifics. I don't have the right clearance."

He squared his shoulders and his mouth hardened. "We completed our assignment. If we hadn't, I wouldn't have been captured."

"Was that assignment worth five years of your life?" She was pushing them both toward an argument, yet she couldn't seem to hold back.

Eyes narrowed, he held her gaze for a long moment, then turned away to look out across the Potomac River toward Washington. He didn't say anything at all.

Kristin needed to know. "Well?"

Without turning to face her, he shrugged. "I don't know. If I could have foreseen..." He didn't finish.

"If you'd known you'd be captured, you wouldn't have gone?"

He took a deep breath. "I had to go. That was my responsibility and my duty. But I would have been more...careful...with you."

Kristin had to concentrate on his words to realize the full implications. And then she went cold. Even if he'd known that he would be gone for five years, he would have left. But he would have been "careful" with her. What did that mean! Careful not to get too involved with her? Careful not to have sex with her?

So there wouldn't have been a baby...Erin. There would have been no reason to marry Luke. That meant Jenny wouldn't have been born, either.

What in the world would her life have been without them?

"Well, that certainly clears things up." Straightening away from the tree, she drove her shaking hands into her pockets. "Where do we go from here?"

"Kris—" He reached toward her.

But Kristin turned her back and started walking, toward the parking lot, she hoped. She needed a chance to consider Matt's feelings about their child. Though he loved Erin, and wanted her to know him as her father, he obviously thought of her as a mistake. Or at least an error in judgment.

So was their marriage his attempt to take care of the problems he considered his responsibility? As soon as possible after his return, Kristin had told him that Erin was his child, and had promised their daughter would know that fact, one day. Not long afterward, Luke had moved into a house by himself, when the comfortable, careful marriage they'd built crumbled under the burden of Kristin's guilt. At that point, Matt had obviously felt bound to take his brother's place as father and husband. Less than a year after her divorce from Luke, he'd asked her to marry him.

So here was the understanding she had wanted to reach. Her marriage was based on great sex and a very dependable man's sense of obligation. At least now she knew where they stood.

Matt caught up as she reached the road. He didn't try to talk on the long hike back to the van. Kristin was very glad of that.

THEIR RIDE out to Manassas, Virginia, was just as quiet. In the visitors' center, she studied exhibits of war memorabilia while Matt made a short tour of the battlefield area. They skipped the cemetery and the memorial to Confederate dead.

"I reserved a room at an inn in Boonesboro, Maryland." Matt hoped to break the silence with something non-controversial. "From there we can get to Antietam and Gettysburg with short drives."

Kristin didn't turn away from the side window. "That's nice."

Not exactly encouraging. And he wasn't sure why she was so angry. She knew his father, knew that the Army tradition went back in their family for generations. One of his great-grandfathers had died at Gettysburg. This trip was about family history as much as war itself.

Of course, for the Brennans the two were pretty much the same thing. Or had been, until Luke broke the mold, ditched college and joined the police force. Little brother was definitely not a chip off the old block.

Matt's thoughts skidded to a stop. Was his career part of the problem? Did Kristin regret giving up her marriage to a man who stayed in town and came home every day? Sure, a cop faced dangerous situations all the time, but usually on his home ground. Not five thousand miles away in a foreign country so that you never even knew what happened to the body.

"Dad's really pushing me to rejoin the unit," he said, trying to explore the issue.

"I noticed." She didn't move, didn't uncurl from her withdrawn position.

He would have to be more direct. "Maybe it's time I made a decision—change careers or go back to the one I had. What do you think?"

Kristin sighed and turned back to the window. "We've

had enough change, Matt. Let's just leave things the way they are.''

He didn't attempt to start another conversation for the rest of the drive.

BOONESBORO WAS a small town, mostly a cozy main street crossed by a few short lanes. The bed-and-breakfast inn—Chisholm's Rest—overlooked the village from atop a hill. Matt stopped the van in the circular driveway.

"This looks nice," Kristin said as they climbed the steps.

"I hope so." Matt rang the bell. "A guy in the unit recommended it. He used to live in the area."

She touched the petal of a bright red flower in the window box, but didn't reply.

The door opened and a tall woman peered through the screen door. "'Afternoon, folks. What can I do for you?''

"I'm Matt Brennan and this is my wife, Kristin. We made a reservation."

"Sure you did! Come right on in!" She pushed the door wide open. "I was wonderin' if you'd get here afore suppertime."

The hall of the house was dim and cool and smelled like roses. Kristin appreciated the gleam of dark woodwork and polished floors. "Your inn is lovely, Mrs...."

"Chisholm. Sadie Chisholm." She put out a hand to Kristin, and then Matt. "M'husband's George. He's asleep right now, but he'll be up in a little while. I was fixin' him a snack. You folks hungry?''

Before they could say yes or no, Sadie swept them down the hallway into a bright white kitchen. "Sit down at the table. I got some iced tea, here, and just a few sandwiches." She put a platter piled high with crustless triangles of bread and cheese in the center of the table. "And some cookies, when you're finished."

Kristin sipped from the tall glass of tea. A cold, sweet trickle soothed her throat and eased the headache behind her eyes. "This is wonderful, Mrs. Chisholm."

"Sadie, honey. Everybody calls me Sadie. You folks come up from Washington today, is that right?"

"Yes, ma'am." Matt had already finished two sandwiches. He took another. "We're going to Antietam tomorrow, then Gettysburg."

Arms crossed over her ample bosom, Sadie nodded. "We get lots of folks wantin' to see the battlefields. And when there's one of them reenactments, you won't find an empty bed this side of Philadelphia."

"Sadie?" A man's voice, lighter and thinner than hers, came from the hall. "Who in the world are you talkin' to?"

"It's the Brennans, George, come to stay."

The man stepped into the kitchen and looked them over. He was as thin as his wife was plump, with iron-gray hair and bright blue eyes. "Pleased to meet you." He shook hands with Matt and nodded at Kristin as he sat down across the table. "See you've got 'em fed already, Sadie."

"Well, the poor things looked half-starved, standin' out on the porch. Here's your tea, George." She rested a hand on his shoulder as she set the glass down. Observing the tenderness of a long-standing marriage, Kristin blinked against the sting of tears.

"Thanks, Mother." He helped himself to four sandwiches and began to eat. In between bites he asked the same question about where they'd come from and where they were going. "Country gets real crowded when they have them reenactments around here. Hardly room to walk.''

Kristin couldn't resist a glance at Matt, and found him hiding a smile, his blue eyes dancing.

George finished the tea and three more sandwiches, wiped his chin and stood up. ''Let me get you folks's bags to your room. I'll move your car round to the back while I'm at it.''

Matt got to his feet. ''That's okay, Mr. Chisholm— just show me where to park. I'll get the bags.''

''That's George, young man. You just sit here with your pretty wife a while.'' He started down the hallway. ''I'll be back in a jiffy.''

But Matt followed. ''George, you really don't have to—'' The screen door slapped shut. ''George!'' The door opened and closed again.

Chuckling, Sadie wiped her hands on a towel. ''Since that man of yours is well occupied, I'll show you to your room and give you a chance to put your feet up while I make us some dinner.''

Kristin wasn't sure she could eat anything else. ''Can't I help with dinner?''

''Nope.'' Sadie led the way up the staircase. ''All I got to do is set the chicken to frying and take out the biscuits.'' Opening a door, she ushered Kristin inside. ''You got time for a little nap while I do that.''

The room evoked another century, with lace curtains at the windows, rose-colored velvet on the armchairs and a crocheted canopy draped over the four-poster bed. Kristin stroked a finger over the mahogany dressing table. ''This is beautiful, Sadie.''

''Glad you like it.'' She turned back the blue-flowered quilt, fluffed the pillows and tucked the sheet more tightly. ''This was my mother's room, and her mother's afore her.''

Sadie obviously did not plan to leave the room until Kristin laid down. Feeling suddenly sleepy, she decided to cooperate. The sheets were cool, and the light dimmed as Sadie pulled down the shades.

''There now. We'll call you in plenty of time for supper. You rest easy—gotta take care of that baby you're carrying.'' She closed the door softly.

Kristin barely registered Sadie's exit. *A baby? What is she talking about? I'm not pregnant....*

She sat bolt upright on the bed. ''Am I?''

CHAPTER FIVE

JOY BLOOMED inside her like a perfect rose. Kristin closed her eyes and held the expectation close, feeling the tender weight of a baby in her arms, remembering the sweet smell, the soft skin, the tiny sounds. Matt would be so...

Surprised. Maybe even angry. He'd told his mother on Memorial Day that the girls were enough of a family for now. He wasn't ready for more children.

Jerked out of her celebration, she lay back against the pillows, then curled onto her side and pulled the blanket up to her shoulders. She couldn't really be pregnant. Kindly older women often believed all younger ones should be having babies. Sometimes they were right, sometimes not.

She thought backward over the last few months. Matt had spent a week away at the beginning of April, on maneuvers with the Army. He'd come back late on a Sunday night and slipped into their bed. Before she had fully awakened, her nightgown was gone and his warm hands were stroking her skin, driving her from dreams straight to the heart of desire. She'd taken him inside her without thought, without hesitation.

And, Kristin realized now, without preparation. She didn't remember noticing her monthly cycle had stopped...but she couldn't remember noticing it start, either. Chances were that Sadie Chisholm was right. Matt and Kristin Brennan had made a baby that night. *Another* baby.

"Oh, Lord." The tears she'd fought off and on all day long won the battle, and came pouring down her cheeks.

The future loomed ahead, suddenly more of a threat than a promise. She and Matt had lost most of their common ground. So far, this trip had done little to restore it. She felt more distant from him today than ever before. Even when he'd been missing, presumed dead, she'd carried his image with her, a part of her mind and soul. And she'd had Erin as a remembrance.

Now he was back, with wariness in his eyes and a guardrail around his heart. Babies brought enough strain to a family at the best of times. What would happen when everything was off balance?

Kristin didn't realize she'd fallen asleep until she felt a hand on her shoulder and heard Matt's voice. "Kris, want to wake up? Dinner's ready."

She felt the stiffness of dried tears on her face as she opened her eyes. Matt leaned over her, his gaze tender, a faint smile just visible on his mouth through the dark. "I'll make your apologies if you'd rather sleep," he said. "You do look tired. Sadie's been beating me up about that."

Sadie had *told* him? Kristin sat up quickly, forcing Matt to straighten. "W-what did she say?"

"Just that I ought to think more about you and less about a bunch of dead soldiers." He sat down beside her and put a hand on her knee. "And she's right. I've dragged you through enough history. We'll find other things to do while we're here—antique shops, national parks, whatever. We could go in to Philadelphia for a play, or some museums. What do you say?''

Tears threatened yet again. She remembered crying through the first three months of expecting Erin, and then Jenny. Luke would have recognized what was happening.

Thank God, Matt didn't. Yet.

''That's sweet, Matt. Maybe we can do some of that, too.'' She slipped out from underneath his hand and crossed to the dressing table. Opening her purse, she pulled out the comb and makeup she'd bought in Fredericksburg. ''But I think we should stick to your original plan. You've waited a long time to see these places.'' Kristin switched on the glass-shaded lamp and turned to face him, hoping the powder hid her secret as well as the tear tracks.

Matt studied her from across the room. Something had changed. He'd seen her just an hour ago, but he was now looking at a different woman. ''Everything okay?''

She gave him a smile—that tilt of her mouth that substituted for a real expression these days. ''Still a little groggy, I admit. What did you and George do while I was being lazy?''

''They've got a little pond out back. We watched a couple of worms do water aerobics.'' He felt more and more as if he were part of a play, saying lines written for him by someone else. ''We can walk down there after dinner. It's a pretty place.''

''Sounds good. Shall we go down and get some fried chicken?''

Matt stood up, feeling weary himself. ''After you. I hear there's strawberry shortcake for dessert.''

Kristin laughed as she left the room. ''I may be shopping for a size larger clothes before we leave.''

With Sadie and George at the table in the dining room, dinner conversation kept up a comfortable pace.

"Our three daughters still live in Georgia," Sadie volunteered as she passed the mashed potatoes. "George and me wanted to get out of the heat, so we headed north when he retired from the railroad. The girls and their fam'lies come at Christmas and the end of the summer. With all their younguns—nine grandkids in all—twice a year's plenty." She surveyed the table. "I'd better get another pitcher of tea. You folks go ahead."

As the door to the kitchen closed, George turned to Kristin. "Your man here says you two have little girls of your own."

Kristin smiled and helped herself to a piece of chicken. "Yes, sir. Erin's almost eight and Jenny's five."

"He'd showed me a pi'ture. Pretty things. Thinking about havin' another one, are you?"

Matt, watching, saw Kristin freeze, then swallow hard. After a measurable second, she finished cutting a slice of tomato. "Maybe in a little while. The girls are getting too old to be babied."

"And you've got a lot of babyin' left over, that it?"

She nodded, chewing.

George nodded, too. "My Sadie was that way. We had them three girls, but she said we were gonna try again, see if we could get us a boy."

"And did you?" Matt asked, as Kristin took a sip of tea.

"We did." Sadie came back into the dining room. "Andrew George Chisholm. Andy. Cutest little rascal there ever was. Always up to somethin'." She rounded the table, refilling glasses. "But he was born with Down's syndrome. His heart was weak, and it just plain wore out when he was nineteen.'' She dabbed at her eyes with her napkin. ''Ten years ago, that was. We still miss him, don't we, George?''

''Yes, Mother, we do.'' He helped himself to a couple more biscuits.

Kristin put her hand on Sadie's arm. ''I'm so sorry.''

The older woman smiled and patted Kristin's fingers. ''Lord bless you, we all are, missy. But Andy packed a lot of livin' into his time here. And I know I'll be seein' him again someday. We just have to wait, don't we, George?''

''That's right, Mother.''

Matt saw Kristin's stricken face, then looked into the hollow that suddenly filled his own chest. ''Sadie, would you mind if, after dessert, we used your phone for a long-distance call?''

Friday night
Dear Diary

Today we went on a picnic at the top of the mountains. Daddy said we were almost a mile higher than our house at home. Jenny was scared and didnt go close to the wall on the side of the road. I did. It was a long long way down.

After lunch Sarah read Jenny a story. Daddy and Buster and me went walkin in the woods. We saw a bunny and some birds and a snake. Daddy said it wouldnt bite. I was pretty glad. When we came out of the woods, Sarah and Jenny were asleep on the picnic blanket. We played ball with Buster til they woke up.

Then we went to a park with rides and stuff. We rode the train and the roller coaster. Sarah held

Buster and Jenny. Sarahs really nice. She doesnt get mad at Jenny for whyning. She doesnt put mushrooms in her spugetty sauce. If Daddy cant be married to Mommy Im glad hes married to Sarah.

The phone rang a minit ago and it was Mommy. Shes in Marlund at a nice ladys house. I told her about the castle we saw. That was cool. And the dinosaur museum. And the rock museum and the train. Jenny started cryin as soon as she said hello to Mommy. She wouldnt let Sarah hold her. Only Daddy. Mommy said she has a cold. Her nose is all stuffy and she talks ruff. I said I hope she feels better.

Daddy talked to her and to Daddy Matt. Then I said goodby to Mommy. Im almost eight and I cant be a baby like Jenny. But I have a hurt inside, like bein afraid when I jump off the divin board only not the same. I think its time to go home. Good Night.

Your friend
Erin Elena Brennan

KRISTIN LAY AWAKE in the darkness of Sadie Chisholm's best bedroom, shivering. She could hear Jenny's sobs in the silence. Her throat closed and her eyes filled. Again.

Beside her, Matt rolled over and put a hand on her arm.

"Kris, you're going to make yourself sick like this. Let me hold you."

She stiffened as he slipped an arm under her head and the other around her waist to pull her back against him. If Sadie was right—and Kristin thought she was—there was a baby under his hand when he did that. She should tell him. Tell him right now.

A long time later, Kristin was still silent, still tense. The words wouldn't come. All she could think about was Jenny. And Erin's quiet little voice. Luke had assured her things were going fine. But her girls had to be hurting as much as she was. They belonged together.

Matt kissed the top of her head. "You know, when I was in Africa, there were certain guards I stayed awake for. If they found you asleep, they got their fun kicking you awake. Or dumping water and garbage over you."

She squeezed her eyes shut. "Matt, you don't have to…"

"Ssh. That's over." His hand smoothed her hair back from her face. "It wasn't so bad during the day, but when they worked the night shift, I struggled to keep my eyes open. So I'd sit there and stare at the western wall. I imagined I could look through it, all the way across the ocean to Myrtle Beach and into your room. I'd watch you sleeping, and in my mind I'd crawl in behind you, like this, and just hold you until dawn. I didn't want to go to sleep then, didn't want to miss the chance to be with you." He gave a slight laugh. "Worked every time."

And while he was imagining them lying together, Kristin reminded herself, she had been married to his brother, starting a new family. She'd endured her own sleepless nights, of course, her own brand of nightmares. After two years of a platonic marriage, those horrible dreams had finally driven her into Luke's arms, where she'd found a measure of comfort, a chance to rest. And where Jenny had been conceived.

Whatever Matt might think, Jenny was not a mistake. Neither was Erin, nor the baby Kristin felt sure was growing inside her. And yet the four of them seemed to be fighting each other, and forcing her to choose sides. How long could she ignore Matt's need for the truth in order to protect Erin from the hurt that truth would bring? Erin and Jenny would have trouble adjusting to the idea of yet another new person taking their mother's attention. Should she sacrifice them...or the child yet to be born?

Like a spear of iron through her chest, she heard that last thought.

Oh my God. I can't believe it even crossed my mind.

She had to stop thinking. Had to stop considering the options, weighing the alternatives. She would go crazy. She would make yet another hurtful, disastrous mistake.

"Matt." She turned in his arms, her mouth seeking his. After a second of surprise, his arms tightened and his kiss deepened. Gratefully, Kristin gave herself over once again to the distraction of desire.

THE SUN SHONE on Antietam Battlefield, on mile after mile of gentle green slopes, wooden fences, shady stands of trees. Matt drew imaginary lines of battle on their picnic blanket, explaining the course of the battle.

"You make it sound simple," Kristin said finally. "Maybe if I'd had you for American history in high school, I might have learned something."

"Or you might just have gotten me into trouble as the teacher who ran away with his underage student." He leaned over to kiss her. "School boards tend to frown on that kind of thing."

She linked her arms behind his neck. "I was chubby, and I had braces in high school."

"And I'm Robert E. Lee." He got to his feet, reached down and pulled his wife to hers. "I remember hearing

Luke talk about his friend Kristin, back when he was in high school. 'Fox' was the term I believe he used.''

"Oh, he did not." She was blushing—the color in her cheeks was nice to see.

"Sure he did. In fact, we had to have a talk about that before I took you out the very first time. I didn't want to break up something he had going."

"But we never—"

She stopped, and Matt saw awareness flood into her eyes—the knowledge that she and Luke had, in fact, been together, as husband and wife, as parents, as lovers.

Damn. There didn't seem to be anything they could talk about that wouldn't lead back to exactly the subjects they wanted to avoid.

Maybe now was the time to settle this once and for all.

He laid his palm along the line of her jaw. "Kris, stop worrying about the past."

She dropped her gaze, but didn't reply.

With a gentle pressure, Matt forced her to look at him. "I was mad, when I got home from Africa. Mad…and jealous as hell. But that's over. You did the right thing, marrying Luke."

As she stared up at him, her wide eyes filled with tears.

"You had a baby to take care of. You gave her a dad who loved her. I'm slow, but I have realized that much. Don't punish yourself anymore."

"Erin…"

"We'll tell her together, one day soon. I know we can't rush it. I've been a jerk about that, too. I'm pretty amazed you've put up with me, as a matter of fact."

He put his arms around her and drew her close, felt her tears wet his shirt. This was as close as he could come to asking the questions that tortured him—Why are you still with me? I'm not the same man I was before Africa. Do you love me…or the memory of the man I was?

He was afraid to put that question into words.

THE PHONE RANG at the Chisholms' that night while they still sat at the dinner table listening to George's railroad stories. Sadie answered the call, then poked her head around the doorway. "Kristin, Sarah Brennan wants to talk with you."

She felt suddenly sick. Sarah and Luke wouldn't call unless something was wrong. Her hand shook as she took the receiver. "Hello?"

"Kristin, it's Sarah. Don't be upset—everything's okay with the girls. But we wanted to tell you that we're heading back home tomorrow."

Her brief moment of relief died. "Is somebody sick?"

"No, oh no. But…well, Jenny's not happy. Erin's dragging a little bit, too. Maybe we should have realized ahead of time that two weeks would be too long for them."

Kristin *had* known. And yet she'd let her need to settle things with Matt override her knowledge of her daughters. "I'm sorry you won't get to stay."

"We've had a great week, but I won't mind being at home again, myself. I don't want you and Matt to hurry straight back, though. I think Jenny will feel better in her own room at our house, with her own bed and all her toys. We'll be glad for them to stay with us until you finish your trip. Are you and Matt…having a good time?"

"Of course." The automatic reply covered her feverish

thoughts. If they left tonight… "When are you planning to be home?"

"Tomorrow evening. But please, Kristin, don't rush. You two need this time together."

Matt's hands came to rest on her shoulders. She hadn't even realized he was there behind her. "I know. We'll talk about what to do and leave a message on your machine about when we'll be back. Can I talk to Jenny?"

"Luke took them to the pool while I spoke to you. We can call back when they come in."

"No, that's okay." The girls would probably get upset. They would see each other tomorrow night. The next morning at the latest. "Y'all have a safe trip home."

"You, too. We'll see you soon."

The phone went dead. Kristin stood gripping the handset, willing her heartbeat to slow down, trying to keep her eyes dry.

Matt came around to face her. "What's wrong?"

"Luke and Sarah are taking the girls home tomorrow." She explained what Sarah had said. "I'm sure she's right. Just being back where she's comfortable will make Jenny feel better."

When she looked up, Matt was watching her with an expression she couldn't interpret. Holding his gaze, she saw him come to a decision.

He brushed back her bangs with his fingertips. "I think we should go home tomorrow, too."

Irrationally, she protested. "But your trip—"

"Will wait for another time. Gettysburg hasn't fallen into the ocean in over a hundred years. It'll still be here next fall, or next summer…whenever I get there. Erin and Jenny are more important."

Than what? Than battlefields and monuments, sure.

But were the groundless fears of two little girls worth more than her marriage?

Kristin didn't know the answer, couldn't consider the right thing to do. She could only follow her heart.

"Thank you." She reached up and kissed his cheek. "I do think this will be for the best."

As they went back to finish dinner, she realized her priorities had now been set. Her daughters came first.

She could only wonder if doing her best for them would destroy her relationship with Matt.

Sunday
Dear Diary,

We didnt stay in the mountains as long as we were sposed to. Jenny was bein real whyny, and she didnt want to eat. I was nice to her. I let her sleep with me and Buster and I read her stories and made her peanut butter sanwitches just like Mommy does. Nothin helped.

So now we are drivin home. Mommy won't be there. She and Daddy Matt are still on vakashun. Ill be glad when I can see her. Sarah is nice. I love bein with Daddy.

But Mommy just kinda makes things right.

Your friend
Erin Elena Brennan

MATT DROVE the eight hours from Maryland to Myrtle Beach as fast as legally possible. Beside him, Kristin seemed to wind tighter and tighter the farther south they got. She barely ate the lunch they stopped for in Richmond. She didn't fall asleep at any point, though Matt knew she hadn't slept much the night before, because he hadn't, either. They'd waited through the darkness side by side, locked separately into their own thoughts.

He really didn't mind cutting the trip short. Kris would have been miserable knowing the girls were home and she wasn't. He still had a few days of leave left—the four of them could have some fun together. A real family vacation.

If he was lucky. Very lucky.

When they finally pulled up on the curb in front of Luke and Sarah's house, they found luggage piled on the driveway. The travelers couldn't have been home too long, themselves.

"Mommy!" Jenny flew out the front door and across the grass, straight into Kristin's hold. Arms tight around her mother's neck, she burst into tears.

Luke and Erin stepped outside, and in another second, Erin was locked onto Kristin, too. Keeping his brain carefully empty, Matt crossed the front lawn to meet Luke on the driveway.

His younger brother saw too much. The understanding in his eyes was almost more than Matt could take.

But Luke didn't address the issue. "How was your trip home? Much traffic?" He bent to grab the handles of an ice chest. Matt picked up two of the clothes bags and followed him into the house.

"Not too bad, until we got off the interstate."

"Believe me, the traffic coming into town was light compared to what we drove through on I-40. Between construction and crazy drivers, getting here in one piece was a real challenge."

Matt laughed—sort of. "Don't let Kris hear you say that. She'll never let them get into a car again."

"She's not that unreasonable." Luke set the cooler beside the kitchen sink.

"She wasn't, before this trip." He realized he was discussing his wife with her ex-husband. That he was, in fact, close to admitting how unhappy Kristin seemed to be these days.

Wrong. Matt set the bags on the floor out of the traffic path. "But everything will settle down again now that we're all home. How's Sarah?"

"She's just fine," Sarah said, coming out of the door to the back hallway. "But I wish you hadn't cut your trip short."

"No problem. We've seen enough battlefields and museums to hold us for a while."

They all turned toward the front door as Erin came into the house, followed by Kristin carrying Jenny.

"Well, munchkins." Luke tilted his head, surveying them. "Does this mean you're not spending the night here after all?"

Jenny hid her face against Kristin's neck.

Erin nodded. "You got us all week, Daddy. It's Mommy's turn." After a beat, she added, "And Daddy Matt's."

"Fair enough. We'll get your stuff into the other car and you'll be ready to roll."

Matt bit down on his automatic reaction to having his brother directing the situation. "Sounds good." He passed Erin on his way outside, and allowed himself to brush his hand over the top of her head. "Thanks, Erin."

She flushed and dropped her chin. With a pat on Kristin's shoulder, he followed Luke outside to transfer his *family's* belongings so he could get them all home.

Kristin shifted Jenny on her hip, then looked at Sarah.

"I hope this isn't a problem. Matt thought we should come back."

The other woman's smile looked a little sad. "Not for us. I'm sure the girls will be glad to get settled right away. And they're welcome here anytime. You know that, right, Erin?"

"Right." But her grip on Kristin's hand was tight. "We get to have two moms and two dads. Most kids don't have that many."

Sarah gestured to a chair. "Do you want to sit down for a few minutes? We can talk about what we saw on our different trips."

Fighting down the impulse to rush out the door and get her daughters home as fast as possible, Kristin sat. "We spent our anniversary night in Washington, D.C., at a very fancy hotel," she said. "That was really special."

"As fancy as the one at Walt Disney World?" Erin asked.

"Fancier. Can you imagine?" She could tell by the dead weight on her arm that Jenny had fallen asleep.

"The castle we saw was pretty fancy, too. We ate lunch there." Erin went on to describe their trip in great detail. But Sarah didn't say much. She would be tired, of course, at this stage in her pregnancy, after having the girls all week. Kristin felt more than a little worn out, herself. And she was taking these two high-energy children home with her! No one would expect her to be exhausted by their demands, though. She couldn't hope to be pampered or taken care of. She would step right back into her regular duties taking care of everyone else.

Because no one knew about *her* new baby.

CHAPTER SIX

A WEEK AFTER the abrupt end of their vacation, Kristin knelt to tie Jenny's soccer shoe, made sure her leg pads were pulled up, then gave her a smile. "You're ready to play."

Her daughter stared at her with doubt in her big brown eyes.

"Come on, Jenny." Erin stood at the edge of the soccer field, hands on her hips. "Practice is startin'!"

The little girl's thumb crept toward her pouting mouth.

"You go on, Erin," Kristin called. "I'll walk her to her team." Standing, she took Jenny's hand. "Let's go see what they're doing, okay?"

The youngest players were standing in a circle, kicking a ball across and back. The coach glanced at Jenny and waved. "Come play with us, Jen!"

Kristin got down on Jenny's level again. "Remember how you wanted to play, like Erin does? Don't you want to give it a try?"

Jenny stuck her thumb in her mouth and shook her head.

"Okay. We'll sit and watch." She found an empty space on the bleachers, helped Jenny to climb, then sat down with the little girl in her lap. The tension left Jenny's body immediately. She swung her feet gently, obviously happy with the way things had turned out.

Kristin rested her chin on her daughter's blond head and closed her eyes.

So tired.

She could have fallen asleep on the wooden bench, given half the chance. If Jenny had wanted to play with the rest of the five-year-olds, Kristin might have gone back to the car and taken a nap. An hour with her eyes closed would be heaven.

"What have we got here?" Matt's voice came from right beside the bleachers. "You don't want to play, Jenny?"

Kristin lifted her head as Jenny shook hers. "I think the idea of imitating big sister was more appealing than the fact."

He grinned. "Yeah, that happens a lot. What if I went out with you, Jenny? Would you play if I played, too?"

Jenny stared up at him. Matt waited patiently, didn't push or prod. He really was a good father.

Finally, Jenny made her decision. She wiggled down off Kristin's lap, took Matt's hand and marched onto the soccer field. Matt glanced back at Kristin, and she gave him a thumbs-up sign. Then she settled as comfortably as she could to watch.

Out in the middle of the field, Erin's team ran through a series of demanding drills. Boys and girls played together, so Erin had learned to be aggressive in order to compete successfully. She was often the high scorer of their Saturday-morning matches.

Chin on her hands and elbows on her knees, Kristin let her eyelids droop. Shouts of children, occasional laughter, a whistle now and then—familiar soccer sounds blended with a pleasant breeze off the ocean, making her even drowsier. Maybe they would stop at a hamburger place for dinner on the way home. She could spend the evening finishing up laundry…or doing nothing more strenuous than reading the girls a story. They were well into a "Little House" book—

"Kris!"

At Matt's shout, she snapped her eyes open. The first thing she saw was a clump of children in the center of the field, then Matt carrying Jenny and running in that direction.

Erin?

Kristin raced across the grass with her heart standing still in her chest. Trying to be gentle, she eased the children out of the way until she could see Erin's coach kneeling on the ground, with Erin curled up in a ball in front of him.

"Erin, love?" She dropped to her knees and put a hand on Erin's hip. "Erin? Can you say something?"

The coach brushed back Erin's hair. "She tripped just as Greg kicked at the ball, and he got her in the stomach instead."

Matt knelt at Erin's head, with Jenny standing beside him. "Has she moved?"

Kristin bit her lip when the coach shook his head. "Erin, sweetie, please. Let us help you. Where are you hurt?"

Finally, Erin's chin lifted. "My tummy," she gasped, then curled back into a ball.

"Okay." Matt moved in closer. "I'm gonna pick you up, Erin, and get you off the field. Don't worry about moving." He looked at Kristin. "You bring Jenny."

She nodded. The circle widened as the children backed up. Matt lifted Erin and got to his feet in one easy movement, without changing the little girl's position at all.

Kristin swung Jenny onto her hip and followed him to the van, using the remote key to open the door just as Matt got there.

By the time she reached them, Erin had uncurled a little bit as she lay on the back seat. Her face was pale, though, and tears trembled on her lashes. "That hurt," she whispered.

"I bet." Matt was on his knees by the seat. "Can you straighten a little bit more?" Erin dropped her knees another few inches. "How's your breathing?"

She winced when she took a deep breath. But the second one was easier. "Okay." Her voice had strengthened.

In another few minutes she was sitting up and talking. "Can I go back to practice now?"

Kristin took a quick breath of her own. "I don't think that's a good idea. Why don't we go on home for today?"

Erin frowned. "I'm fine, Mommy. I want to play."

When Kristin looked at Matt, he shrugged. "If she feels okay, I'd say let her play. But take it a little easy, Erin."

"Uh-huh." She hopped off the step of the van, dashed toward the field, leaped over the low chain border and joined the team.

With Jenny still locked around her neck, Kristin sat down on the floor of the van. "Do you think she's all right?"

Matt climbed out and stood watching the practice. "I think so. She's moving okay. We'll keep an eye on her tonight."

Kristin was reassured by Erin's willingness to get back in the game, and even more so by her appetite at dinner.

Bath time went smoothly, though she flinched from the ugly bruise forming underneath Erin's ribs. She read the girls a chapter of their book, tucked them in, kissed each good-night.

Then she stood for a few minutes outside their rooms, listening to the peace. And realizing—again—that she must tell Matt about the new baby. Now. Nothing would improve if she waited.

When she went down to the family room, though, she found her husband asleep on the couch, a military manual of some kind propped on his chest. She knew he hadn't been sleeping well. Neither of them had, since the trip last week. While their relationship seemed smooth on the surface, the currents of doubt and misunderstanding below affected them both.

Kristin sat down in the recliner with one leg crossed underneath her and her arms folded. Head back, she let her eyes drift shut. From there, sleep was a very short trip.

Until a cold hand closed over her wrist. "Mommy?"

She jerked her head toward the voice. Her vision blurred when she opened her eyes, then slowly cleared.

"Mommy, I don't feel good." Erin had one arm over her waist. "My tummy hurts."

"Come here, love. Let me see." Erin climbed into her lap as Matt sat up on the couch. One touch of a palm on the girl's forehead drove Kristin's heart into a pounding beat.

Cold, damp skin, pale beneath the tan. Fast, panting breaths. Erin's whole body trembled.

When Kristin looked up, Matt was leaning over them. He met her eyes, nodded, and went to the kitchen.

Kristin drew Erin back against her chest. "You know,

I think we should get a doctor to check out this stomachache of yours. There might be some medicine we can get to make you feel better.''

Erin shook her head. "Don't want to." She sounded winded, as if she'd run a long race.

Matt came across the room. "Dr. Petersen's not on call tonight. The answering service said we should go to the E.R.''

"What's that?''

"The hospital, love." Kristin smoothed her hair. "When you get sick at night, that's the easiest place to find a doctor.''

Erin started to cry, silently, helplessly. "Do I hafta get dressed?''

"Nope." Matt reached down and gently took Erin in his arms. "It's a nice warm night and you get to go for a drive in your pajamas. When I was little, we lived one place where we could go to the movies in our pajamas.''

"Huh?''

"You drove your car in and parked and watched the movie without getting out." He shouldered his way out the door while Kristin went up to get Jenny. When she reached the car, Matt had buckled Erin into the center of the second seat. "I figured you could ride next to her.'' He put Jenny in the car seat while Kristin climbed in next to Erin for the drive through the hot summer night. They got to the hospital in just a few minutes.

But Erin was already clearly worse. She lay listlessly against Matt's chest when he picked her up. Holding Jenny tight against her breast, Kristin followed them into the emergency room.

The woman at the desk took a look at Erin and stood up. "I'll get a doctor.''

In minutes there was a stretcher and people coaxing Erin to lie down, then taking her through a double swinging door. Erin didn't say anything at all. Kristin wanted to cry. But her tears had frozen.

"Come sit down." Matt put an arm around Kristin's shoulders and led her to a chair in the emptiest part of the waiting room. She seemed to be holding herself upright by sheer force of will.

And he couldn't promise everything…anything… would be okay. Erin was in bad shape. He should have taken her to the hospital right after she got kicked. He'd thought she was fine, since she wanted to go back into the game…but he'd been wrong. Stupidly, blindly, criminally wrong.

Kristin raised her head. "Luke."

He didn't understand the word at first. When he did, he felt the floor drop out from underneath him. "What's that, Kris?"

"We should call Luke. He'll want to be here if he can."

"Sure." Matt stared blindly in front of him for a second. Then his brain kicked in. "I'll go get the cell phone from the car. I'll be right back."

She nodded, then buried her face in Jenny's hair.

He strode out to the car as fast as he could, grabbed the phone and dialed as he went back into the hospital.

Sarah answered in a sleepy voice. "H'llo?"

"Sorry to wake you up, Sarah. It's Matt. Is Luke there?"

"He went to work about an hour ago." She woke up a little more. "What's wrong?"

"Erin…" He had to clear his throat. "Erin got kicked

at soccer this afternoon. She started feeling bad about ten. We're at the hospital.''

''Oh, God, Matt.'' She drew a deep, shuddering breath. ''Luke will want to know. I can call him—''

''That's okay, Sarah. I'll call the station.'' He sat down next to Kristin again. She hadn't moved. Thankfully, Jenny had barely waked up at all. ''You go back to sleep.''

''Matt…'' Sarah gave a gasping laugh. ''Tell Luke I'll meet him there.'' She hung up before he could say anything else.

He dialed information to get the number at Luke's precinct headquarters. Lieutenant Corporal Brennan had just checked in and was still in the building.

''Brennan.''

''Luke, it's me.''

''What's wrong?''

Matt explained again, this time feeling Kristin flinch beside him as he went over the accident. ''Sarah said to tell you she'd meet you here.''

''I'll get my shift covered. See you shortly.''

The call disconnected. Matt glanced at Kristin. ''He's on his way.''

White-faced, she nodded. ''We probably ought to call my mom and dad…they can come get Jenny and put her to bed.''

''Good idea.'' He didn't suggest his parents—he doubted his mother would be much comfort in a situation like this.

Irene and Frank Jennings had come and gone—taking a whimpering Jenny with them—before they received a report on Erin from a small, slight man in green scrubs. ''Mr. and Mrs. Brennan? I'm Dr. Walsh.''

Matt kept his hand under Kristin's elbow as they both stood. "How is she?"

The doctor gestured toward the double doors. "Let's go back here."

And with that invitation, Matt knew the news was going to be bad.

The doctor leaned against the wall in the back hallway, arms crossed over his chest. "All indications are that Erin's spleen was torn with that kick this afternoon. We're stabilizing her now. We need permission from you for blood tests, a CT scan and a vaccine against pneumonia. The CT scan will tell us how bad the bleeding is and then we'll know if we need to take her to surgery."

"Can I see her?" Kris's voice was small.

Walsh smiled gently. "Not just now. We're still working. Nurse Lee has the paperwork, and I'll talk to you again when we know what's going on."

They were led to a small room with a table and chairs and handed a sheaf of papers. The nurse sat down with them. "I'll go over these with you." She explained the CT scan and its reasons, then pointed to a bottom line. "If you'll sign here, Mr. Brennan, as Erin's legal guardian..."

"I'll sign," Kristin said. She took the pen from Nurse Lee's hand and turned the paper toward herself. "Here?"

"Um, yes."

Kristin signed the rest of the permission forms without comment. Matt sat back in his chair and thought about not being his own daughter's legal guardian.

Footsteps approached on the tile floor outside the room. The receptionist peeked in. "Officer Brennan is here."

Luke and Sarah came through the doorway. Sarah

knelt beside Kristin's chair. "I'm so sorry. What can we do?"

"We're signing some papers." Kristin rubbed her eyes. "They're going to get a CT scan. Her spleen may be ruptured."

Luke muttered a rude word. "When did she start feeling bad?"

Matt bit back on an urge to be defensive. "She was fine until about ten. We brought her over as soon as we realized something was wrong."

Sarah nodded. "Sometimes it does take a while. Back when I was a photo journalist, a reporter I knew was fine for several days before he realized he needed medical attention."

Kristin's smile was shaky. "The doctor said they would know from the scan whether she would need surgery." She slid the stack of papers across the table to Nurse Lee.

"Thank you." The slim young woman got to her feet. "I'll get these to all the right people. If you'll go back out into the waiting room, someone will find you just as soon as a decision has been made."

As she left the room, Sarah put an arm around Kristin's shoulders. "How about a trip to the rest room?"

On her feet, Kristin nodded. "That's a good idea." She looked toward Matt for a moment, and in her eyes was the fear she tried to control. "I'll be back in just a minute."

He took her hand. "Sure. Take your time."

Out in the waiting room, he and Luke sat across from each other on facing rows of chairs. Matt propped his elbows on his knees and rubbed his face. "What a nightmare."

"Sick kids break your heart."

"I'm wondering why people put themselves through this."

Luke laughed a little. "Something to do with populating the planet?"

"Yeah, but how about limiting your exposure? We've only got two little girls to worry about. If there were more…" Matt shook his head. "I don't think I could take it."

"But there will be, soon. Right, Sarah Rose?"

Matt looked up and saw that Kristin and Sarah had returned. Sarah sat down in the curve of Luke's arm. "Right." Sarah looked at Matt. "You worry about children, of course. But I have to believe the love and joy they give are worth that worry."

Kristin sat down without saying anything. She stared down at her hands as she twisted the diamond engagement ring she wore around and around on her finger.

Matt put his hand on her arm. "Hey. Are you okay?"

"I'm trying." She looked at him, but her eyes didn't seem to see his face.

He would have held her hand, but as he reached out she got to her feet. "I need to stand up for a while. No—" She shook her head as he started to rise. "No, don't get up. I'm just going to stand at the window. I'll be fine." With her arms folded, she went to the window to stare into darkness.

Some unmeasurable time later, Dr. Walsh crossed the waiting room. "Mr. Brennan?" Matt and Luke stood up. Kristin returned from the window.

"How is she?" Matt asked.

Walsh nodded. "Stable enough. The CT scan shows what I expected—blood in the space around her spleen.

Sometimes we watch these for a while, say twelve hours, to see if the bleeding will resolve on its own. But—''

''Not Erin?'' Matt finished.

''No. We're prepping her for surgery now. I believe we'll be able to repair the spleen instead of removing it. But I think it's best if we go ahead and fix the damage rather than wait for healing.''

Kristin took a shaking breath. ''Can we see her... before?''

The doctor smiled. ''Sure. Come on back.'' When all four of them started to follow him, he stopped. ''I think only her parents should see her now. She can have visitors after she wakes up.''

Aware of Kristin's gaze on his face, Matt looked at his brother. The conflict of the last four years lay between them... *Whose daughter is she?* He knew what *he* wanted. He knew what Erin would want.

''You go on,'' he said to Luke, stepping back. ''I'll wait with Sarah.''

Dr. Walsh's eyebrows wrinkled and his tired eyes asked a question. But he only nodded. ''Fine. This way.'' He led Kristin and Luke back through the double doors.

Matt went to stand at the window. He discovered that the only thing he could see was a reflection of the room behind him. Sarah approached, and slipped her arm around his waist.

''That was good of you,'' she said. ''Luke would have let you go in.''

''Erin will want to see him.'' His throat hurt, saying the words.

''She'll change over time.''

''We're working on four years, Sarah.'' He hesitated,

then voiced the agony in his mind. "And we might have run out of time."

"No, Matt. Don't think that way. She's going to be fine again in just a few days. Dr. Walsh seemed confident."

"I don't know. This branch of the Brennans hasn't been getting many good breaks recently."

"So you deserve a big one. Erin's recovery will be that break." Her arm dropped away. "They're back."

Kristin was white. Luke had his arm around her shoulders. Matt swallowed his fear and went to his wife's side. "How is she?"

"Groggy," Luke answered. "But she knew who we were. And she said the nurses had promised her ice cream when she woke up." His grin looked forced.

"The surgery waiting room is on the third floor," Kristin said quietly. "They'll look for us there if…when it's over."

Matt put his hand on her back and moved her out from under Luke's hold, directing her toward the elevator. "Let's go," he said as firmly as he could.

No one else spoke for a very long time.

LIKE A NIGHTMARE, the hours of Erin's surgery seemed disjointed, confused. Kristin kept glancing at her watch, expecting time to have passed, and finding it hadn't. The four of them were the only people in the waiting room. They'd agreed not to wake the Colonel and Mrs. Brennan until they knew definite results.

Jenny was sleeping again, Kristin's mother reported when called. God would be on Erin's side.

Kristin prayed her mother was right.

At 3:00 a.m. Dr. Walsh came to find them. His face

was drained of all color and energy, but he smiled. "Erin came through very well. She's in recovery, and you can see her in an hour or so."

Wiping tears off her cheeks, Kristin smiled at him. "Thank you so much."

Beside her, Matt extended his hand. "We really appreciate your help."

Walsh nodded. "My pleasure. Let's sit down a minute and I'll explain what we've done."

When Sarah and Luke joined them, Dr. Walsh put up a hand. "I know this isn't my business, but I'm confused. Who is Erin's father?"

Matt's fingers around Kristin's stiffened.

After a long pause, Luke said, "Kristin and I are divorced. Matt is Kristin's husband, and Sarah is my wife. In a way, Erin has four parents."

"We're all concerned." Matt's voice was gruff.

"Okay." The doctor relaxed into his chair. "Erin's spleen was damaged—a fairly deep wound. She'd had a lot of bleeding into her abdomen. We cleaned all the blood out, repaired the tear in the spleen and gave her two units of blood to replace what she'd lost."

Fear poured into Kristin like an icy river. "A transfusion? You gave her a transfusion?"

His expression became wary. "Yes. You gave us permission with your signature."

"But isn't that dangerous these days?"

"The blood supply is monitored very closely and screened for any possible risk of disease. We give transfusions all the time. You don't need to worry about that."

Matt's hand tightened. "What do we need to worry about?"

"We're going to keep Erin a few days to monitor the

function of her spleen and her overall condition. I fully expect her to recover completely. There's a small chance the spleen won't perform well, and if that's the case, we'll go back in and remove it. But I really don't think that will be necessary.''

He got to his feet. ''Someone can stay in her room with her tonight, and every night, if she's more comfortable.'' He glanced from Luke to Sarah to Matt to Kristin. ''I'll leave it up to you to decide who that'll be.''

As he turned toward the door, a nurse stepped into the waiting room. ''Erin is awake, Doctor. She'd like to see her mom.''

Dr. Walsh nodded. ''Sounds like a good idea. You folks take care.'' He left before they could thank him again.

Kristin looked at Matt, and he grinned. ''You'd better get in there.''

''Give her our love,'' Sarah added.

Luke made a thumbs-up sign. ''Tell her I'll see her tomorrow morning.''

With a nod, Kristin followed the nurse down the hallway. She wasn't sure she'd be able to speak when she finally reached Erin. Between fear and gratitude and exhaustion, she felt as though she might break into pieces if she did anything besides breathe.

In the recovery room, Erin lay on a stretcher, covered with blankets and pink sheets. At the sight, Kristin recovered her ability to talk. ''Hello, love.'' She took Erin's free hand. ''How do you feel?''

Erin opened heavy eyes. ''Sleepy. My tummy still hurts. I thought you said I could have medicine, Mommy.''

''You can.'' The nurse stepped over and adjusted one

of the IV lines. "At least it hurts for a different reason now. The doctor fixed up the part that got torn."

"My s-sp-spleen." Erin nodded. "He told me about what it does."

"So now all you have to do is go to sleep. When you wake up, you'll feel a whole bunch better."

Erin's hand clutched hers. "Are you going home?" Her voice held an edge of panic.

"No, no. I'll be right here all night long. I promise. Right beside your bed."

The child's hand relaxed. "Okay. Where's Jenny?"

"She's with Grandma Irene and Granddaddy Frank. I'll make sure they know you're getting better."

"Is Daddy here?" Her eyes drifted shut, and she opened them with difficulty.

Kristin bit her lip. She knew Erin meant Luke. "Luke and Matt are both here, sweetie."

"Can I—" Erin yawned.

Supplying the answer to Erin's question was beyond Kristin's ability at this point. "Luke said he'll see you in the morning. Matt will go home and bring back some of your books, first thing."

"'Kay." With her next breath, Erin was fast asleep.

Kristin sat by the bed, not thinking beyond the moment and the chance to watch her little girl sleep. Lying so still, with the bright blue eyes closed, Erin looked less like Matt. She reminded Kristin of herself as a child— the rounded cheeks, the blond hair, the turned-up nose.

But where the pictures in her mother's albums featured a laughing, carefree eight-year-old, Kristin's photographs of Erin showed a serious, slightly detached little girl. So much had happened to Erin in just a few years, so many changes. Would she grow up trusting in the goodness of life?

"Mrs. Brennan?" The nurse put a hand on her shoulder. "We're going to take Erin to her room. Number 320. Give us a few minutes and then you can join her."

Out in the hallway again, Kristin hardly knew what to do. The floor felt uneven beneath her feet, and she had to walk very carefully. She made it back to the waiting room without falling, and leaned against the door frame to stay standing.

Matt had been pacing. He turned, saw her, and came straight across the room. "Is she okay? Are *you* okay?"

Kristin managed a nod. "They're taking her to a room." She cleared her throat to give her voice some sound. "I told her I'd stay the night. And that you'd bring some of her books tomorrow morning."

"Sure. But I'll stay with you until she wakes up again."

"Um…" She put a hand to her aching head. "I don't know if that's allowed. Maybe only one of us can stay." Looking beyond him, she saw Luke and Sarah. "I told her you'd see her tomorrow."

Sarah came over. "Then we'll clear out and do just that." She closed Kristin in a hug. "Take care of yourself," she whispered.

Luke lifted his hand in salute and they left.

Alone with Matt, Kristin wanted to lean into his chest and let go of the sobs she held in her throat. She longed for his arms around her, his low voice soothing her fears, his warmth making her warm again. He was her husband, and she needed him.

But he was also the man she'd heard earlier tonight talk about "limiting your exposure" to the worry chil-

dren caused. Living with Erin and Jenny, dealing with
the problems they posed, was as much as Matt could
handle. Kristin didn't blame him. The girls had been ret-
icent at the very best of times. That wasn't their fault, of
course. Her daughters had been happy with the life she
and Luke had made for them. They had never understood
the need for change. And they saw Matt as the agent of
that change.

But her daughters were wrong. Kristin had engineered
the chaos in their lives. Instead of making the best of a
wonderful man and a lovely family, she'd let old emotions eat at her, tearing away the happiness she'd enjoyed. Given the resurrection of her dead love, she'd
somehow thought she could resurrect all their dead
dreams. A more selfish, shortsighted goal would be hard
to find.

And so Kristin didn't lean into Matt, didn't seek solace
in his arms. She straightened up and put every ounce of
energy she had left into her voice. "I really don't think
you need to stay the night. You go home and get some
sleep, stop by to see Jenny tomorrow morning, and then
bring Erin her books."

His big warm hands closed on her shoulders. "You're
exhausted. You should be the one who gets some sleep."

"I will." She turned out of his grip and led the way
down the hall to room 320. The door was ajar, and she
stepped inside. "See, there's a nice recliner, but only one.
I promised Erin I'd be here all night. You go home and
rest. Oh, and call your parents tomorrow morning.
They'll be angry we didn't let them know tonight."

"That's the truth." He stood with his hands on his
hips for a minute, staring at Erin, and then at Kristin.

Finally, he shook his head. "I hate leaving you here alone. Call me if you want to talk."

"I will." She closed her eyes as he stepped near enough to bend for a kiss. It was a sweet kiss, comfortable, gentle, supportive. This time she knew she was going to cry.

"Good night," Matt whispered. "Give Erin part of that kiss for me."

He left just before the tears dropped onto her cheeks. Kristin fumbled to the recliner, sat down with her elbows on her knees and her face in her hands, and gave in to the anguish she'd held in check.

Crying solved absolutely nothing. But at least it wore her out enough to sleep.

CHAPTER SEVEN

THE COLONEL AND Mrs. Brennan, early risers, arrived at the door to Erin's hospital room before nine o'clock. "What have we here, young lady?" The Colonel went to sit on Erin's bed. "You're supposed to stay out of the way when somebody kicks the ball!"

"D.J. tripped me," Erin muttered. "That's the reason I fell."

As Kristin pushed herself out of the recliner, Elena Brennan confronted her. "I have always thought soccer a dangerous game for little girls." She didn't bother to lower her voice. "Perhaps now you'll agree with me."

Kristin brushed her hair back and took hold of her temper. "Soccer is as safe for girls as it is for boys. This was just...an unlucky accident."

"She could have—"

"Please!" Kristin held up a hand. "I'm not saying it wasn't serious. But she could have been hurt on the playground or in the backyard, too. She's going to be fine. Let's just be grateful."

Mrs. Brennan's blue eyes snapped with a cold anger. She turned to the bed, which meant turning her back on Kristin. "How are you feeling, Erin dear? We brought you a book about ballet dancers that I'd been saving for you."

"Thank you, Grandmom."

Kristin went to stare out the window. She'd gotten

about two hours of sleep before the nurses started their morning rounds, followed by the doctors. And she'd been entertaining Erin ever since. Matt had come by at about eight with lots of books, but when he volunteered to replace Kristin, Erin's reaction bordered on a tantrum.

"Maybe I'll go home when Luke comes," Kristin had told Matt, knowing how much that would hurt him, but unable to protect him.

"Yeah." He'd nodded, avoiding her eyes, and left soon after.

Now his parents arrived, questioning her decisions as a mother. Kristin suddenly remembered why she'd been so afraid when she found out she was pregnant and Matt was gone. The Brennans would have tried to take her baby away. And she'd known even then that she wouldn't allow anyone else to raise Matt's child. Not if there was some other way.

Just then, that other way Luke walked into the hospital room. "Well, looks to me like you're ready for another soccer game, Erin Bear!" He stood at the end of the bed and gave her a wink. "How's it going?"

"Okay. What did you bring me?"

"Erin!" Kristin protested.

Mrs. Brennan clicked her tongue and shook her head in reproval. But Luke just laughed. "Boy, have you got this hospital thing figured out. Everybody brings presents, don't they?" He presented the box he'd been holding behind his back. "I figured you'd need to make a little bit of noise, if you couldn't run around like crazy."

"Cool!" Wincing, Erin eased higher up in the bed to unwrap some kind of colorful computerized toy. "I wanted one of these for my birthday!" She began to play, and the toy gave off electronic noises that sounded vaguely like music.

"Thanks, Luke," Kristin said. "That'll certainly make the days shorter for someone."

He glanced at her and grinned. "I should have brought you some ear protection." After watching Erin for another minute, his gaze came back and lingered on her face. "You haven't been home yet?"

"Um, no."

"I thought Matt was coming back early."

"He did." From the corner of her eye, she saw Mrs. Brennan listening. "But Erin was a little...fussy then. So he went on to work."

Luke nodded. "Well, I'm here now, and I deserve the punishment of listening to this monstrosity I bought. You go home and get some rest."

The word fell on Kristin's ears like a blessing. "Are you sure? You couldn't have gotten much sleep yourself."

"Some is better than the none I'm betting you got. Go home. Sarah's coming by in a couple of hours. We'll keep the Bear here occupied until this afternoon. I promise. And we'll call if anything comes up."

With her mother-in-law standing there, Kristin felt she should insist on staying to fulfill her responsibility to her child. But that toy seemed so *loud*. And the "comfortable" recliner had definitely not been. She could hardly see for the burning in her eyes.

"Okay."

Mrs. Brennan sniffed, whether in comment or just coincidentally, Kristin decided not to wonder. "I'll call my mom and ask her to pick me up. Matt took the van."

"Nope." Luke shook his head. "If your mom comes, she'll probably bring Jenny. Then you'll be caught up taking care of Jenny instead of getting some sleep. Mom and Dad can drop you at your house.'' He turned to his parents. ''Right?''

The Colonel stood up. ''Sure we can. We'll come back this afternoon and see how Erin's getting along.'' He put a hand on the little girl's head. ''You stay quiet for Granddad, sweetheart.''

Erin sighed. ''Okay.''

Mrs. Brennan bent over for a kiss. ''We'll talk about your book this afternoon, Erin. I love you.''

That last sentence melted Kristin's anger. Yes, Elena Brennan was difficult. But she really did care about Erin and Jenny.

That knowledge didn't make the ride home any more comfortable. The Colonel drove, pipe between his teeth and eyes on the road. Mrs. Brennan said nothing, even about Erin. Kristin sat in the back seat, trying to stay awake, trying to ignore how carsick she was feeling.

At the house, she opened the door to fresh air with relief. ''Thank you for the ride,'' she told the couple in front. ''I always hate to bother Matt at work. I'm sure he'll appreciate the favor.'' She stood up out of the car.

Mrs. Brennan's window rolled down. ''If Matt will call us, we can schedule our visit when he's there,'' she said.

''I'll tell him.'' Kristin lifted a hand and then turned toward the house. If she was lucky, she would get inside before she was sick.

The front door was locked. She fumbled with her keys, sensing the Brennans in the driveway behind her, feeling her stomach on the very edge of revolt. At last she got the lock turned and managed a wave toward the car. Then she bolted for the bathroom off the hall.

A shower and five hours of sleep later, she awoke with Matt's hand along her cheek. ''Hey there, sleepyhead.'' His grin was soft, his eyes tender.

"Hey." She stretched a little, feeling warm and safe. His hand eased to her throat, to the hollow of her collarbone, slipping under the soft cotton of her nightshirt.

Her husband leaned closer. "I always did want to play out that scene in *Sleeping Beauty*." He covered her mouth with his own, warmer than warm, insistent, completely irresistible. Kristin moved into the kiss, tilting her head to perfect the fit.

"Yes, indeed," he murmured. His hand cupped her knee, slid up her thigh. Underneath the nightshirt, he stroked her flank, then skimmed her waist and the edge of her ribs with the backs of his fingers—a familiar journey to them both. Kristin knew where the path would lead, and she arched in anticipation of his hand on her breast, her belly...

A rush of fear flooded her mind and heart. Her body was changing. Her breasts were fuller, firmer now, her stomach more rounded with the first growth of their baby. In daylight, making love slowly and deliberately, Matt would notice. He would discover the secret she was hiding. There would be no way to explain her deception. She couldn't let him find out like that.

She drew back from his kiss. "Matt." With a shift of her hips, she impeded the progress of his hand. "Matt, I..."

Tell him. Now.

She should. God, she knew she should.

How?

He nudged aside the neck of her nightshirt, pressing hot kisses over the top of her breast. Kristin nearly forgot to be afraid.

But not quite. She put her hand on his hair. "Matt, stop."

On a deep breath, he lifted his head. "Stop teasing? I

can get real serious, if that's what you want." This grin was sexy, a little wicked. His blue eyes had darkened with his arousal.

"I—" *Say it. Say it!* "Y-your parents were at the hospital this morning. Your mother said if you would call her, they would meet you there this afternoon."

He nodded as he unfastened the top button on her nightshirt. "I'll call later." He pressed a kiss where the button had been.

"But—" Kristin closed her hands tightly around his biceps. "She was very upset this morning about Erin. She'll be waiting to talk to you."

This time when he looked up, confusion had replaced some of the desire in his eyes. "Erin's doing okay?"

"She was when I left. Luke said he would call if anything changed, and the phone hasn't rung."

With his brother's name, the fire in his gaze burned even lower. "That's good." He dropped his chin, then gave a weary shake of his head and sat up. "What you're saying is that I should call my mom *now*. Right?"

"I—I think so."

"Well, sure. Why not?" His voice was bitter. He jerked off the bed, then rubbed a hand over his face and neck. "I'll do that. This very minute." His shoulders were stiff, his spine straight as he stalked out of the bedroom.

Kristin couldn't believe she had tears left to cry.

But she discovered that she did.

MATT'S PARENTS were waiting in the hospital lobby when he and Kristin arrived. They rode the elevator together, with Kristin silent in one corner and his mother disapproving in the other. Dr. Walsh opened the door to Erin's room just as they approached. With a wave of his hand, the doctor stepped back and held open the door. "Y'all come on in. Everything looks good and she's doing just great."

"So, Miss Erin." The Colonel went to stand by the head of the bed. "What have you been doing since this morning?"

"Playing games. Talkin' to Daddy."

"You probably should have taken a nap," her grandmother said. She sent an irritated glance toward Luke, who stood on the far side of the room, with Sarah sitting in the recliner beside him.

"I wasn't sleepy. Daddy was telling me about blood. What blood type are you, Mommy?"

A warning bell went off in Matt's brain.

At the foot of the bed, Kristin grasped the railing with white-knuckled hands. "O-positive. Why?"

"That means you can give blood to everybody. Sarah is O-negative, so she can take blood from anybody. Grandmom, what are you?"

"Why, B, I believe. B-negative."

Kristin put a hand to her eyes. Luke took a step forward. Matt saw understanding, then dismay, dawn in his eyes.

"Granddaddy?"

"I'm A-positive, Miss Erin."

Beside Luke, Sarah stirred, and reached for his hand.

"So our family has A's and B's and O's. Daddy says he doesn't know about his. Daddy Matt, do you know?"

Though it had to be his imagination, Matt felt as if the whole world stopped, waiting for his answer.

Elena Brennan forestalled him. "Luke is B-negative, dear. I remember from the time he fell onto the spike of an iron fence when he was ten. And Matt is A-positive.

So now you have all your questions answered. Did you ask the doctor what your type is?''

Erin hesitated, thinking. She was an extremely bright girl, and Matt knew her brain was racing beyond the facts to the implications, like a locomotive with the throttle tied down.

''Erin, dear?'' His mother did not like to be ignored.

''A-positive,'' his daughter said slowly. ''That's what he said. I'm the same as…'' she looked up, her eyes puzzled, a little afraid ''…as Daddy Matt.''

Matt heard the words, but couldn't seem to hold on to them. His mother straightened up from the bed, but she still kept her eyes on Erin. When he looked at his father, he found the Colonel staring back at him, confusion growing in his face.

''That doesn't sound right.'' The Colonel turned to Erin. ''Are you sure you understood?''

Erin nodded.

Matt's mother put a hand to her throat and took a step back. ''But that would mean—'' She glanced at Luke, then her gaze crossed Kristin to rest on Matt. Her posture stiffened, and her eyes froze. After a silent moment, she looked at the Colonel. ''I believe we should leave, William. Now.''

No one ever questioned Elena Brennan when she used that tone of voice. Erin's granddad bent and gave her a gentle hug. ''We'll see you tomorrow, Miss Erin. Sleep tight.'' The little girl barely returned the embrace.

''I'll call you later, Mom.'' Matt stepped forward to kiss her cheek.

''I'll be waiting.'' As he drew back, he got another stab from the cold blue eyes before she stalked into the hallway. The Colonel followed and closed the door behind them.

The tension lessened only slightly. Matt turned to Kristin and put a hand on her shoulder. "Kris, maybe we should—"

But she slipped out from underneath his touch. For the first time since they'd come in, she got close to Erin, sitting on the bed and taking the little girl's hands in hers. "Are you feeling okay, love? I got a little sleep and I'm doing much better. Shall we read a story?"

Erin shook her head. Her gaze, fixed on Kristin's face, was deeper, wiser than an eight-year-old had any right to own. "Mommy, is Matt my...real...daddy?"

Luke took a short, shocked gulp of air.

"Yes, Erin. Matt is...your father." Her voice was low, and sounded steady. But Matt heard the fear vibrating underneath her words. "That seems weird, doesn't it?"

"You lied." Erin never ignored facts.

Kristin pulled in a shaking breath. "Yes. We did."

"Why?"

"Because..." Kristin stopped, lifted Erin's hands to her mouth and kissed the knuckles. "We're gonna talk about this, love. But why don't we let Luke and Sarah get some rest?" She looked around then, and Matt was jolted by the despair in her face. "Thanks for taking the time, Luke. I—we'll call you tonight, okay?"

"Sure." Luke was pale, his eyes blank. He stepped to the bed and bent over. "Don't worry, Bear. It'll all turn out okay. I love you." He kissed her forehead.

Erin didn't move.

When Luke and Sarah were gone, Matt acknowledged his own responsibility to leave. "I'm going to take a walk," he said. He hardly recognized his own voice. "I'll be back in a little while."

Kristin nodded. Erin didn't move.

The air in his chest felt like lead as he stepped into the

hallway. He was running from a battle, something he'd never even thought about doing before.

But only one person could get Erin through this. Kristin would have to handle the situation by herself.

And then he would pick up the pieces when *she* fell apart.

Matt only prayed he could put them all back together the right way.

Tuesday
Dear Diary

Matt brought you to the hospital in case I wanted to write about bein hurt. I got kicked at soccer. DJ is so dum. The doctor fixed my spleen and I got to have a popsikle for lunch.

Everybody was here for awhile sept Jenny and Grandmommy Irene and Granddaddy Frank. We talked about blood. People have difrent kinds. I havethe same kind of blood Matt does.

Mommy says thats coz Matt is my father. He went away and got caught by the ennemy before I was born. Mommy was scared and she wanted me to have a daddy so she got married to Luke.

I get tired thinkin about that. My head kinda gets it. But somewhere inside, I feel bad. Really bad.

Everybody went away but Mommy. Shes sittin in the chair watchin cartoons on tv. Does she know she is cryin?

Id like to cry. But Im to tired.

Your friend
Erin Elena Brennan

KRISTIN GLANCED OVER and saw that Erin had fallen asleep while writing in her diary. Getting out of the re-

cliner, she picked up the book and closed it without looking at the words on the page. Erin deserved her private
thoughts. God knew, the rest of her world had just fallen
into chaos.

She was surprised that disaster could be this calm. The
Colonel and Mrs. Brennan had left quietly. Luke and
Sarah and Matt had slipped away without causing any
fuss about what had happened.

And Erin had listened as Kristin explained the facts
about her father—*Matt*. Funny how the words she'd worried over for so long seemed to come easily enough, once
the most important point had been made. What she'd
done didn't sound stupid or cowardly as she explained it
to her daughter. Just another example of an unlucky accident, the kind that happened to everybody.

But the darkness in her daughter's blue eyes told Kristin that damage had been done. Erin hadn't said much at
all, after that one important question. Kristin hadn't attempted to pry. If Erin wanted to talk, she would.

Back at the window again, Kristin stared across the
rooftop and its air-conditioning vents. She hadn't seen
Jenny all day. She had a sudden desperate desire to hold
her little girl close, smell the sweetness of her skin, see
the clarity in her eyes. Was a five-year-old allowed to
come into a hospital room? If so, her mother could bring
Jenny after supper, and see Erin.

"Kris?" Matt's soft voice came from the doorway.
She turned around. "How's Erin?"

Kristin shrugged. "Pretty quiet. She didn't have a lot
of questions. I guess she's...thinking."

He nodded. In the low light he looked tired, a little
dazed. Not at all the take-charge military commander she
was used to. "I-I'm sorry."

"We planned to tell her."

"Not like this."

She gave a small laugh. "Maybe our plan wasn't such a good idea. At least this way it's done."

He leaned back against the wall on the other side of the room. "What do we do now?"

Definitely *not* take-charge. Kristin shrugged. "We'll have to wait and see what Erin wants, I guess. I think I'll call the counselor we worked with before…when you first came back. I'll make an appointment. Erin might need to talk to somebody who's not…involved." Another hollow chuckle escaped her. "I've driven my own daughter into therapy." The never-ending tears burned her eyes, reminding her she had a headache.

Matt watched from across the room as Kristin wiped her eyes with her fingertips. He wanted to hold her, but she seemed so far away. Talking wouldn't accomplish much—they knew all the facts. The unpredictable element was Erin's reaction. Life had become a maze, and he kept running into dead ends.

"I stopped by your mom's house," he said finally, just to fill the silence. "Jenny seemed to be okay. They went to the library today, and shopping for shoes and a new dress that has a doll outfit to match. Jenny was very pleased with herself."

Kristin's smile flashed and was gone. "I imagine she was. Mom's been really amazing. She's a little too worried sometimes, but she does come through. I wonder—"

When she didn't go on, he prodded. "What are you thinking?"

She shook her head. "Sometimes I just wonder if I hadn't panicked when I found out I was pregnant, if I'd told my mother and asked her to help, what would have happened. I know she would have been disappointed. It seemed so terribly important at the time, that she not be unhappy with me." With a sigh, she crossed to the bed and reached out to brush Erin's hair back from her eyes. "Now I think of all the unhappiness I've caused Erin, and Jenny, and Luke..." She looked at Matt suddenly and he saw her cheeks stained with tears. "...and you. I sacrificed so many people, so my mother wouldn't be ashamed of me."

He cleared his throat. "You were young, Kris. Facing a hard choice."

"Which choice was that?" She left the bedside and went back to staring out the window. "The one where I told my mother?"

Matt straightened up from the wall. "Well—"

"Or the one where I should have told you *no* that very first time?"

If she'd slugged him, he wouldn't have felt it for a second or two. But then he recognized the slow burn of anger in his belly. "You could have. You've really gotten good at that lately."

Her hand tightened on her elbow. But she didn't say anything else.

Nothing had changed when Irene Jennings arrived with Jenny fifteen minutes later. "Jenny wanted to see her big sister," she started in a cheery voice, which lowered as she saw Erin still asleep. "I called and asked the nurse if we could come and she said it would be all right."

"Mommy!" Jenny had no reservations about making noise. She ran across the floor into Kristin's arms as soon as her grandmother released her.

"Jenny, love." Kristin buried her face in the little girl's hair. "I missed you so much."

Erin stirred. "What's going on? Who's here?"

Within a few minutes, Jenny had climbed onto the bed to see Erin's stitches, and then to play the computerized game Luke had brought. Kristin watched them with almost fierce concentration, her arms wrapped around her waist. Matt stayed where he was, watching his wife's misery, until Irene stepped up beside him.

"Kristy doesn't look at all well."

Matt shifted his gaze to his mother-in-law. "It's been a tough twenty-four hours. We appreciate your taking care of Jenny, though. That's a big help."

Irene waved away his thanks. "I'm always happy to have the girls. But if Erin's going to be fine, why is Kristy so upset?"

Matt hesitated. He hated to lie. But should he tell the truth? Now?

He glanced toward Kristin and found her watching him. When their eyes met, she tilted her head, and gave a small shrug, as if to say *Go ahead. She has to know sometime.*

Maybe the best way he could help Kris right now was to take the burden of telling her mother off her shoulders. "Let's go outside," he suggested, and opened the door.

The waiting room was full of parents and rambunctious children. Matt ended up at the end of the hallway in front of a large window, with Irene beside him. He stared outside, but she faced him.

"What is it, Matt? Something about Erin?"

He pulled in a deep breath. "Well, yes."

"She's not doing well?" Her gentle voice tightened with anxiety.

Matt realized how poorly he was handling the situation. Turning toward Irene, he put a hand on her shoulder. "She's fine. The doctor says she can go home by Thursday at the latest."

"Then…?"

Okay. Just do it. "Erin discovered something today

that you need to know, too. Somehow she got interested... No. That doesn't matter." He braced himself
against the questions in Irene's gaze. "Luke isn't Erin's
biological father. Kris was pregnant when I left for Africa. Erin is my daughter. By blood, anyway."

Whatever he'd thought to see on Kristin's mother's
face, the relief he found there was totally unexpected.
After a moment, she even smiled.

"I wondered," Irene said, laying her palm over the
back of his hand, "when you and Kristy would decide
that you could tell me the truth."

ELENA REFUSED to lose her temper. She did not intend
to exhibit her emotions for the strangers in the hospital
hallways. No matter how furious she was, any comment
would wait until she and William had privacy.

She didn't say a word until they were safely inside
their own house. Putting her purse down on the kitchen
table, she moved automatically to the refrigerator for a
pitcher of cold water. As she poured two glasses, she
heard William pull out a chair and sit down.

He cleared his throat. "I guess we just found out something we weren't meant to know."

Elena brought the glasses to the table. "Yes." Her
voice shook on the one word.

"Kristin must've been expecting when Matt was pronounced dead. She married Luke to give the baby a father."

"It would seem so." The fewer words she spoke, the
better she could contain her rage.

"I can't figure out why they didn't tell us, though.
Especially after Matt came back."

"I have no doubt that Kristin would do anything to
escape censure of her conduct. Surely that's the reason

she forced Luke to marry her—to avoid the disapproval of her family and friends.''

''I don't know, m'dear. I think she was concerned for the baby, wanted it to have a good home with two parents.''

''Then why Luke? Why not some other man of her acquaintance? I imagine there were many.'' Trying to relax, she sat down at the table in her accustomed chair.

''Well—''

''She wanted to be sure a Brennan baby would have a Brennan father. She probably realized that Luke would agree quite easily to such a quixotic plan—he has always come to the aid of the weak and needy.'' Elena realized she was fidgeting with her rings. Getting up again, she went to the dishwasher and began to put away the clean dishes.

When she glanced over, William was staring at her, his eyebrows drawn, his eyes worried. ''However it happened, the fact is that Matt is Erin's dad. And she knows now. I think that'll be hard for her to deal with.''

''Deception is difficult for anyone to deal with.'' Elena knew too much about the pain a parent's lies could cause. Her father's drinking and gambling—and the deception he practiced to conceal them—had made her childhood a nightmare of uncertainty.

''We'll have to help them pick up the pieces,'' William said. ''Maybe we can have the girls over to stay for a while. We could give Erin a chance to talk about what she knows with somebody besides her parents.''

''I doubt she will confide in us...unless we tell her we didn't know about her father, either,'' Elena retorted.

''That doesn't sound like a good idea. Let's just have her over and give her the same love and attention we always have. I imagine that's what she needs more than anything else.'' William got up from the table. "I'm going to take a walk on the beach. Come with me?" He put his hand on her shoulder.

She covered his fingers with her palm. "No, thank you. I think I'll stay out of the sun this afternoon. You go ahead.''

With a kiss on her temple, he left through the door to the deck. Elena carefully restored the dishes to their proper place, then went to the family room and took up her needlework. She was making a cover for one of the chairs at church, and had fallen behind with the project.

But with her needle raised, she found herself staring at the latest portrait of Matt, Kristin and the girls instead of stitching. Taken by Luke's wife at Christmas, the picture glowed with love. Elena had been so pleased with the image at the time.

Now, though, she could see what she never had before—the resemblance between Matt and Erin. The same blue eyes, like Elena's own. A similar set to the mouth and chin. Other evidence came to mind—Erin's long legs and arms, her curious mind and studious inclinations. The clues had been there for anyone to see.

How could she and William have been so blind?

More important, though—how could Kristin Jennings have been cruel enough to hide such an important truth?

CHAPTER EIGHT

MATT QUIETLY STEPPED BACK into Erin's hospital room. Kristin glanced at him, then focused her gaze. He looked stunned, and yet almost as if he wanted to laugh.

"You need to talk to her," he said, tilting his head toward the door and, by implication, her mom.

Kristin couldn't tell from his face what she should expect to hear.

In the hallway, her mother turned as she approached. "Hi, Kristy."

"Matt said I should talk to you. What's going on? What did he say?"

A rueful smile curved Irene Jennings's lips. "He told me that *he* is Erin's father. I told him I've known that for several years now."

The world started a crazy, off-center spin. Kristin closed her eyes and fought for balance.

"Kristy? Are you all right?" An arm came around her waist, and her mother's cool hand gripped her wrist. "There are chairs over here. Come sit down."

She let herself be led, and sat when her mother told her to. The spinning hadn't stopped, and a black cloud was forming in her brain. With a gasp, Kristin folded up and put her forehead on her knees.

"Is something wrong?" A strange voice, probably a nurse.

"I'm not sure." Her mother, obviously worried. Kristin drew a deep breath, trying to settle reality inside her head again.

"Honey, look at me." The nurse's voice, close in front of her, and a soft hand on her hair. "Let me see your eyes." When Kristin didn't reply, she felt a breeze as the nurse stood up.

"I'll get a room for her to lie down. And I'll call Dr.—"

"No." Pushing her palms against her knees, Kristin sat up. She opened her eyes. "I'm fine, really. I got...dizzy. It's been a long day."

The nurse stared at her for a minute. "You're awfully pale. When'd you eat last?"

She gave a weak grin. "I honestly don't remember."

"Well, then, maybe you should go to the cafeteria, get something in that stomach of yours. Food's important, you know." She patted Kristin's shoulder before heading down the hall.

Kristin watched until she couldn't see the nurse's clown-printed smock anymore. Then she turned to her mother. "Maybe she's right. Let's go downstairs."

She had to concentrate on walking steadily, because the dizziness still buzzed in her head. But she made it through the cafeteria line and to a table without falling and without dropping her tray of food.

Not that she had any desire to eat. She looked into her mother's face. "You knew about Erin? How?"

"I was surprised when you married Luke. You were so in love with Matt. I couldn't imagine you turning to another man so quickly. And then you were pregnant. I knew you better than that—I couldn't believe you would...be with...more than one man." A soft blush colored her mom's cheeks, and she lowered her eyes. "But when you had Jenny, and you and Luke seemed so happy, I thought I had to be wrong.''

Kristin stabbed a fork into her salad. ''What changed your mind?''

''Watching Erin grow up. She looks so much like Matt. Her eyes…the way she runs. Once she got to be five or six, I was almost sure. And seeing her in the same room with him…'' The other woman shrugged. ''It's so obvious. I don't know why the Brennans haven't realized.''

''They know now.'' Head propped in her hand, Kristin forked another piece of lettuce, slid it back into the bowl and went for a carrot. ''But when Luke and I got married, they were completely devastated about Matt, too devastated to really think…or count. We were depending on that.''

''I'm sure.''

At the dry tone of her mother's voice, Kristin looked up. ''I know I should apologize for lying. I was confused. And scared.'' She was just as scared right this minute. Somehow, keeping yet another secret—the new baby— suddenly seemed safer than having the truth revealed.

''I just wish you had trusted me enough to let me help you.''

Kristin stabbed another carrot. ''Does Dad know, too?''

Irene Jennings pursed her lips in reproof. ''He's my husband, Kristy. I don't keep secrets from him.''

Pushing her tray away, Kristin stood. ''I…I need to visit the rest room. I'll be right back.''

Alone in the cold, tiled room, she leaned back against the wall and fought for control. The temptation to tell her mother about this baby was powerful. But Matt should know first.

Matt didn't want to know. He had all the children he could handle. He might change his mind. And he might not.

Telling Matt would mean telling the girls.

Kristin thought of Erin's face when she'd asked, "Is Matt my real daddy?"

She was a small, scared little girl in a world where the sunshine had disappeared. Expecting her to handle another huge adjustment right now was impossible. Kristin couldn't do it.

The new baby deserved to be greeted with joy, expected with love. Not resentment, not dread, not stress. Until the rest of their lives made sense, this pregnancy would remain a secret.

She pressed her hand against the baby. *Only a few weeks,* she promised. *Only a little while, until everybody settles down again. That's not too much to ask for.*

She hoped.

IRENE VOLUNTEERED to stay with Erin, so Kristin and Matt took Jenny home with them. She wanted to know why Erin couldn't come, too.

"Erin has to stay another day," Matt explained. "The doctor wants to be sure she's well again. Then we'll bring her home."

"She can play with Clara."

Matt managed a grin. The chance to play with Jenny's favorite doll was a frequent source of arguments. "I know she'll like that, Jenny. You're really a good sister to offer." He glanced at Kristin, who hadn't even smiled. "Should we order a pizza for dinner?"

"Yippee!" Jenny bounced in her seat. "Pepperoni! Pepperoni!"

"You got it." He used the cell phone to place the

order. "You'll have just enough time to wash your hands and face before the pizza gets there. Pretty good, huh?"

"I like pizza," Jenny volunteered.

Matt laughed. "I know."

The laugh surprised him. After the tension of the afternoon, he wasn't sure humor should be an option. But Jenny always made him laugh. Kids were good at that.

He sobered, thinking about Erin. *She knows.* He had thought it would feel good to have his daughter recognize him, understand that she was a part of him. A celebration should have been appropriate, balloons and streamers and a heart-shaped cake saying I Love Erin.

Matt didn't see that happening any time soon. Judging from Erin's eyes, all of them had a long road ahead. Kristin, maybe, longest of all.

She'd fallen asleep by the time they reached the house. Unbuckling Jenny's car seat, he put a finger to his lips. "Mommy's really tired. Let's be quiet so we don't wake her up, okay?"

"'Kay." Jenny's little-girl whisper was only a fraction softer than her normal voice.

Matt unlocked the house and then went back for Kristin. She didn't stir when he picked her up to carry her inside. Even Buster's excited whining didn't wake her. Jenny closed the front door behind him.

"Thanks," he said. "You're a big helper."

She nodded. "I know."

Chuckling, Matt climbed the stairs and took his wife to their bedroom. She'd never been heavy, but today she felt especially fragile.

He set her gently on the bed, eased her shoes off, then pulled the blinds. The room held sunshine all day. He didn't think she'd be cold.

At the door, he looked back, watching Kristin sleep.

The vacation trip hadn't solved their problems the way he'd hoped. There were issues they hadn't talked about. And now…Erin.

Not to mention Luke, he thought as he went downstairs. His brother hadn't been prepared to lose a daughter this afternoon. Then there was the Colonel and their mother. Matt didn't try to imagine the scene ahead.

Instead, he found Jenny, got her hands washed, and paper plates ready. The doorbell rang. "Pizza!" she cried. "Pizza's here!"

They raced to the front door and then came back to the kitchen, with Jenny—and Buster—practically prancing in delight at the prospect of their meal. Matt grinned wearily.

At least there was one person he'd made happy today.

KRISTIN RETURNED to the hospital at nine that night, after Jenny had gone to bed.

Her mother rose from the recliner as she opened the door. "Let's go outside. She just nodded off."

The hallway light was bright and revealing. "You got some sleep," Irene said. "But you don't look rested."

Kristin tried to look lively and awake. "I'm much better, Mom. Thanks for staying with Erin. Did she…say anything?"

"No. We played cards and read a couple of stories, and watched TV until just now. Whatever she's thinking, she's not ready to talk to anybody yet."

"Did she seem okay?"

"Kristy, I can't read minds." Her mother's cool hands closed on her shoulders. "What's done is done. Let go of the worry for tonight. Tomorrow will take care of itself." She patted Kristin's cheek. "You should know the

Bible references for those particular ideas. Look them up. I'll get my purse and go home to your father.''

A nurse looked in on them at eleven and then the hospital night got quiet. Kristin dozed in the recliner, waking often just to look at her child's face in the dim light. Once when she woke, she found Erin's eyes open.

"Erin, love? Are you okay?" She went to the bed and took Erin's hand. It lay warm and motionless in hers.

"I'm okay." Her whisper didn't sound as if she was in pain. Just...far away.

"What are you thinking about?"

After a long silence, Erin turned to meet her mother's gaze straight on. "Nothin'."

And Kristin knew, with a shiver of fear, that serious trouble lay just ahead.

Dr. Walsh stopped by on Wednesday morning. "Looking better all the time," he pronounced. "Eating well, going to the bathroom, sleeping...you're doing all the right things, Miss Erin. What do you say to going home this afternoon?"

"Really?" Erin was pleased, if not jubilant.

And Dr. Walsh noticed. "We'll let you stay, if you'd rather do that."

"N-no. That's okay. I want to go home." She started to slip out of bed.

"Wait just a little while, okay?" The doctor tucked her back in. "Hospitals have paperwork that has to be filled out. When we get that done, you can leave."

"Okay." Obediently, she leaned back against the pillow.

At Dr. Walsh's glance, Kristin followed him into the hallway. He leaned a shoulder against the wall and crossed his arms over his chest. "Most kids start swinging from the ceiling when they get to go home. I was betting on Erin doing the same. What's happened?''

Heat flooded into Kristin's face. ''Yesterday…the discussion about blood typing…''

''There was a discussion?''

''Erin likes to know how things work.''

He nodded.

''She found out that…that her dad isn't Luke. Her biological father is…is my husband, Matt.'' Would that sentence ever get easier to say?

''I…see. That's going to be tough on everybody.'' The doctor looked at his watch. ''Erin's going to be a little emotional for a while because of the surgery and being in the hospital. I would tell you to treat her gently, but I gather that's already on the agenda. She should come to my office in ten days for a follow-up. In the meantime…'' He gave her a long list of warning signs to watch for and what to do if something seemed wrong.

''I'll remember,'' Kristin promised.

He put a hand on her shoulder and squeezed. ''I know you will. And…good luck.''

''Thank you.'' She watched him walk away, almost dreading to go back into Erin's room. Being cheerful, being gentle…being a *mother*…just seemed to require more energy than she had right now.

But there was no one else who could do that for her daughter. So Kristin squared her shoulders, smiled and opened the hospital-room door. ''Isn't that great, Erin? You get to sleep in your own bed tonight!''

Wednesday night
Dear Diary

Im back at home. I got to have barbecu chiken for supper and ice cream. Jenny said I could play with Clara all night. I couldnt beleeve she said that. She never lets me play with Clara. I put her on the chair so I could see her when I wake up.

Matt was here with Jenny when I got home. I dont know what to say to him. I cant call him daddy. Hes bein nice to me. I dont know if I like that.

Luke called me on the fone. I dont know how to talk to him anymore. He said he would come to see me. I wish he wouldnt.

I wish DJ didnt kick me. I wish it was last week. I was happy last week.

> Your friend
> Erin Elena Brennan

MATT CALLED his parents after he'd carried Erin upstairs so Kristin could read the girls a story before bed. The Colonel answered.

"Hi, Dad. It's Matt." He waited through a long moment of silence for an answer.

"Matt. How's Erin?"

"I wanted to let you know she came home late this afternoon. She's doing fine."

"That's good to hear."

Matt broke the next silence. "Dad, we need to talk."

"I'd say so. Your mother's quite upset."

"Would you and Mom like to come over sometime tomorrow to see Erin?"

"I'll talk to her. We'll call you in the morning."

"Great. Good night, Dad." He put the phone down and put his head in his hands. Could the situation get much worse?

Kristin's step sounded in the hallway. As he looked up, she stopped on the threshold. "What's wrong?"

"I called my parents. Sounds as if Mom's pretty worked up."

She passed him on the way to the kitchen. "I didn't expect anything else."

Matt followed. "Are the girls asleep?"

"Jenny is." She took a pitcher of lemonade out of the refrigerator. "Erin wanted to read for a while. Would you like a drink?"

"No, thanks. How's she doing?"

With her back to him, Kristin shrugged. "I don't know. She hasn't said anything."

He felt as if they were talking through a sheet of glass. "She needs time to sort things out."

"Yes." Still with her back to him, Kristin sipped her drink.

Matt closed the distance between them and put his hands on her shoulders. "We need time, too, Kris. Time to talk and plan. I didn't mean for things to happen this way." He pressed a kiss onto her hair.

"I know." As close as they were, the glass still divided them.

"Why don't we sit down and do a little of that? I feel like I haven't seen you for a week."

He wasn't surprised when she shook her head. "I can't, Matt. Not tonight. I guess…I guess I'm like Erin. I've got to get this sorted out in my own head first."

I thought husbands and wives helped each other with sorting things out. Not the right thing to say. "Sure. Finish your drink and we'll just call it a night." He ran his hands over her arms to her elbows, then slipped them around her waist. "We could get into bed and relax." Her soft flower scent met him as he bent his head to the curve of her shoulder. "Make some distractions of our own."

Kristin stiffened like stone in his hold. After a second, he felt her deliberately relax. She reached up and back to put a hand on his cheek. "You're sweet." With a sigh, she stepped out of his arms. "But I'm so exhausted. Maybe…maybe tomorrow?"

"Sure." Matt was almost relieved. He didn't know what he would have done—what he would have been forced to think—if he'd made love to her and the damn barrier stayed between them. "I'm pretty beat, too. Let's get some rest."

Kristin's smile was the brightest he'd seen it since Erin got hurt.

"Thanks," she said. "I'd love a good night's sleep."

MATT'S PARENTS visited with Erin in her room, then came downstairs. Matt suggested the living room for their discussion. "We can close the doors and the girls won't hear."

The Colonel chose the armchair in the corner. Mrs. Brennan sat across from him near the window. Kristin eased down on the love seat and clasped her hands tightly to keep them from shaking. She'd dreamed about this meeting last night. The ending wasn't nice.

Matt remained standing, almost at military attention. "I'm sure you've figured out the truth. Luke is not Erin's father. I am."

"How long have you known?" As in Kristin's dream, Mrs. Brennan took the initiative.

"Kris told me about six months after I got back from Africa."

The older woman took a breath. "That long!"

Colonel Brennan stirred in his chair. "You didn't think you could tell your parents?"

"It was a tough call, Dad. Erin believed Luke was her

father. He and Kristin were separating. None of us thought a little girl needed more to handle than that.''

"We could have been trusted not to tell her.'' Mrs. Brennan's stiff back and sharp voice conveyed her outrage.

"I'm sure that's true, Mom. But the more people who knew, the greater the chance that something would slip. Besides...'' He cleared his throat. "Luke and I weren't exactly getting along. There was just too much conflict in the whole situation.''

"Luke.'' Mrs. Brennan's stern gaze turned to Kristin. "A great deal of misunderstanding and misery could have been avoided if we had been told the truth at the very beginning.''

Kristin tightened her grip on her fingers. "Matt was dead. I was scared, not thinking very clearly. I went to Luke, and he suggested a solution.''

"A solution that involved lying to the people most closely concerned! Not to mention a surreptitious wedding.''

"It was the best I could do for my baby at the time.''

"We would have helped you,'' the Colonel said. "That was our grandchild.''

"And still is,'' Matt pointed out. "Does all this history really make a difference? Erin is her own person. She has two dads—the one who raised her and the one who wants to get to know her. Everything else is the same.''

Kristin took a deep breath. As if he'd heard it, Matt glanced over and gave her a smile.

"I think deceit matters.'' Mrs. Brennan stood up and turned to look out the window. "I hardly like to think of my granddaughters being brought up in an atmosphere of half-truths.''

"Enough, Mother.''

"Elena, that's uncalled for."

Matt and his father spoke at the same time, their voices equally stern.

"You never asked if Luke was Erin's father," Kristin said, struggling to keep her voice steady. "You just assumed that I would get...involved...with Luke so soon after Matt. You believed he would seduce his brother's fiancée."

Mrs. Brennan's glance was scathing. "Accurately, it would seem."

Kristin fought the instinct to shrink back. "Luke and I were friends for a long time before we got married. And after."

"You had a child together."

Drawing on all her resolve, Kristin met the other woman's stare. "We made a life together."

No one said anything for a moment, but the silence throbbed with recrimination and blame.

"What has Erin said about all this?"

Matt looked at his father. "Nothing, really. We're giving her a chance to think things over before we try to talk." Finally, he came to sit on the love seat beside Kristin.

"Have you spoken with Luke?" The Colonel, again.

"No. He called to talk to Erin last night after she got home."

"I expect he's pretty broken-up about this."

Matt clasped his hands between his knees. "Probably."

"I can imagine how betrayed Erin feels," Mrs. Brennan said. "She's been deceived by everyone she loves. She may not believe that even her grandparents weren't told." She focused on Kristin again. "I suppose your parents have known all along?"

Something inside Kristin snapped. She got to her feet. "Yes, they've known for a couple of years."

"I'm not sur—"

"Because my mother *guessed*. She looked at Matt and at Erin, she thought about what kind of people we are, and she knew without being told what the explanation must be."

Elena Brennan wasn't so easily beaten. "The explanation being that you and Matt were unable to exercise basic self-control." She looked at her son. "We did not bring you up to sleep around."

Matt stood. "Damn right you didn't. Kris and I were getting married."

"All the more reason to practice restraint. Some promises should be sacred."

"Mom—"

"It seems to me that Kristin lacks a real understanding of that concept. Marriage is a lifetime commitment." She paused, then looked directly at Kristin again. "To *one* person."

Kristin felt as if she'd been slapped. "That's un—"

"If you had confided in us at the very beginning, we could have at least seen to it that our grandchild was raised with honesty and an understanding of responsibility. As it is—"

"Elena, that's enough." The Colonel was standing now, with his hand on his wife's arm.

She ignored him. "As it is, I'm surprised the child has any sort of moral compass at all. Her mother's example is one of total self-involvement."

Since the accusation was completely true, Kristin had no argument to offer.

Matt strode to the door and opened it. "Mom, I don't want to ask you to leave. But I'm not going to listen to you insult my wife. I would appreciate it if you'd offer Kris an apology.''

Chin lifted, Elena Brennan surveyed her son. "I have no apology to make."

"Then I think you should go home."

"I agree." Colonel Brennan used his grip on her arm to start his wife toward the door. "We all need some cooling-off time."

Matt's mother stopped as she reached him and put a hand on his shoulder. ''Both you and your brother have been victims of a woman whose only real loyalty is to herself.''

Matt stepped back from his mother's touch. "Dad, please.''

''We're going, son.'' The Colonel continued to propel Elena into the hallway.

But she refused to leave her point unmade. ''I can't even urge you to end this marriage. My granddaughters need one dependable parent. Poor Erin won't be the only one hurt. What will Jennifer think when she discovers she's only a half sister?''

With her face buried in her hands, Kristin heard the front door open, then close with a forceful thud. The absence of argument felt like a blessing…and like a curse.

She looked up as footsteps padded across the carpet. Jenny stood just in front of her. ''Mommy?''

Crawling out of the tunnel of her own misery, Kristin sat down again and drew her daughter close. "Yes, love?''

The little girl had been crying recently. Her cheeks were still damp. But today there was no leaning, no clinging, no climbing into Mommy's lap. Jenny stood solidly on her own two feet.

''Mommy, what's a half sister?''

Friday
Dear Diary
Jenny and I had a fight. She wanted her doll back. I wasnt finished playin. She yelled at me an I told her I didnt have to do what she said coz she's only my haf sister.

I think Mommy will be mad. Thats okay. I'm mad at her to.

Your friend
Erin Elena Brennan

Dear Diary
I take it back. Im not mad at Mommy. I was just bein dum.

CHAPTER NINE

KRISTIN TOOK IN a deep breath that hurt. "Where did you hear that word, love?"

"Erin told me. She says she doesn't have to do what I want 'cause we're only half sisters. What's a half sister?"

Pulling Jenny close, Kristin tucked the little girl's head under her chin and closed her own eyes. "Sometimes people say that two girls who have the same mother but different daddies are half sisters."

"Erin's daddy is the same as mine."

"Well, no, Jenny. Luke is your daddy, you know that. But...but Erin's daddy is...is Matt."

After a long silence, Jenny sat up and looked into Kristin's face. "Huh?"

"Daddy Matt and I were going to get married a long time ago." She felt as if a wild animal were clawing at her breast, trying to get out. "But he had to go away with the Army, and then we all thought he had died. Remember how we talked about that with Granddaddy Brennan?"

Jenny nodded slowly.

"Erin was Matt's baby. But *your* daddy, Luke, and I got married because we thought Matt wouldn't come back and we wanted to take care of the baby the best we could." Why didn't the words get easier with each repetition? "And then we had you, and we were a family, the four of us."

"Now we aren't."

"Oh, yes, we are. Now you have two daddies, and Erin has two daddies. And each of you has two mommies—Sarah *and* me. So we're really an even bigger family, all together."

Jenny's brown eyes were doubtful. "So Daddy Matt is Erin's, and Daddy...Luke is mine."

Matt crossed the room to kneel beside them. "Jenny, I love you. You are my daughter, just like Erin. And Luke loves Erin. She's his daughter the same way you are. I promise."

Pushing against Kristin's hold, Jenny eased herself to the floor. "Okay." She went to the doorway and stopped there for a second. Kristin thought the little girl would turn back to ask another question.

Instead, she continued into the hall. The soft patter of her feet headed toward the kitchen. The door of the refrigerator rattled open, then closed. A chair at the table scraped the floor. Jenny had gotten herself a drink.

Matt propped his elbow on his knee and wiped a hand over his face. "Well, at least now everybody knows everything. We can begin to repair the damage."

Afraid that if she let herself react, she would lose control, Kristin gave a tiny nod. "Of course." Her dry throat produced barely a whisper. "We can start making things right."

ON MONDAY MORNING, the phone rang. For a long moment after Kristin answered, no one spoke. "Hello?" She was about to hang up when an icy voice came on the line.

"Good morning, Kristin. How is Erin today?"

If there had been another adult in the house, Kristin would have handed off the call. But Matt had already left for work. She would have to deal with his mother alone. "She's doing well, thank you."

"That's good. I wanted to remind Matt that our Fourth of July party is tomorrow and we do expect him to be there."

"I'm sure he remembers." She didn't know whether to invite herself or not.

On the other end of the line, the Colonel said something. "And, of course," his wife said, her voice as smooth and cold as ice, "we'll look forward to seeing the girls." Again, Colonel Brennan said something Kristin couldn't distinguish. "And you," Mrs. Brennan added.

Kristin didn't have the courage to refuse. "Thank you. We'll be happy to come." Yet another lie to add to her collection.

"Until tomorrow," Matt's mother said, and hung up without waiting for a reply.

Matt couldn't believe his ears when Kristin reminded him about the party late that night. "No. We don't have to go."

She sighed and sat down on her side of the bed with her back to him as she rubbed lotion over her hands. In the soft light her hair shone like sunshine. "Of course we do. How would your parents explain our absence to their friends?"

He turned off the light on his side table and lay down facing her, his head propped on his arm. "I don't give a damn what they say. My mother, at least, owes you an apology. We're not going over there again until you get it."

Kristin turned out her light but she didn't lie down.

"Your family doesn't need any more divisiveness. Your mother was upset—with good reason. We've lied to her for the whole of Erin's life."

Matt moved close enough to curl his hand over her shoulder. "I got over it. Why can't she?" He massaged the stiff muscles at the curve between her neck and shoulder.

"Are you? Over it?" She sighed again, and tilted her head.

On his knees behind her, he started working on both her shoulders, easing, pressing, stroking, from the hollow behind her ears to her elbows and back again. The lotion scent reached him, berries and cream. "I was a jerk about it for a long time. Then I grew up. I wanted Erin to know, but I was willing to wait. And I told Jenny the truth—I love them both the same. They're yours. They're ours."

She made a sound like a purr and dropped her head forward. "This feels so good."

"Glad to hear it." He spread his fingers wide, moved his palms down over her collarbone, just brushing her nipples with his fingertips. "What else can I do?"

"Oh, Matt." Her throaty whisper drove his pulse into double time. He eased closer, bringing their bodies into contact, rocking his hips against her spine, and let his hands roam farther to cup the fullness of her breasts. Kristin dropped her head back against his shoulder and turned to press her mouth against the pulse in his neck. Her palms covered the backs of his hands, pressed them closer into her softness.

"Kris," he groaned, coming apart. "I love you so much."

At his words, she turned in his arms to meet him on her knees, mouth to mouth. Her hands wandered over his bare chest and back, leaving shivers of heat in their wake.

He didn't realize until much later, when she'd fallen asleep in his arms, that Kristin had not said she loved him, too.

WALKING INTO the Brennans' beach house felt like walking into a tiger's cage. For Kristin, anyway.

Mrs. Brennan's eyes were as cold as a big cat's when she greeted them. "Thank you for coming. Most of the guests are out back." She turned immediately to the girls. "How are you feeling, Erin? Jenny, you look very sweet in that new dress."

Matt touched Kristin's shoulder. "Would you like a drink?"

Recognizing the invitation for an escape tactic, she nodded. They moved together into the kitchen, leaving grandmother and granddaughters to talk.

As Kristin poured ginger ale, Luke and Sarah stepped through the door from the deck. "That looks good, Kristin." Luke himself looked as if he hadn't slept for days. "Would you pour one for me?"

"Of course. Sarah?"

"If you don't mind." Luke's wife came to stand beside Kristin at the counter. "How is Erin feeling?"

"Really good." Kristin handed Sarah her glass and extended one to Luke and then to Matt. "She's staying pretty quiet, but she's eating well and she says her stomach doesn't hurt at all anymore."

"Kids can recover really quick," Luke commented.

"Good thing," Matt said.

An uncomfortable minute passed as the four of them sipped their drinks and avoided each other's eyes, as well as the subject uppermost in all their minds.

Sarah, direct as usual, finally broke the silence. "Has

Erin said anything about..." She stopped, looking flushed.

Kristin sympathized—there was no easy way round this predicament. "Not yet."

Luke set his glass down with a snap. "Don't you think she should?"

"She doesn't need anyone forcing her to talk." Matt's voice and his posture stiffened. "She'll know when she's ready for help."

"Unless she keeps it all bottled up inside because there isn't really anybody she can turn to who wasn't part of the lie."

Luke rarely gave in to impatience. Sarah put her hand on her husband's arm, and he relaxed a little. "None of us will let Erin go for too long without talking."

"I've already called the counselor," Kristin added. "She said to give Erin a couple of weeks, and if she still hasn't said anything we should make an appointment."

Luke rubbed his eyes with the heels of his hands. "Sorry. I'm not handling this as well as I wanted to." Dropping his hands, he drew a deep breath. "What did the parents have to say about it?"

Kristin looked at Matt, saw him shake his head slightly. "They're upset," he said. "What else would you expect?"

"Expect from whom?" Colonel Brennan joined them. "And why are the four of you inside playing it safe, instead of outside doing your jobs?"

When the Brennans hosted a big crowd, as they were today, Luke and Matt—and, by extension, Kristin and Sarah—were expected to entertain the guests.

Matt was the first to reply. "Sorry. We were just trading news about Erin."

His father nodded. "She looks pretty good, for a little girl who had major surgery only a week ago."

And for a little girl who's had her whole world rocked. Kristin saw the same thought in Sarah's face.

Luke straightened up. "Yeah, she does. I think I'll say hello before I go outside."

He glanced at his wife and got a smile. "You go ahead," she said. "I'll catch up." With a nod, he rounded the counter and crossed the family room to the sofa where Erin and Jenny sat on either side of their grandmother, looking at a book. As Luke approached, Jenny and Elena raised their heads.

"This isn't going to work." Sarah pressed her fingers over her lips as she stared at Luke and the girls. Matt turned toward the family room. Kristin followed her sister-in-law's gaze.

Luke sat on the coffee table across from the sofa, facing his mother and Erin and Jenny. What he said was hidden by the voices of others in the room. But Kristin could see him holding one of Jenny's hands, and one of Erin's. After a moment, Jenny climbed onto Luke's knee. He put one arm around her and kept hold of Erin's hand with the other.

But Erin didn't lift her gaze from the book as he spoke to her. When she did answer a question, she nodded or shook her head. No words.

Mrs. Brennan said something, and Luke appeared to stiffen. He spoke to Erin, who only averted her face.

Luke stood, still holding Jenny, and turned to come back to the kitchen. He was smiling, but his face was set like stone.

"Jen and I are going to walk on the beach." He cleared his throat. "Want to come, Sarah?"

"Of course." She set her glass down and joined them at the door. "What about Erin?"

"She's too tired," Luke said.

"He's *my* daddy, not hers." Jenny spoke at exactly the same moment, flinging her arms around Luke's neck. "She doesn't wanna go with *my* daddy."

Without a word, Luke pulled open the door and stepped out into the hot afternoon. Sarah glanced at Kristin, deep worry in her green eyes, and shut the door behind them.

"I'll have to talk with her," Kristin said. "She'll kill him if she keeps on treating him like that."

"I doubt it." Matt was watching her with an unreadable expression. "I'm still alive."

The comment sliced into her heart. Kristin stared at him through the tears burning her eyes. "I'm sorry. I...I know they've done the same with you. You just..." *Seem so much stronger.*

But words were beyond her. She hurried across the kitchen, sidestepping as he reached out. "Kris—"

Matt grabbed onto thin air. Cursing himself, he watched Kristin slip through the family room and into the hallway leading to the rest of the house. He'd driven her into hiding.

Two steps into the family room, a firm hand grabbed his arm. "Major Brennan! Good to see you!"

He turned and automatically stood up straighter. "General Reeves. How are you?"

"Fine, just fine. Your dad tells me you'll be back in Special Forces soon."

Choking down a denial, Matt managed a grin. "I'm thinking about it, sir. If you'll excuse me, I need to find my wife. She's not feeling well."

The general let go. "By all means, son. Sorry to have kept you."

Matt made it across the room and up the stairs without any further delays. Of the five bedrooms in his parents' house, only one had a door closed. He approached the room Erin and Jenny shared when they stayed over.

"Kris? Kristin, I'm sorry. Let me in so I can talk to you."

Silence replied.

"Kristin, please. I..." God, there was no excuse for what he'd just done. However he felt, however things looked, he should have the discipline to keep his mouth shut.

He stood outside the door for an eternity, waiting. He would not force Kristin to see him. She deserved her privacy.

She deserved a husband who didn't hurt her.

Once out on the deck again, he listened with half an ear to the military reminiscences of his dad's friends. Matt had heard all the tales a dozen times before. He could have told the stories himself.

When Luke and Sarah and Jenny came up the steps from the beach, he crossed to meet them. Luke had recovered some of his color, but his face was unnaturally grim. Sarah and Jenny seemed fairly relaxed.

"Will you do me a favor?" Matt pulled Sarah to the railing, out of the crowd's way.

"If I can."

"Kristin's upstairs in the girls' bedroom. Could you check on her? Make sure she's okay?"

"What happened?"

He propped his hands on his hips and hung his head. "I said something stupid, as usual. She was already upset about Erin, and I made it worse. She wouldn't answer when I spoke to her through the door. Please?''

Her hand closed over his upper arm. ''Sure, Matt. I'll be down in a few minutes.''

She came back in less than that. ''Matt, we need to get Kristin to a doctor. Now.''

Heart pounding, he followed her up the stairs, ignoring the curiosity of the party guests. ''What's wrong?''

He stopped at the door to the girls' room. Kristin lay curled on Jenny's bed, her arms clutched around her waist. ''Kris?'' Matt knelt by the bed. ''What's wrong, sweetheart? What can I do?''

She shook her head and closed her eyes, which squeezed tears out onto her cheeks. More scared than he'd ever been in his entire life, Matt looked up at Sarah.

Luke's wife took a deep breath. ''She's having some bleeding, Matt. And some pretty bad cramps.''

He could only stare in bewilderment. ''Somebody's going to have to explain. I'm not making the connection.''

Sarah dropped her gaze to her hands. ''Kristin may be having a miscarriage.''

TELLING HIS PARENTS only that his wife was feeling sick and he would take her home, Matt drove to the hospital with Kristin lying in the back seat of the van. Sarah came along and went into the examining room with Kristin, which left Matt sitting alone in the waiting room. With nothing to do but think.

Kristin was pregnant. He prayed that she would be okay, prayed that the baby wasn't hurt. Knowing zero about babies and pregnancy, he couldn't begin to guess what was going on. His rational mind told him that Kristin looked okay—not good by any means, but not in danger of losing her life.

His gut didn't believe anything his mind had to say.

What if she died? What would he do? His life had been built around her for so many years now…how could he keep going?

How had Kris kept going, when she thought he was dead?

By marrying Luke. By having her baby—Erin. By taking care of Matt's daughter to the best of her ability and making a life she could cope with.

Matt only hoped he had that kind of strength.

"Mr. Brennan?" Another tired-looking doctor in scrubs and a white coat. "I'm Jim Abbott, from Obstetrics."

He got to his feet. "How is my wife?"

Dr. Abbott smiled. "She's going to be fine. The baby, too. These episodes occur, occasionally, early in the pregnancy. They're scary, but not necessarily a problem. I got a nice strong heartbeat on the baby. Would you like to hear it?"

He followed the doctor back through a maze of hallways to a room where Kristin lay on a gurney, her arm over her eyes to protect her from the overhead lights. Sarah gave Matt a relieved smile as he stepped in. "I'll wait outside."

"I told your husband he could hear the baby's heartbeat, Kristin. I think that will make him feel better about both of you." Abbott picked up a strangely shaped microphone and pulled the sheet down from Kristin's shoulders. "Just let me find it now." Lifting the hem of her knit shirt, he moved the rounded end of the mike across the smooth skin of Kris's tummy. In the merciless light,

Matt could see a roundness there he hadn't noticed before, by sight or by feel.

"There. How about that?"

Matt concentrated. In the silence, he heard a very definite *whoosh-whoosh-whoosh*. He couldn't stop a grin. "That's really fast."

"One hundred forty beats a minute. Perfect." The doctor took the mike away. "I want Kristin to stay for a couple of hours, so we can be sure everything is fine. Then you can take her home and put her to bed for the rest of the day." He picked up Kristin's hand. "You need to take things easy. Get somebody else for the heavy cleaning and carrying. Don't pick up anything that weighs more than your purse. I don't think any of this is really necessary, but you have obviously been working too hard and you need to give yourself a break. Okay?"

Kristin lowered her arm and nodded. "Okay." Her voice was subdued and a little hoarse. Her eyes were swollen with tears.

Abbott nodded. "Good. I'll check in from time to time. Pull up that stool, Mr. Brennan. Have a seat."

When they were alone in the room, Matt did as the doctor had suggested and pulled over the rolling stool. He sat down beside the gurney and took Kristin's limp hand in his, bringing her fingers to his mouth.

"I don't know how to make it better, Kris. Just when I think I've finally got a handle on everything, we get into a situation with Luke and the girls and…and I completely screw up. But you've got to believe me. I think you've done the very best anyone could have. Our daughters are sweet and smart. They'll get everything figured out one day, and we'll all be good together. You and me and Erin and Jenny…and our new baby."

He stood up and braced a hand on the other side of

the bed so he could look into Kristin's pale face. ''I have to admit I'm a little surprised. I thought we'd been pretty careful.''

She swallowed. ''Not…not at the beginning of April.''

''April? Oh…when I came back from that training exercise.'' Matt bent and pressed a kiss on her forehead. ''I was pretty desperate that night—it seemed like I'd been gone for months. I guess I didn't give either of us time to think.'' He remembered the heat of that night and grinned. ''When will the baby be born?''

''December.''

''That means you're about three months, right? And you hadn't realized?''

The quality of Kristin's silence got his attention, and he thought back. ''Wait a minute. Sarah said…'' He took a deep breath. ''You knew you were pregnant?''

Kristin nodded.

''When?''

''Sadie Chisholm…figured it out.''

''So you've known since the middle of June. Almost three weeks.'' Matt sat down on the stool again. ''You didn't tell me.''

She didn't say anything.

''Why not?'' No answer. ''Why not, Kris? When did you tell Sarah?''

''Just today.''

''So…nobody was supposed to find out about this baby. Why is that?''

She rolled to her side, with her back to him.

''You have to talk to me, Kristin. I'm your husband and this baby's father. I deserve—'' He stopped as a thought struck his mind. ''I am, right? The father?''

Without warning, Kristin sat up and turned around and

slapped him, all in one quick motion. "How dare you? How dare you even think I'd been unfaithful to you?"

Appalled at his own question, he wasn't surprised at her reaction. He rolled the stool further from the bed. "I don't know anything anymore. What's true, what's not. Where your mind is, who your heart belongs to. The idea that you could keep this baby a secret for three *hours*— let alone three *weeks*—just blows my mind. I don't get it. I would never have believed it—until ten minutes ago."

Dr. Abbott stepped into the room. His grim face advertised how much of their argument he had heard. "Kristin, you should lie down. Mr. Brennan, I think you can wait outside. More emotional stress was not what I had in mind for Kristin while she's here."

Matt faced the doctor across the gurney. He debated arguing—Kristin was *his* wife and he damn well had a right to be here.

But he heard Kristin's shuddering breaths and knew he wouldn't protest. "Right. I'll be in the waiting room when she's ready to go home." With two fingers, he touched her shoulder lightly. And then made himself leave.

ONCE MATT LEFT, a nurse dimmed the light and gave Kristin a blanket. She awoke sometime later and realized with surprise that she'd simply dropped into sleep. As good a way as any to avoid thinking.

Dr. Abbott stepped into the room. "I'm glad you got a nap. I've checked your pulse and the baby's heartbeat a couple of times and everything looks great."

Kristin sat up slowly, aided by his hand behind her shoulder. "So I can go home?" At home, she'd be in her own bed with her own nightgown and her children sleeping down the hall.

And a husband who could believe she would cheat on him. With his brother, of course. Who else would Matt suspect?

The doctor gave her a worried look. "Your husband... Will you be okay? I can make arrangements to keep you at least overnight."

Her marriage might be falling apart, but Matt would never physically hurt her. "No, no. I'll be fine."

A nurse came in and helped her dress, gave her some medicine Dr. Abbott had prescribed and walked her to the waiting-room door. Kristin stepped outside, disoriented to see that the sun still shone. She was sure it must be night by now.

Matt and Sarah sat together, and turned their heads as the door swung shut behind her. Sarah came quickly across the wide room, Matt, more slowly.

"You look much better," Sarah said, putting an arm around Kristin's waist. "I bet a good night's sleep will put you back to normal."

Matt arrived at her side. Kristin didn't look at him. After a few seconds he said, "I'll go get the car." Kristin only glanced up once he'd turned away.

Sarah urged her to sit down while they waited, and held her hands. "I called Luke. He said that Mrs. Brennan explained to Erin and Jenny that you weren't feeling well. She asked them to stay with her for the night, and they were excited. So don't worry about them."

"The fireworks," Kristin said weakly. "Jenny's afraid of fireworks."

"Luke remembered that. He said to tell you he would stay inside with Jenny while Erin goes out onto the beach with his parents. Everything will be just fine."

Kristin couldn't help a laugh. She looked at her friend. "Will it? Will anything ever be right again?"

"Oh, Kristin—"

Matt stepped into the waiting room. "I've got the car outside. Ready?"

With a nod, Kristin got to her feet. Sarah stepped back and Matt put his hand under Kristin's elbow to walk her outside. She would have pulled away, but she didn't want to fall and hurt the baby.

Matt's baby.

They rode silently over to the Brennans' beach house to drop Sarah off. "Thank you," Kristin said through the window. "Tell Luke I'm sorry. And I'm grateful that he's taking care of them."

Sarah smiled and squeezed her hands. "I will. You take care of yourself and don't worry. I'll call tomorrow." She backed up, waving, then turned and went around the house toward the beach.

Matt didn't say anything as they drove home. Kristin didn't have anything to say. She didn't wait for him to open her door once they'd reached their own driveway. The house was locked, though, and he'd brought the only set of keys.

So she waited for him to open the kitchen door. He stepped back, she went inside and crossed the family room toward the stairs. All she wanted was sleep.

"Kristin?" His cool voice stopped her at the foot of the stairs. "Do you want something to drink? Something to eat?"

"No, thank you." She didn't look around. He didn't say anything else, so she started up the stairs, much slower than usual.

In their bedroom she closed the blinds and pulled a gown out of a drawer, all the time keeping her mind a careful blank. A warm shower made her feel even more exhausted. Still, she managed to dry her hair before she collapsed.

And then came the moment when she sat down on *their* bed, the place where her new baby had been conceived. Automatically, she reached for her lotion, smoothing her hands and elbows in familiar routine. Anything at all to keep from thinking.

Once again, she didn't remember lying down, or going to sleep. For the second time that day, she awoke surprised. This time, though, night had definitely fallen, leaving the bedroom dark. She turned to look at the clock. Three a.m.

The space beside her was empty. Matt?

From the top of the steps she could tell that all the lights were off downstairs. He might have fallen asleep on the couch in the family room…but that usually meant the TV would be left on, and it was not.

Already knowing what she would see, Kristin turned to the end of the hallway where they'd set up Matt's office in the guest bedroom. He was so neat and organized that he hardly disturbed the comfortable look of the room. They hadn't had any guests so far, anyway.

And there she found him, arms folded against his chest, legs straight, as he slept on his side. The moonlight through the windows showed her the furrows in his forehead.

He had chosen to sleep in a separate bed. Was he so convinced of her deceit that he couldn't bring himself to lay down beside her?

Pulling the door almost closed, Kristin went back to their…her…room. She pulled Matt's pillow against her back and curled up under the covers.

She'd never felt less like sleep. But the sun would be up in two hours or so. The arrival of morning would give her a reason—an excuse—to get out of this damn empty bed.

CHAPTER TEN

THREE WEEKS of silence from her daughter, Kristin decided, was more than enough. "Erin, love, do you remember Dr. Rose?"

"Yeah." She didn't raise her face from the book on whales she was studying. Kristin decided to ignore the absence of "Yes, ma'am."

"I'd like to give her a call and make an appointment to talk to her."

At that, her daughter looked up. "Why?" The reserve in her blue eyes said she knew perfectly well why.

But Kristin would explain anyway. "Because finding out that Matt is your father is a pretty important thing to have happen. You haven't talked to me about it, or anybody else. I thought Dr. Rose might be a more comfortable person to listen to how you're feeling."

Erin shrugged. "I'm not feelin' anything."

Kristin tightened her fists in her lap. "Okay. So you can tell her about whales when you see her next week."

Erin shrugged again, and didn't say anything at all.

After leaving Jenny with her mother on Monday afternoon, Kristin drove to the office of Rose Howard, the therapist they'd seen a few times during Kristin's divorce from Luke. Warm and solid, with dark skin and dark eyes and a penchant for bright colors, "Dr. Rose" had been easy for all of them to talk to. Kristin hoped she could work the same magic with Erin now.

She greeted them in the waiting area. "Well, hello, Erin Brennan. Give me five."

Erin put out her hand and, looking surprised, grinned.

"Good to see you." Dr. Rose gave Kristin a one-armed hug. "Have a seat. Erin and I are gonna arm wrestle." She ushered the little girl into her office and shut the door. In a few minutes, Kristin heard shrieks of laughter she identified as Rose's and Erin's. She relaxed a little into her chair.

At the end of the session, Rose called Kristin into the office. "Have a seat, Mom." She folded her hands and looked over at Erin. "Our girl here really doesn't feel much like talking. That's okay—nobody has to share their thoughts if they don't want to. I've told her that I'll be glad to listen even if she wants to call me late at night and talk on the phone." Rose handed Kristin a card. "She can reach me at the number I wrote on the back anytime. If I do happen to be busy, I'll call her back as quick as I can."

Kristin took the card and swallowed her disappointment. "Thanks for your time today, Rose."

"My pleasure. Erin, you know that candy jar out in the waiting area? I think there's a piece that's got your name on it."

"Thanks!" Erin hurried out.

Rose partially closed the door and looked at Kristin. "She's feeling very isolated. Doesn't want to talk about Matt or Luke or you at all."

"That sounds terrible. Can't we do something?"

"Just be there. Let her know you care and you'll listen. She did say you gave her a diary and she's writing things down. That's something. Her anger is going onto the page, at least a little." She put a hand on Kristin's shoulder. "This is tough for all of you. We knew it would be, when you were here three years ago. Just don't give up. There's plenty of love to go around, and I do think we can get this worked out. Bring Erin back in a couple of weeks and we'll try again. How's Jenny?''

They went into the waiting room to say goodbye. Erin waved, since her teeth were enclosed by a big ball of taffy. In the car, she extracted the taffy. "Do you have a tissue, Mom? This is too sticky."

"In the glove compartment." She waited until Erin had thrown the wrapped taffy away. "So...you're keeping what you're thinking to yourself these days."

No reply.

"I'll be glad to listen, if you ever do want to talk."

"'Kay."

They reached a traffic light. Kristin put on the brake and reached out to place her hand over the small brown one on the console between them. "I love you, Erin. Always and forever."

No answer to that, either. But at least she didn't pull her hand away until they got back home.

KRISTIN AWOKE on July 29th—the day of Erin's birthday party—as she had every day since the Independence Day party—alone. Early each morning, Matt came quietly through the bedroom, showered and shaved behind the closed bathroom door, then took his clothes out of the closet and went down the hall to dress. He pretended he didn't know she was awake. She pretended she was still asleep. Sometimes they didn't see each other at all until late in the afternoon. They were polite, even friendly sometimes.

Just not...married.

She lay in bed for a few minutes after he left, gathering her energy and her thoughts. Today would be a real chal-

lenge—hosting Erin's birthday party with all the grandparents present and with Luke and Sarah standing by.
They'd all kept their distance from each other since July
fourth. This would be the first meeting with Matt's
mother since Kristin had left the Brennans' party for the
hospital. She was not looking forward to the encounter.

At her request, Matt had not told his parents about the
new baby, and she had not told hers. Luke and Sarah
knew, of course, but promised to keep the secret from
everyone else. Nothing had been settled with Erin so far
as Matt was concerned. Kristin didn't think a new baby
would improve the situation.

Downstairs, she found the girls had gotten their own
breakfast. Erin ate milk and cereal in the kitchen with a
book propped on the table in front of her. As Buster
watched every move of her hand, Jenny munched dry
flakes in front of *Sesame Street.*

Kristin bent to kiss Jenny's head as she went by.
"Morning, love."

Jenny ducked her head, which was about as much
greeting as she ever gave before 9:00 or 10:00 a.m. Jenny
was not a morning person.

In the kitchen, Kristin put a hand on Erin's shoulder.
"Happy Birthday, Nine-year-old. How do you feel?"

Erin shrugged off her touch. "Okay."

Kristin accepted the rebuff. "You didn't want to wait
for special birthday pancakes?" Luke had instituted the
tradition of chocolate-chip pancakes for birthday break-
fasts when Erin was three.

"Yuck." She stuck out her tongue and grimaced. "I
hate those things. They taste awful."

"Okay, Erin. I get the message." Kristin poured herself a glass of juice. The message had nothing to do with

chocolate chips and pancake batter, but everything to do with the fact that Luke was not her father.

She had not asked to see him, to talk to him, or even mentioned his name since the party at the Brennans'. When he came over, Erin stayed in her room while Luke played with Jenny. The one time he'd gone upstairs to find her, the door to Erin's room had been firmly closed, with a hand-written Not Here sign taped to the panel.

Luke had left the house pretty fast that day, his face set in grim lines.

But if Erin had frozen Luke out, she certainly had not accepted Matt in his place. Dinner conversation was practically nonexistent at their house these days. Most nights Matt cleaned up after the meal while Kristin bathed Jenny and read her a story. Erin had announced that she was old enough to take a shower by herself. And she could read her own stories.

In the midst of despair, Kristin sometimes reminded herself that she'd known all along how bad this would be, how terribly the news would affect them all. Especially Erin. Seeing her predictions come true one by one was satisfying, in a twisted, heartbreaking way.

But today was not one of the times she could allow Erin the luxury of ungoverned reactions. Kristin pulled out a chair at the table and sat down across from her daughter. "Erin, we need to talk."

The book standing between her face and Erin's didn't move. "Okay."

"Put the book down, please."

"But I'm reading."

"Not while we're talking you're not."

Erin heaved a sigh and closed the book. "What?"

Fists clenched, Kristin ignored the deliberate rudeness.

"I want to be sure you know how to treat your guests politely this afternoon. *All* your guests."

She rolled her eyes. "Don't grab, say thank-you even if it's a stupid present. Walk everybody to the door to say goodbye."

"That's a good start for your friends. But I'm concerned about the way you act with your family. Especially Luke."

Erin turned in her chair, giving Kristin a view of her profile, so like Matt's. "I won't say nothing to him."

"That's the problem." Kristin got up and went to kneel in front of her daughter. "Erin, love, it's not Luke's fault. He was just trying to do what was best for me and for you. He has loved you from the very beginning, even before you were born. Nothing is ever going to change that."

"He's havin' a baby with Sarah."

"Having more children only makes more love. Nobody loses anything."

"He doesn't have to be my daddy now. When he has a baby of his own, he won't have to come over at all. He can leave Jenny and me alone."

"That is not what Luke wants, Erin. If you let them, things with Luke and Sarah can be just the same as always. Nothing has to change."

Erin hunched a shoulder and pivoted back to the table. "Can I read now?"

Kristin sat back on her heels and dropped her chin to her chest in frustrated defeat. "No, you can't read. I want you to listen. I expect you to be polite to all the grown-ups at your party this afternoon—Luke and Matt and Sarah, Granddaddy Frank and Grandma Irene, and Granddaddy William and Grandmom Elena. That means no sulks, no pouts, no ignoring what anyone says to you.

Even if you don't feel happy, even if you don't like that person, I expect you to be nice to them. Do you understand?''

''Yeah.''

''Excuse me?''

''Yes, ma'am. Can I go?''

Kristin gave up. ''Yes. Do you want to help me decorate the porch later?''

Erin grabbed her book and slipped off the chair. ''Maybe,'' she tossed over her shoulder as she left the kitchen.

Kristin eased over onto her knees again, braced her arms on the seat of the chair Erin had left and buried her face against them.

After a few minutes, Jenny came into the kitchen. She put a hand on Kristin's arm. ''What are you doin', Mommy? What's wrong?''

On a deep breath, Kristin straightened up. ''Nothing, Jenny, love. Just resting. What are you doing?''

''I want more flakes.'' She held out her bowl.

That Kristin could handle. ''Want some milk with those flakes? Or a banana?''

Jenny shook her head. ''Just flakes. I'm going to give some to Buster and he doesn't like milk.''

''Good point.'' Ignoring a twinge of pain in her right hip, Kristin stood to get more cereal, thankful that at least one of her daughters would talk to her.

THE DAY FLEW BY, filled with errands and decorating and tussles with Erin. No, she didn't want to help set up the party. No, she didn't want to wear a dress. No, she didn't want to take another shower. No, she didn't want her hair braided. Following her older sister's example, Jenny also refused to have her hair braided. She would, however, wear a dress. Jenny always chose to wear a dress.

At four o'clock, the first of Erin's friends arrived. Soon a pile of bright presents waited on a table in the corner of the deck and the backyard was filled with little girls and one excited dog. Because of Erin's recent surgery, Kristin kept the games quiet, but the laughter level remained high.

Matt appeared on the deck at the start of the party, wearing a yellow knit shirt and khaki shorts, his hair still damp from a shower. He worked Saturdays now, citing "paper pushing" to be done. Kristin kept one eye on the game of Statues in progress and the other on her husband. He seemed almost like a stranger.

And yet her heart beat faster just looking at him, so tall, so powerful, with broad shoulders and a flat belly and long, tan legs. He stood with his feet slightly apart and his arms at his sides. Kristin remembered with a deep breath how those arms felt holding her, how gently his warm hands could touch...

She jerked her gaze back to the game. Not appropriate thoughts for a child's birthday party.

Or when your weren't sleeping with the man you wanted so much.

Luke and Sarah stepped through the backyard gate a few minutes later and came to stand beside Kristin.

"This looks like fun," Sarah said with a smile, the shutter button on her camera clicking away. "I always loved playing Statues." She paused a moment and lowered the camera. "You know, that instant when you freeze in position is kind of like taking a photo shot, isn't it?"

Kristin laughed. She noticed that Luke barely smiled.

"I hadn't thought of it before, but I suppose that's true. How are you feeling?"

"Wonderful." Sarah placed her palms gently at her waist. "I'm wishing I usually wore tight jeans and skinny skirts, just so I could make the change to maternity clothes and let everybody see. But most of my clothes were pretty loose to begin with. I guess I'll have to wait a while yet."

With a pang of fear, Kristin thought about the tightness in her own waistbands. Soon she would need to wear different clothes…and explain to Erin. But she said, "I remember that stage. You could get one of those T-shirts that has an arrow on the front pointing down and the sign Baby."

"Good idea! We'll look for one tomorrow. Right, Luke?"

He shifted his gaze to her face, and his eyes softened. "Sounds good, Sarah Rose. I'll be there."

Sarah put a hand on Kristin's arm. "How are you feeling? Doing okay?"

Kristin nodded without looking at her friend. "I went to the doctor last week because I'd been having some pain in my hip. Everything was normal. He even did a sonogram, and said the baby looked just fine."

"Do you have a copy? I'd love to see it. My doctor is waiting until twenty weeks."

"No…I didn't ask." This baby got so little attention.

Beside them, Luke leaned back against a tree trunk, still watching the game. Kristin searched for a neutral comment. "How's the cop business?"

"Quiet," he said, his eyes on Erin. "Is she feeling okay these days?"

"I think so. She looks pretty normal, doesn't she?"

Luke nodded without speaking. When Kristin looked

at Sarah, her sister-in-law indicated that this was not unusual behavior. Luke, the restless, high-spirited brother,
was suffering. And Kristin couldn't see how to make
things any better.

Up on the deck, Matt waved and held up the boxes of
tacos she'd ordered delivered from a local restaurant.
Kristin turned to the kids.

"How about something to eat and drink?"

The little girls—with Buster in the middle—stampeded
toward the deck. Sarah stepped to the side, still taking
pictures. Following more slowly, Kristin saw that her parents and Matt's had arrived and were standing in the
kitchen. She took a deep breath.

"Have you talked with them again?" Luke asked.

"No."

"Matt?"

She shook her head.

"This is a real mess." He ran a hand over his hair. "I
never expected any of this back then." His eyes were
bleak when they met Kristin's. "I really thought we were
doing what was best for everybody."

She couldn't comfort him because she had no idea if
their situation would ever get straightened out.

Above them on the deck, Matt was handing out tacos.
Kristin climbed the steps and started pouring drinks.
Once the girls were all busy with food, she straightened
her shoulders, lifted her chin and joined the grandparents
in the house.

"Hi, Kristy." Her mother gave her a hug and a kiss.
"Feeling okay?"

"Just fine. Hi, Dad." Her father, always quiet, always
withdrawn, had become even more so as he got older.
She hadn't talked to him yet about Erin. She wasn't sure
he wanted to discuss the problem at all.

"How is Erin?" Mrs. Brennan asked the brisk question as she gazed out the glass-paned door at the party.

"She looks good," the Colonel volunteered. "Those young ones heal fast."

"The doctor checked her over and said she's just great." Kristin moved to the refrigerator. "Can I get y'all something to drink?"

"Let me do that, Kristy." Her mother bustled in and took the pitcher of tea. "You've been working all day, I know. Why don't you sit down and rest a minute?"

Out on the deck, Matt and Luke stood by the railing with Sarah between them. It looked as if she was trying to keep the conversation going single-handedly. Kristin knew she should help. But she just couldn't make herself go out there. "That sounds like a good idea, Mom. I think I will."

With an impatient glance at Kristin, Mrs. Brennan opened the door. "I'll see if Matt needs any help."

When Kristin looked at the Colonel, he was shaking his head and feeling in his pockets for his pipe. He caught her eyes on him. "I'm going to step out front for a puff. Want to join me, Frank?"

Her dad followed silently. The older men seemed to get along well—maybe because the Colonel had a lot to say and Kristin's father almost always simply listened.

"You look tired, Kristy." Her mother sat down across the table. "What's going on?"

She wasn't ready to mention the new baby. "Erin. Matt. Luke. I don't know what to do."

"They have to do some of this themselves, you know. You're not the only source of the problem."

Kristin looked at her mother. "Yes, I am."

"Kristy—"

"I didn't say no, years ago—not to Matt, and not to

Luke when he suggested getting married. I didn't say no to Luke when he offered to move out, or when he suggested a divorce, and I didn't sat no when Matt asked me to marry him. Five points at which I could have changed what has happened. Five crucial mistakes.''

''Honey—''

Kristin got up and walked to stand where Mrs. Brennan had stood, staring out the same pane. ''For which *they* have to suffer. But now—when I see so clearly, when I would do anything to make a difference—there's nothing to be done.'' She rested her forehead on the window glass. ''Nothing.''

Irene Jennings came up behind her and held her shoulders. ''Straight through, Kristy. When there's no way around, you go straight through. And you get there in the end.''

But Kristin was very sure that she did not want to arrive at the destination she saw looming before them all.

MATT FELT like an observer at the birthday party rather than part of the family. Hell, he felt like an observer in his own life—watching the whole thing fall apart and being too far away to do anything about it.

Kristin stood at the door from the kitchen to the deck, looking just about as excluded as he felt. *His* wife—and he couldn't reach her. His daughters—and he couldn't talk to them. His baby—and nobody had bothered to tell him.

Of course, when he'd finally found out, he'd done the unforgivable. The idea that Kristin would be unfaithful had never crossed his mind until the words came out of his mouth. There was no way to call them back. And she'd denied him any chance to apologize. When he'd awakened in the guest room that morning and realized

Kris hadn't come to bring him to their bed...well, the message was loud and clear. He'd managed to leave her alone since then. He wasn't getting much sleep. But those were the breaks.

He watched her whenever he could without getting caught. The circles under her eyes said she wasn't sleeping any better than he was. She'd lost some weight, too. That couldn't be good for her or the baby. He'd called her doctor after her checkup, just to confirm that she was, indeed, okay. Even tired and sad, she was everything Matt wanted, or needed, and so much more than he deserved.

Which might be why he was losing her.

His mother's shadow fell across his feet. "Erin seems to be well again."

Matt nodded without meeting her eyes. "Kristin's taken really good care of her." That should be adequate opening for an apology from Elena.

Evidently not. "Your father and I would like to have the children stay with us during the first week in August. I thought we might do some school shopping—"

"I don't think so, Mom." He finally turned to watch her during a minute of silence, as her eyebrows rose and her mouth thinned.

"I beg your pardon?"

He met her cool blue gaze. "This isn't the right time for Erin and Jenny to be visiting."

"And why..." She paused and turned away to cough "...would that be?"

Matt tilted his head.

"Matthew?" Another cough, rougher than the first. Matt knew he should ask if she was sick. He did care how she was feeling.

But he didn't ask. "I don't have to explain. You know what the problem is."

"Because I recognized some unflattering truths—"

He faced away from the party so his voice wouldn't be heard. "Because you insulted my wife. Because you let your prejudices and your arrogance override your judgment. And because you haven't apologized to me or, more important, to her."

"Well." He heard her deep, hoarse breath. "I didn't realize I was present at this party on sufferance. You should have warned us, and neither your father nor I would have presumed to attend."

"I'm trying to avoid dividing the family any further."

"You should have thought about that before making the mistake of becoming involved with *your wife* a second time." She turned on her heel and crossed the deck, gave a kiss to Jenny and to Erin, then disappeared into the house.

With his parents gone, the tension in the adult atmosphere eased immediately. Luke managed a couple of jokes for Sarah to laugh at. Kristin and her parents came outside and talked with some of the children. Kris served birthday cake, for the first time looking as if this might actually be a celebration instead of a heartache.

Then, during the moment of general goodwill, Jenny knocked over her drink.

A tide of punch flowed over the table, into her plate and down onto her lap. As the closest grown-up, Matt grabbed a handful of napkins and began to mop as Jenny started to cry.

He put his hand on her shoulder. "It's okay, Jenny. There's lots more cake, lots more to drink."

"My dress!" she wailed. "It's purple!" Indeed, her yellow cotton dress wore a huge grape blot.

"I'm sure it'll wash." Matt pressed a napkin to the stain. "Your mom is—"

"No!" She pushed his hand away. "You go away. You're not my daddy. My daddy takes care of me!" Turning toward Luke, she held out her arms. "Daddy…Daddy…"

Matt stood still as Luke drew his daughter away from the table. "Okay, Jenny Penny. I'm here. Let's go up and get something else on so you can come back and have cake, okay?"

Jenny put her thumb in her mouth and dropped her head onto his shoulder. With a shake of his head and a shrug, Luke carried her into the house.

Avoiding Kristin's eyes, Matt dropped the napkins into the trash bag she'd set out for the purpose. He glanced at Erin and found her staring toward the kitchen door as if she could watch Luke carry Jenny up to her room, help her change, read her a story. The longing on the older girl's face said more than Matt wanted to know.

He made himself useful during the rest of the party—helped with the presents, picked up wrapping paper and ribbon, even conducted a few rounds of Red Light, Green Light. And when the last guest had left, when the toys had been carried inside and Erin sat on the couch between her mother and grandmother, reading a book about juggling while her grandfather dozed in the recliner and Luke and Sarah sat nearby…

Matt picked up his keys off the kitchen counter. Without saying goodbye, he stepped quietly through the door into the garage, started up his truck, and ran away.

"NICE PARTY."

Elena glanced across the front seat of the car at her

husband as they waited for the light to change. "I suppose so."

"Er...Kristin works hard to make things special for Erin and Jenny."

Unclenching her teeth, Elena managed to say, "Yes."

William pressed the gas pedal and they accelerated through the intersection. "You're damn hard on her, you know."

She did not want to discuss this, not with Matt's reprimand ringing in her ears. Especially not with her head aching and her chest hurting. "Kristin has been, to put it mildly, irresponsible."

"The girl has done her best to handle some pretty tough situations."

"All of which might have been easier had she, at any point along the way, simply told the truth!" Elena gave in to the need to cough. William drew a deep breath, but didn't speak again until they'd reached home and entered the house.

He came up behind her and put his hands on her shoulders as she poured them both a glass of tea. "This cold of yours is hanging around too long, if you ask me."

Elena patted his hand. "I'm fine."

"Well, then." He hesitated. "If you can't bend a little, when it comes to Kristin, you're going to be sorry."

"I am already sorry that Matt ever met that woman."

"He loves his wife and she loves him. If you force him to choose, he'll choose her."

Elena closed her eyes. She tried to picture Matt's grim face as he requested an apology. But what she saw instead was a thinner face, topped with a wave of black hair like Luke's, split by a rueful, ingratiating grin.

"Sorry, darlin'," Gray Calhoun would say. "There's no money for debutante doin's this year..." or private school or even a secondhand car…never any money for the advantages she should have claimed as a Calhoun of Charleston.

Or even the necessities, sometimes. How many dinners had she eaten at her grandmother's house because there wasn't food at home? And how many times had that been her only meal of the day?

But there was always money for liquor, and for women, and for gambling. For fine suits and soft shoes, for the horses her father kept at the most expensive boarding stable in Charles County.

"Elena, sweetheart?"

She realized she hadn't heard a word William had said. "I'm sorry. What did you say?"

The pressure of his hands turned her to face him. "I said that you could lose Matt and his children if you don't settle this…disagreement with Kristin. Do you see that?"

She put a hand to her throbbing temple. "What I see, William, is the extent to which you and I have been made fools of. Kristin Jennings has difficulty telling the truth. I wonder if, even now, we know everything."

"We don't have to know everything."

"A family doesn't keep secrets."

"You kept one from our boys for more than thirty years."

Elena felt her face flush. She stepped out from underneath his hands and walked across the kitchen. "We had no reason to tell them about…about Melody. Being unaware that we'd lost a child did no harm to Matt or Luke."

Behind her, William sighed. "You're being stubborn and unreasonable. I guess I'll just hope that you realize it before the damage is beyond repair." He started to leave the kitchen.

"I'll have supper warmed up in a few minutes," she said. Even though she'd never felt less like eating.

At the doorway to the dining room, he stopped and shook his head, without looking back. "Don't worry about me. I'm not at all hungry tonight."

Saturday night
Dear Diary

This was my birthday. I got a klideskope from Trina an a whale puzzle from Dee an a dum purse with lipstick and perfume and stuff in it from Ashley. I didnt tell her it was dum. I said thanks very much.

Matt and Mommy gived me a new bike coz Im too tall for the old one. Grandmom and Granddad Brennan gave me a box of paints an paper an colored pencils. Its kinda okay, if it rains or somethin'. Granddaddy Frank and Grandma Irene gave me a book of storys from the Bible. It has piktures an everything. I read about a guy named Joseph, who got throwed in a pit by his brothers and then somebody took him to a difrent country an he got to be famous.

Jenny spilled grape drink when we were eatin cake an she cryed. I wish I could put her in a hole. Her an Matt. An other people to. Maybe somebody would take them away. If they becomed famous, I wouldnt go see them.

Your friend
Erin Elena Brennan

CHAPTER ELEVEN

"A DOWNTOWN BAR is a strange place to find a family man at almost midnight."

Matt didn't look up from his mug as Luke slid onto the stool beside him. "The problem with the situation lies, I believe, in your characterization of me as a family man."

"You looked like one this afternoon."

"I don't think you were paying attention."

"Your wife is worried about you."

"She worries about everybody."

"True. But you more than most."

"I've been a bastard." He emptied the last of his beer down his throat.

"Probably. Still, you owe it to her to be home."

"That was mistake number one. If I'd stayed home nine years ago, none of this would have happened."

"Well...maybe. Who's to say that would be good for anybody? Jenny wouldn't have been born. Sarah and I wouldn't be married. I love Kristin, but I hate to think about that."

"Everything I do only makes things worse."

"Maybe you're trying to do too much?"

Matt shrugged. "I'm just trying to be a husband and father. That doesn't seem like such a big deal."

Luke laughed. "Spoken like a raw recruit."

"Meaning?" He signaled for another beer.

"Being *just* a husband and father is the hardest job you can ask for. In fact, brain surgery is easier, to perform or to live through, than parenthood. In the very best of situations, being a dad means twenty-four hours a day attention to every detail. The one you miss is the one that's going to cause problems."

"Like not taking Erin straight to the hospital after she got kicked." That memory still gave him nightmares, when he managed to sleep.

"Yeah. You don't get to stop thinking. Most people, even in the Army, get to leave work at some point. Parents never do. When the kids leave home for good, I figure we'll still be worrying, wondering, trying to cover all the details."

"How did you learn so much?"

"On-the-job training, bro. Nobody is born knowing this stuff. You realize it as you go along…getting woken up every night for a year to feed a baby, getting woken up for years after that to change wet beds…or worse than wet. Panicking at fevers and ear infections and rashes, holding them when they get booster shots. Just the day-to-day stuff of having kids."

Taking the top off the beer the bartender had placed before him, Matt sighed. "I've been working on this for over a year now."

"You're fighting an uphill battle. Nothing is easy when you start out with your handicap."

"Following your footsteps, you mean?" And didn't that sound petty?

Luke chuckled. "Uh, no. That's not what I mean. I made plenty of mistakes, mistakes Kristin and the girls were kind enough to forgive me for. What I mean is, you're trying to be a dad to little girls who can think for themselves and talk and deliberately refuse to cooperate.

Babies just want to feel good—a much easier assignment than convincing Erin that you want to be her dad.''

"I don't know what else to do."

"Me neither."

Finally, Matt looked at his brother. "What do you mean, 'me neither'? After shoveling out all this advice, you're supposed to provide the answer."

"You watch too many movies. I'm as stumped as you are."

Matt signaled the bartender one more time. "Great. Join me in a drink?"

"No, but I'll drive you home. You can get your truck in the morning." Luke threw a few bills on the bar. "Let's go."

Matt thought about protesting, then gave in. No sense in making a fool of himself. He could mope at home in the guest room as well as anywhere. And the bathrooms at home were cleaner.

PARKED IN THE DRIVEWAY of his house, though, Matt hesitated. Kristin must still be awake. The lights downstairs lit up the windows like a jack-o'-lantern's grin. How would he explain taking off from his daughter's birthday party?

Then he laughed at himself. Why would an explanation be necessary? Erin had probably not even missed him.

"Kristin doesn't bite," Luke commented. "But I think you two need to talk."

"Thanks for the advice." The tone was more sarcastic than he'd intended. Matt hopped down from the truck. "And for the ride. I appreciate it."

"No problem. See you later." His brother's taillights vanished down the street before Matt made it to the front door.

He let himself in, walked into the living room to turn off the lamps, and did the same in the dining room. With a tightness in his throat that felt a lot like fear, he went down the hallway to the family room.

Kris had fallen asleep curled up on the sofa. Her hair was loose and shining, her cheeks tinged with rose, her mouth pouting the way it did when she slept. Yet she looked far from relaxed. A little line had formed between her eyebrows. The shadows under her eyes weren't caused by her long, thick lashes. And her hands were held against her chest, clenched defensively.

Matt shook his head. This was not the way it was supposed to work. Being together should make them happy. Not defensive. Not in need of protection. They ought to protect each other.

He knelt by the couch and put his hand on her cheek. ''Kris? Kris, honey, you need to be in bed.'' She didn't stir. Sliding his hands under her knees and shoulders, he got to his feet, cradled her against his chest and started for the stairs.

In the bedroom, he lowered her gently to the bed and then stayed on his knees, just looking at her. The dim light deepened the circles under her eyes and the hollows under her cheekbones. She shouldn't be so sad. She should feel cherished and treasured and safe.

Leaning close, Matt pressed a kiss to his wife's forehead…then lingered for several more as the smooth texture and sweet scent of her skin snared him. They hadn't been this close in weeks. He brushed his mouth across hers, testing the shape and softness of that pout. He felt Kristin's smile, and made the kiss real.

His hand shook a little as he stroked from her wrist to her elbow to her shoulder, under the short sleeve of the gown she wore. With his stupid pride and thoughtless words he'd almost thrown away this privilege—the right to lie down on their bed, to take his wife in his arms and mold her against him. She was soft where he was hard, and the fit was perfect. Sweeping his palm along the sweet slope of her thigh, Matt pushed the short nightshirt up to her waist, then leaned back far enough to take the hem with both hands and ease it over her head.

As he gazed at her, at the roundness of her breasts, the dip of her waist and the flare of her hips, it was all he could do to harness his desire. Kris deserved more. He wanted her with him when he exploded inside of her. Breathing hard, he lowered his head and kissed the velvet skin on the slope of her breast.

Kristin shivered as cool air flowed over her skin. She shivered again as she felt Matt's mouth moving on her, the welcome weight of his body above hers. She gasped in shock and pleasure as he licked and bit and suckled. Such heaven, being loved by him, loving in return. She shifted her hips, adjusting to the press of his. Her hands reached for him, finding clothes in the way.

And then she woke up.

This gasp was dismay, quickly stifled. All the warmth, all the pleasure drained away as her mind began to function. They hadn't spoken to each other in any meaningful way for weeks. How could they make love as if that hadn't happened? They couldn't. They would simply be having sex. In all her life, Kristin had never had sex. She hated the idea of such an intimate joining of bodies without an equal meeting of minds and hearts.

But Matt was her husband. Perhaps she could pretend, could give him what he wanted simply because she loved him. Her own response really wasn't important...

After a few moments, he lifted his head. "Kris? What's wrong?"

"Nothing." She put her hand at the back of his neck and drew him close for a kiss. "Nothing."

He drew away. "Don't lie to me." With his back to her, he swung his legs off the bed and put his head in his hands. "There have been too many secrets already, too much left unsaid."

She sat up as well. "I'm just tired. You disappeared so suddenly tonight…we haven't talked to each other…"

"What's there to say?" He stood up. "You made your point three weeks ago when you left me asleep in the guest room. And every day since, by avoiding my eyes and any chance we might get to be alone together. Believe me, Kris, I get the message."

She watched in disbelief as he crossed to the door. "You're leaving?"

"I'm tired, too," he said without turning around. "We both need a good night's sleep. See you tomorrow." His footsteps padded toward the other end of the hallway. The mattress on the guest-room bed squeaked.

Kristin was alone again.

THREE DAYS LATER, Kristin was halfway through reading "Cinderella" to Jenny when the phone rang. "Excuse me, love. I'll be right back."

But the conversation took longer than she anticipated. And when she did return, she closed the book. "We need to go get Erin at Trina's house, Jenny. We'll finish the story when we get back."

"I don't wanna go!"

Kristin picked her up and carried her downstairs. "I know. But this is an emergency." She strapped the frustrated little girl into her car seat and climbed in behind the wheel. "The trip won't take but a few minutes, I promise."

At Trina's house, Kristin tried to apologize while Erin put on her shoes. "I'm sorry. I don't know why Erin would be so hard to get along with. She's been looking forward to playing with Trina all week."

"Well…" Trina's mother glanced at Erin, then beckoned Kristin to step outside and pushed the door almost closed behind them. "I haven't said anything because I didn't want to upset you and I thought it would pass. But Erin's been difficult for a while now. Demanding her own way in the games she and Trina play, refusing to help pick up unless I interfere. She's said some pretty mean things to Trina, too. She gives an apology when I ask for one, but…this isn't like her. She's always been high-spirited. But not cruel."

Before Kristin could muster up a word, Erin opened the door behind them. "I'm ready, Mommy." She didn't look up as she slipped by—just walked down the steps and straight to the van.

Kristin called her back to the porch. "Aren't you forgetting something?"

"I didn't bring anything with me."

"Did you say thank-you to Trina's mom?"

Erin hung her head and mumbled.

"We didn't hear you, Erin."

She flung her head back and gazed up at the other woman with resentment. "Thank you for having me over."

Trina's mother nodded. "Have a good afternoon, Erin." For the first time in the four years Trina and Erin had played together, there was no suggestion of a return engagement.

At that omission, Kristin understood how badly Erin had behaved. "Thanks," she said, feeling her cheeks heat

up. "Tell Trina we'll be thinking about her." Then she
hurried Erin out to the van.

She didn't trust herself to maneuver the car and talk
with Erin, so she didn't say a word on the short drive
home. In the house, Jenny clamored to resume her story.
"I wanna read. Come on, Mommy!" She tugged at Kristin's shirttail.

Kristin knelt to meet her daughter face-to-face. "I will
finish the story, Jenny. But first I need to talk to Erin. If
you'll go to your room and read by yourself, I'll be there
just as soon as I can."

Jenny's lower lip quivered. "But you said we would
read when we came back."

"And we will. But I have to talk with Erin right this
minute. Can you be a big girl and understand that?" She
leaned forward to kiss Jenny's cheek.

Jenny hunched a shoulder and turned away to trail
slowly up the stairs, disappointment drawn by every line
of her body.

Kristin sighed and started to rise. A sharp pain drove
through her hip, pushing her back to her knees. Panting,
she stayed where she was until the spasm eased.

This time she got up more carefully, slowly, and the
pain didn't come back. Relieved, she went in the direction Erin had last taken. "Erin? Erin, where are you?"

Erin didn't answer, but Kristin found her curled up on
the couch in the family room with Buster. Not reading,
not watching TV, or even talking. Just sitting with her
arms around the dog's neck, her face buried against his
soft fur.

"Erin?" Kristin sat across from them on the coffee
table. "What happened at Trina's?"

"Nothin'."

"Trina's mom wouldn't have asked me to come get you for nothing."

After a long silence, Erin stirred. "She was bein' dumb."

"How?"

"She wanted everything her own way. We were playin' animal doctor, but she had to be the doctor an' the animals had to be what she said they were an' all I got to do was hold them. I wanted to be the doctor."

"You could have taken turns."

"Trina's too dumb to take turns."

"I can understand that you would be upset. What did you do?"

"I don't know."

"Erin, you were there. You do know."

She looked up, flushed, eyes bright with tears and anger. "I tore up her stupid stuffed dog, okay? She wouldn't let it need an operation and I grabbed it and it just tore."

Kristin calmed her own voice. "Was it the one she always brings when she spends the night?"

Erin nodded, her face again buried in Buster's splotched fur.

"Oh, Erin." Kristin closed her eyes. "You know how much Trina loves that dog. She's had it since she was a baby."

A muffled sob concurred.

But the discussion couldn't just end in tears. "Why are you so mad these days, Erin? What's wrong?" Kristin didn't need an answer to the question. But Erin needed the chance to provide one. "Tell me, please?"

Erin shook her head. Kristin waited for quite a while, until she heard Jenny thumping around in her room upstairs, clearly impatient. Finally, she put a hand on Erin's shoulder.

"I want to talk about this, Erin. Whenever you're ready. I think we need to talk because we love each other and we want to make things easy for each other. Just let me know, okay?"

The little girl didn't move or acknowledge Kristin's request. With another sigh, Kristin got up and started upstairs, wishing that Erin's problems could be solved as simply as Cindrella's.

LATE THAT NIGHT, Kristin awoke to darkness and Jenny's whisper. "Mommy?"

"What's wrong, love? Are you sick?"

"Mommy, my bed's wet."

She struggled up on an elbow, still barely awake. "What happened?" The absence of a reply explained the situation. "Oh dear." Eyes mostly closed, she flung back the covers and swung her legs to the floor. "I'm coming."

As she got to her feet, the hall light came on. Matt stood silhouetted in the bedroom door. "Is everything okay?"

She noticed he carefully did not step over the threshold.

Blinking back tears, she said, "Jenny wet her bed."

"Oh." The three of them stood silent for a frozen second. "I'll take care of it."

"That's okay. I can—"

Shaking his head, Matt turned away. "You go back to sleep. Jenny and I can handle this. Right, Jenny?"

Jenny had her thumb in her mouth. She shook her head.

Kristin looked out into the hallway. "That's okay, Matt. Really."

"You get her changed," he said over his shoulder. "I'll fix the bed."

When she and Jenny came into the girl's room after a quick sponge-off, Matt had stripped the bed. He held out a set of sheets on each arm. "Pink or yellow, Jenny?"

Jenny popped her head through the neck of the nightgown Kristin held. "Yellow."

"You got it." He bent to make up the bed.

"Why is everybody up?" Erin stood at the door to the hall.

She took in what Matt was doing. "Jenny wet her bed? What a baby."

"Erin!"

"Mommy, make her take it back! I'm not a baby!"

Matt smoothed the blanket on Jenny's bed. "I remember when I was about seven. One night I had to go to the bathroom, and I got out of bed and went down the hallway and turned on the light and everything. Only then I woke up and realized it was just a dream. Too late." He shrugged casually. "Happens to bigger kids, too. Not just babies."

Erin looked down at her bare feet.

"So, Miss Jenny. Do you want to get into your nice clean bed now?"

Jenny stared at him warily, then climbed onto the bed. Matt pulled up the sheet and blanket and tucked her in. "Sleep tight. Don't let the bugs bite."

She lifted heavy eyelids. "What bugs?"

He smiled. "No bugs. Just a way to hope you have nice dreams." Touching her on the nose with his forefinger, he straightened up. "Good night."

Mesmerized by his sweetness, his patience, Kristin

took a second to realize she, too, should leave. She gave Jenny a kiss. "Love you. See you tomorrow."

"'Night, Mommy."

When Kristin straightened, both Matt and Erin had left the room. Turning off Jenny's bright light, she wondered briefly which end of the hall she should go to. Finally, she went to Erin's room. Her first responsibility lay with her children.

The room was dark. Erin huddled in the center of her bed.

"Erin? Are you asleep?"

No answer. The air felt too lively for Erin to be sleeping, but she obviously didn't want to talk. Kristin decided to leave her alone. Tomorrow would be soon enough to face the situation.

"I love you, Erin," she whispered to the dark. "Sleep tight."

At the other end of the hall, the guest-room door was closed. Matt was sending a message of his own. Kristin returned to her cold, empty bed, where she lay awake until Matt came in some three hours later to get dressed.

When he came out of the shower, Kristin was sitting up against the pillows. "Good morning."

Matt looked away from her tousled hair, her serious brown gaze, focusing on the buttons of his uniform shirt. "'Morning."

"Thank you for helping out last night."

He shook his head. "I only made the bed."

"And made Jenny feel better about what had happened. That's more important."

Just listening to Kristin's sleep-husky voice was tearing him up. This was as much as they'd said to each other since the last argument, three days ago. "I'm glad I could help."

"Matt, we need to talk."

He propped his arms stiffly on the edge of the dresser. "I know."

"Maybe…maybe we should get out of the house. Go somewhere the girls won't interrupt."

"Maybe we should." Hope pounded in his chest, so hard he could barely breathe.

"I'll find out if Luke and Sarah can take the girls."

"Good." He straightened and forced himself to meet her eyes. "Just let me know." He tried a smile.

And found a soft reflection on her lips. "I will."

He left the house feeling better than any time in the last month. Surely Kris was right. With a chance to talk uninterrupted, they could get the issues sorted out.

With the beginning of August, the summer recruiting rush had ended at work. Kids were getting ready to go off to college now. He could expect a new flood when midterm grades appeared in October and some of them realized they weren't ready for college. Or vice versa.

He busied himself with paperwork for an hour or so, then sat back with a cup of coffee and too much time on his hands. A new book on Sherman's march to the sea had arrived. Now was as good a time as any to begin.

As he reached for the book, the phone rang. "Brennan? Colonel Tilden."

His Special Forces commanding officer. "Good morning, sir."

"How the hell are you, son? Haven't heard from you in quite some time."

"I'm doing just fine, sir. And yourself?"

"Never better. But I could use you to keep tabs on this latest group we've brought in. A bunch of wild cards, less predictable than usual. We've got to break them pretty quick. What do you say? It's about time you took your rightful place again. I need men like you.''

Matt rubbed his eyes with his free hand. ''I haven't made that decision yet, sir.''

''So your dad tells me. I figured you just needed a kick in the butt. This is it.''

''Thank you, sir. If that were all it took, I'd be there tomorrow.''

''What's the holdup?''

''I've got a family now, sir. They deserve my time and attention.''

''The Army comes first, son. Your wife should know that. Or she shouldn't have married you in the first place.''

Matt wondered about that, though for different reasons. ''We both understand that, sir.''

'''He who hesitates is lost.' And he's damn sure not right for a Special Forces post. Quit stalling, Brennan. Come back to work or get out. I expect your decision by one September.''

''Yes, sir.''

The Colonel hung up without a goodbye. Matt put his head in his hands. All he needed was a deadline. In a month he would have to know if his marriage would last and if he could make a family with his daughters.

If not, he might as well go back into Special Forces. Maybe he'd be lucky, and really get himself killed this time.

LUKE HESITATED when Kristin called Friday morning and asked him to take care of the girls.

''I don't know. I'm not sure that's a good idea right now.''

''Because of Erin?''

"Well, yeah. She's not talking to me. How'm I supposed to deal with her when she won't look me in the eye?"

"But nothing will get better if we don't try, Luke." That included her marriage. She *had* to have this time with Matt.

"What about your folks?"

"Mom and Dad are out of town this week."

"You could wait until they got back."

"Luke. I can't."

"Damm it, Kristin. I know this is all wrong. She's just a little girl and I ought to be able to handle her. But I'm not doing a very good job. What about my parents?"

"Matt says he's not going to see them until your mother apologizes."

"So hell will freeze over, and you'll still be waiting for a baby-sitter."

"Something like that."

He sighed. "Okay. I'll give it a shot. No promises on either of us coming out unscathed, though."

"I'll talk to Erin first."

"That might help."

But as had become the norm, Erin didn't want to talk. "Okay. I understand. I won't do anything mean."

"It's more than that, Erin. Luke loves you. All he wants is for you to love him back. Is that so hard?"

"He's not my dad. I don't have to love him."

"You don't have to love anybody. But Luke hasn't done a single thing to make you so mad. He doesn't deserve the way you're acting."

"He lied."

"For your own good."

"He married somebody else."

"Because he loves her and she makes him happy."

"They're having a baby."

"Erin, love, the new baby doesn't make a difference." This message had to get through before Kristin could break her own news. "I don't love you any less than I did before Jenny was born. I only love both of you more. Luke and Sarah will love their new baby and that love will just increase what they feel for you."

"Sarah doesn't have to love me. She barely knows me."

They were talking in circles. "Sarah loves you because of what she knows. That's enough. Love is very precious, Erin. Not something to be thrown away when it's offered."

"Love hurts."

The simple sentence drove into Kristin's heart like a sword. "Sometimes it does. But mostly it makes us feel better and act better."

Erin finally raised her gaze to Kristin's face. "You love Matt?"

"Yes. I would never have made a baby—you—with him if I didn't love him with all my heart. We were going to be married."

"You love Luke?"

She drew a deep breath. "Yes. He's been my friend since I was in the seventh grade."

"You made Jenny with Luke."

"We were married. I thought Matt was dead."

"Do you love Luke as much as Matt?"

"In a different way, I did and do."

"But not enough to stay married to him when Matt came back."

Inescapable logic. "Erin, I know it doesn't seem to make sense. I've made mistakes. And I'm really, really sorry. But I want us to make life good again. Can't we do that?''

Erin considered, her gaze still fixed on Kristin's face. Then she shook her head. "I don't think so. It's too hard.''

"Not if we all work together. That's what families are for. To help each other.''

Erin slid off the stool at the counter. "Families are just trouble," she said. "I think I won't ever have kids of my own. Come on, Buster. Let's go outside.''

Without waiting to be excused, Erin walked out on the conversation.

And Kristin let her leave, because she couldn't stand the pain one moment longer.

Friday
Dear Diary

I desided today not to get married or have kids. I dont like what happens when people love each other. Seems like everybody just gets hurt. I hurt enuf already.

Trina hates me and Jenny makes fun of me. I wonder if I can be a animal doctor in sum other country. Then I wouldnt have to see anybody here ever again.

I would run away now but I dont have any money and I wouldnt have anywhere to live. Besides Matt is in the Army. He could get them to find me quick.

So Ill stay home. When they see how bad I can be they wont send me to his house anymore. I can be very bad.

Your friend
Erin Elena Brennan

CHAPTER TWELVE

AFTER LUKE AND SARAH picked up the girls on Saturday morning, Kristin packed a fried-chicken lunch. Matt came home at noon and they headed south to Brookgreen Gardens, one of South Carolina's most beautiful places. August heat blanketed the entire region, but under the live oaks of Brookgreen, their long branches draped with swaying Spanish moss, it was possible to feel reasonably cool.

They found a table at the far end of the picnic area. Few people had braved the one-hundred-ten-degree heat, so they practically had the whole garden to themselves.

Kristin spread a tablecloth and unpacked the food. Matt had said almost nothing on the drive down, and she hadn't tried to break the silence. There was so much to say and yet, in a way, everything had already been said. Today they had to try to put the pieces back together. She prayed they could.

"This looks pretty decadent." He sat down on one side of the table. "Fried chicken, deviled eggs, potato salad? I can feel my cholesterol level climbing." His grin robbed the statement of any criticism. "It may kill me..." Taking a bite of chicken, he closed his eyes and smiled as he chewed. "But what a way to go!"

She laughed. "We can walk the entire garden after lunch. That should help your cholesterol."

"That's assuming I can move." He took another piece of chicken. "You may have to roll me back to the van."

She chuckled again, and they lapsed into silence. The buzz of crickets and cicadas was loud, the still air almost too thick to breathe. A typical low-country summer day.

"I've been trying to figure out how to start," Matt said in a quiet voice, turning a peanut-butter cookie between his fingers. "But I'm not coming up with anything brilliant."

"Me neither." Kristin sipped her lemonade without looking at him.

"I'll start by apologizing. I shouldn't have said what I did at the hospital. I didn't believe it even while the words were coming out of my mouth."

"I know you didn't." Matt was like his mother—in emotional situations, he tended to react first, then think. "It's okay. Don't worry about that anymore. I'm not."

"I still don't understand why you didn't tell me about the baby."

"I—" Tears stung her eyes. "I didn't know if you'd want a baby."

When she looked up, he was staring at her, his blue eyes wide with surprise. "Why would you think that I'd be anything but overjoyed?"

"You told your mother the girls were enough." The deep breath she took trembled. "And when Erin was hurt…at the hospital you told Luke…you said something about limiting your exposure."

"Damn." He reached for her hand. "I was worried Kris, not thinking clearly. But having a baby with you—" His smile was gentle. "I can't think of anything I want more."

She returned the pressure of his fingers, but she wasn't reassured. "I dread telling Erin. She's resentful of Luke and Sarah's baby. When she hears there will be another one, I'm afraid she'll be devastated.''

He nodded. ''Erin's got some adjusting to do. But I think we're being too careful about what she thinks and wants and feels.''

''How can you say that? She's lost Luke as her father, not once, but twice. She'll look at the new baby as a sign she's losing me, too.''

His blue eyes snapped with impatience. ''She's manipulating the situation, Kris. Can't you see? We're all walking on tiptoe around her, trying not to rock her boat. But life is about getting your boat rocked, over and over again. She needs to learn to cope.''

Panic grabbed her throat. ''Erin is nine years old. Not eighteen.''

''Erin's a wonderful little girl who is bright enough to figure out how to stand between you and me. Don't get me wrong—I love my daughter. But that doesn't blind me to the fact that she's using your emotions to drive us apart.''

''You think I'm blind to Erin's behavior? Her motives?'' Kristin drew her hand back into her lap.

''I think you always give your daughters the benefit of the doubt. Sometimes long past the time when you should have recognized the facts.''

''I try to be fair.''

''I appreciate that. But there has to be a kind of… of…solidarity between you and me if this family is going to work. Erin senses that, and she's doing her damnedest to see that it doesn't happen.''

''You talk as if you two are strangers.''

Matt shrugged. ''We are, in a lot of ways. Erin doesn't want to let me into her life. Especially now that she knows I belong there. And believe me, I don't like admitting that she doesn't want me as her dad." The hurt on his face was real.

Kristin took a deep breath to calm down. "So what is your suggestion for solving this problem?"

"I think Erin needs to be told the facts. We should assure her of our love and support and understanding. Tell her we know this isn't easy to accept, but we all have to do just that. And then she needs to realize that she can't do anything that will push me out of her life— or yours."

Too agitated to sit still, Kristin got to her feet and started packing up the food. "I don't think Erin is as…as calculating as you say she is. She's just a confused little girl. I don't want to make that any worse."

"Something in this situation has to give, Kris. It can be Erin's stubbornness. Or it can be our relationship."

She looked up into his face. "You want me to choose between our daughter and our marriage?" Hadn't she expected this all along?

Matt shook his head. "No. I want you to have both. But I think there should be some balance." He was silent for a few moments, then continued. "Kris…" He paused again, struggling for the right words. "I'm fighting for my life, here. I can't let her make all the rules."

She turned on him, her eyes wilder than he'd ever seen them.

"Fighting? Dear God, you're *fighting* your own daughter? For what? Attention? You think I haven't been a good enough wife this last year? That I spend too much time with the children? That I'm choosing my daughter over you because I simply want to cushion her against another blow?"

He held his temper with an effort. "You're twisting my words. And you know it."

"I'm trying to understand. What is it I haven't done for you? What's missing from our life together? What—what the *hell* do you want?"

Hearing that mild curse in her gentle voice snapped his control. "Honesty, for starters. Some hint of what you're thinking, maybe. Why are we married? Where are we going? What does our future look like...or do we even have one together?"

Kristin opened her mouth to answer. The cell phone in his pocket rang at the same time.

Taking a deep breath, he took the phone out and flipped it open. "Hello?"

"Matt, it's Sarah." She didn't give him time to ask a question. "I think you two had better come back to town. Things are going very badly over here. I need to bring the girls home."

He looked over at Kris. She had turned away from him, her shoulders and back stiff, unyielding.

"That's okay, Sarah. We're finished here, anyway. You stay put—we'll be at your place within the hour."

"I WAS PLAYING Candyland with Jenny," Sarah explained on the doorstep of the house she shared with Luke. The girls waited in the van. "Luke tried to talk with Erin. At first she was quiet, and I thought she was listening. But then..." She shook her head. "It was like an explosion. Suddenly, she was yelling at him, accusing Luke of lying and cheating. She told him she hated him and didn't want to see him again. Then she hit him."

Kristin covered her face with her hands. This couldn't get any worse.

"When Luke caught her wrist and tried to deal with the hitting, she picked up that big conch shell we found on our honeymoon and threw it against the wall." Sarah chuckled a little. "That made quite an interesting impression on the wall."

"Did the shell break?" Those were the first words Matt had said since they left Brookgreen.

"Only when it hit the tile floor."

Feeling empty, Kristin looked up. "I'm so sorry, Sarah."

The other woman shrugged. "We can go back to the islands for another shell. But Luke…" She sighed. "This is tearing him up. I think the only thing we can do until Erin adjusts is keep our distance." She placed a hand protectively over her unborn baby. "So I hope you'll understand if we're not around for a while. It's not that we don't care. We care too much."

Kristin backed off the small front step. "I know you do." She drew a deep breath, pushing away the need to cry. "Tell Luke that I'm terribly sorry and I'll do the best I can to bring Erin around. You take care of yourselves and your baby, okay?"

Sarah smiled sadly and waved before closing the door. In the van again, with Matt driving, Kristin leaned back against her seat's headrest, squeezing her eyes shut.

No one said a word on the ride home, not even Jenny. In the house, Kristin told the girls to go to their rooms and stay there. They obeyed without question or protest.

As she stood in the family room, trying to gather her thoughts, Matt's hand came to rest on her shoulder. "Do you want me to talk to her?"

Kristin pulled away from him and walked to the bottom of the stairs. "No. I don't think anything either of us can say will help." She looked at him over her shoulder. "Frankly, I'm beginning to wonder if the right words will ever come."

Saturday

Dear Diary

Mommy sent me to my room until suppertime. Thats okay. I like bein by myself.

I dont have to see Luke anymore. I broke a seashell at his house and Im pretty sure they wont ask me back. Im glad. I didnt want to go in the first place.

Seems like everythings gone bad since that day in the hospital. Nobody talks to nobody, sept for me and Buster. Mommy keeps tryin to make things right, but nothin works anymore.

She shoulda thought about that before she went and messed everything up.

Your friend

Erin Elena Brennan

STILL SHELL-SHOCKED from the weekend, Matt answered the office phone Monday afternoon with no enthusiasm.

"Matt." He'd never heard his father's voice so unsteady.

"What's wrong?"

The Colonel made an audible effort at control. "Your mother...your mother is being admitted to the hospital. She has pneumonia."

"I'll be right there."

For the third time in as many months, Matt sat in a hospital waiting room, grappling with fear. Luke and Sarah arrived shortly after he did, and their company seemed to reassure his dad. But the wait lasted forever, anyway.

By dinnertime, they knew the worst and best of the situation. Elena Brennan had developed pneumonia after a cold, with both lungs affected, which was a serious complication. She would be kept in the hospital for several days to receive IV antibiotics. At home, it might take as much as ten days for her to *start* resuming her usual activities.

Matt and Luke and Sarah made plans while the Colonel sat with his wife. "Your dad won't be able to manage alone," Sarah pointed out. "He doesn't cook or clean. Your mother will go crazy if the house is less perfect than usual."

"So we'll have to take care of it for them." Luke looked at Matt. "Have you told Kristin?"

"Yes." He flinched away from remembering the terseness of that conversation. "She said she'd do anything she could to help." Between the four of them, they ought to be able to manage two grandparents and two grandkids pretty easily.

Matt stayed at the hospital until the doctors agreed to let him visit his mother. She lay propped on pillows in the narrow bed, her face nearly as white as the sheets. When he stepped close, she opened her eyes slowly, as if the lids were too heavy to lift. "Matthew?" Her voice was a whisper.

He took her dry, hot hand between his. "Don't talk, Mom. I just wanted to say hello. Dad's okay," he said in response to the question in her eyes. "Luke and Sarah have taken him to the cafeteria for some food. We'll make sure he gets home tonight."

She nodded slightly and closed her eyes again. Matt started to put her hand down, but her fingers closed weakly on his.

"He'll…need…help."

"I know. We've got everything worked out. Everybody is going to pitch in and take care of Dad, the house, the meals, whatever. You just concentrate on getting better, okay?''

The corners of her mouth lifted a fraction of an inch. ''Yes.'' In another moment, she had gone back to sleep.

It felt wrong to leave the room and leave his mother all alone, so Matt sat down in the armchair, waiting for the others to return. He was still upset with her for the things she'd said about Kristin. But a life-threatening illness put even the serious conflicts on hold. However badly she'd behaved, however difficult she might be to deal with, he wasn't ready to lose his mother.

He didn't fool himself; the next couple of weeks would be tough. Adding sick-room duty to their other responsibilities would push everyone to the limits of their endurance.

Even more complicated were all the personal issues. How could Kristin take care of the woman who had treated her so badly? Sarah couldn't do it all though, she had her photo shop to run. He and Luke had jobs to report to. But Matt didn't trust his mother to behave, even while Kristin was doing her an immense favor. The last thing his marriage needed was one more blowup with his parents.

When he tried to suggest, later that night, that she could help without actually going over to his mother's house, Kristin balked.

''I won't allow her to believe I didn't care enough to come over.''

''But you're just asking for trouble. Mom doesn't mince words at the best of times. When she's feeling bad and frustrated about something, there's no telling what she might say.''

His wife gazed at him, her brown eyes more determined, and somehow harder, than he'd ever seen them.

"Your mother is part of my family. Regardless of what she thinks, I take my responsibilities to my family very seriously and I won't shirk them because of a disagreement. If she asks me to leave, I will. Otherwise, I'll do my share."

Matt couldn't argue with her commitment and dedication. He only wished he, too, wasn't simply another "responsibility" for Kristin to shoulder. He wished he could believe she was his wife simply for the joy of loving him.

But there didn't seem to be much joy left in the world these days.

REGARDLESS OF her brave words to Matt, Kristin approached her first shift with Mrs. Brennan pessimistically.

The Colonel met her at his front door on Mrs. Brennan's first morning home. "I'm glad you're here, Kristin. Luke left just a few minutes ago. Now she's talking about getting up for a shower, sitting in her chair in the family room, writing some overdue letters. She's not listening to reason. I hope you can help."

Kristin put on a smile as she stepped into the bedroom. "It sounds like you're feeling better, Mrs. Brennan. Really sick people usually want to stay in bed."

Always fair-skinned, Elena's face was absolutely white, her lips barely touched with color, her eyes heavy. "I am quite ill." A wracking cough proved her point. "But I refuse to lie in bed and abandon my responsibilities."

The bedsheets were wrinkled and twisted. Kristin bent to smooth them out. "I think women often try to carry on with their work when they're feeling sick. Men, too, of course." She cast an apologetic glance at the Colonel as she straightened the blanket. "But mothers, especially, tend to just keep going. And as a result, they often stay sick longer. Can I smooth those pillows?''

With her mouth in a grim line, Elena sat forward. Kristin plumped and straightened the pillows, then piled them back at a slightly lower angle. ''There. Have you had breakfast?''

''I'm not hungry in the least.'' Another painful-sounding cough.

''Probably not. But some food might help you get your strength back faster. How does a poached egg and a piece of soft toast sound?''

''Like an invalid.''

''Well, if you handle that, we can always make something more adventurous.'' Kristin went to the doorway and managed another smile. ''I'll be back in just a few minutes.''

Once safe in the kitchen, though, she propped her elbows on the counter and buried her face in her hands. The effort of maintaining calm and being pleasant in the face of Elena's rancor had left her shaking.

Sarah clearly expected the worst when she came to relieve Kristin at three o'clock. Her first question was not about their mother-in-law. ''Are *you* okay?''

With freedom in sight, Kristin could grin. ''We both survived. She ate an egg and toast, drank some tea, and has slept the rest of the time.''

Sarah's face relaxed. ''I was so worried. Anything else I need to know?''

''I straightened the guest room that the Colonel's using and washed the clothes in the hamper—they're drying now. I put together some chicken soup. Just let it simmer until she wakes up. Um…'' She tried to think of anything else she could do to help before she left.

But Sarah shook her head. ''Okay, that's enough.

You've done your work and most of mine for the day."
With an arm around Kristin's shoulders, she led her to
the door. "Go home and get some rest, yourself. Hug the
girls for me."

Two days later, the carefully planned schedule fell
apart. Luke was supposed to sit with his mother in the
early mornings after he got off the night shift at the police
department. The third morning, he called Kristin at 6:00
a.m.

"I'm not going to get there today." He sounded
rushed. "We had a domestic-violence incident last night
and I'm still working the crime scene. Can you go earlier?"

She was scheduled to be there at ten, after the girls
had eaten, dressed and been dropped at her mother's. "I
suppose I can rush the girls some, get there by eight-
thirty. Would that work?"

"It'll have to. Gotta go." He disconnected without further wasted words.

Of course, Erin and Jenny didn't want to hurry. "I
wanna watch *Sesame Street*." Jenny sat on the floor in
front of the television with her usual bowl of dry cereal.

"You can watch at Grandma Irene's house." Kristin
knelt and set the cereal bowl aside so she could pull the
nightgown over Jenny's head. She eased on a play dress.
"Grandma Irene has a bigger TV."

"Okay." Jenny's head emerged and she looked
around. "Mommy! Buster's eating my frosty flakes!"

That was the last of the box. "We've got other cereal,
love. I'll get you a new bowl."

Jenny continued to whine. "I wanted frosty flakes. I
always have frosty flakes."

"Baby," Erin muttered as she came into the room, still

wearing her pajamas. "You're always cryin' about something."

"Am not."

"Are too."

"Erin." Kristin sighed. "Go upstairs and get some clothes on, as I asked ten minutes ago. I need to get over to Grandmom Elena's house to take care of her."

"I don't want to go."

"What you want doesn't come first today. Now please go upstairs."

"What I want never comes first."

Kristin kept her hands gentle as she brushed Jenny's hair. Inside, she was screaming. "I know it feels like that sometimes. Maybe especially right now. But we try to do things for you as much as we can and we hope that you can be patient with us when we need to do things for other people."

"I don't want to go. I'll stay home."

"No, you won't." Standing, Kristin faced her elder daughter directly. "You aren't old enough to be here by yourself. Now go get dressed."

Erin stood straight, her hands at her sides, feet slightly apart, and lifted her chin. "No."

There had never been such outright defiance, not since Erin turned three, anyway. Kristin took a deep breath. "Why not?"

"Because I'm tired of bein' with everybody. I want to be by myself."

"You can be by yourself at Grandma Irene's. Just go into the guest room and close the door."

"I want to be in my room."

"Erin." Taking a step forward, she put her hands on her daughter's shoulders.

Erin jerked back, then took another step away for good measure. "I'm not goin'."

Over the fear twisting inside her, Kristin tried to think. "Okay. Go to your room and stay there. I'll make other arrangements."

Those other arrangements didn't fall into place. "I'm sorry, Kristy," her mother told her, "but I have to be home this morning. The men are coming between nine and noon to install a new hot-water heater, and your father is teaching until two this afternoon. I was glad to have the girls here. But I can't leave."

At the photography shop, Sarah's assistant answered. "Ms. Randolph is on location this morning in Charleston. Can I take a message?"

A message would not help. Kristin reached Matt at work. "The recruiting-area C.O. is due in about twenty minutes. I'm sure Dad can handle things if you don't get there, Kris. Don't worry about it. Just a minute." She heard conversation in the background. "The C.O. is early, Kris. I have to go."

And so she called the Colonel. "I don't see how I can get there until Erin calms down. Later in the morning, I hope. Will you be all right until then?"

"Well…I can get her some cereal and juice. Do you think you'll be here before lunch?" The anxiety in his voice was obvious. The Colonel might command soldiers, but he was useless around the house.

"I'll do my best," Kristin promised.

By lunchtime her mother's water heater had been installed and she could come to Kristin's house to stay with the girls. Kristin escaped to the Brennans' beach house with a feeling of relief—handling Elena Brennan was easier than handling Erin these days.

When the Colonel answered the door, his own relief

was clear. "She's feeling better, and that makes her even harder to keep in bed."

"Have you two eaten lunch?" Kristin stepped inside the house, drew a breath…and choked on an acrid odor. "What happened?"

He looked sheepish. "I tried to heat up some of the stew Sarah brought over last night. But it started burning right away, and before I got the burner turned down, the whole batch was black."

She grinned at him as they went down the hallway. "I think we should find you a cooking class to attend. You need the experience." In the bedroom, she found Elena Brennan standing at the dresser, slowly combing her hair. "You must be getting well. How does it feel to be up and around?"

"Just fine, thank you." The slight tremor in her hand as she laid the comb down belied the statement. "I really think William and I can manage by ourselves now."

Kristin nodded. "Probably. But Matt made me promise to stop by every day until you get an all-clear from your doctor. I can't face him if I don't." In fact, Matt hadn't made her promise any such thing—they were still barely speaking to each other.

But she knew the thought of her son's concern would work on Elena when nothing else did. The older woman's face softened. "That's kind of him. Matt always was a responsible, dependable son."

Responsible, dependable…and unreachable. "Why don't you come sit in the family room with Colonel Brennan while I make lunch? You can eat sitting up and spend a few minutes out of bed."

Surprise and a wary gratitude passed through Elena's cool blue eyes. "I think I will." She hesitated. "Thank you."

This time, Kristin's smile was genuine. "You're welcome."

The Colonel helped his wife into the family room while Kristin made plates of vegetable soup and grilled cheese sandwiches. She cleaned up the kitchen as they ate and washed the dishes while they sat for a few minutes in the sun pouring through the windows.

"How are Erin and Jenny?" Back in the bedroom, Elena slipped out of her pink silk robe and eased into the bed Kristin had changed.

"They were a little fussy this morning, which was the reason I couldn't get here earlier. But otherwise, they're just great."

"Erin has...adjusted to the knowledge that Matt is her father?"

Kristin ran a dust cloth over the dresser top and sides, avoiding her mother-in-law's probing stare. "N-no. I don't think so. She's still pretty upset."

"Have you discussed the issue with her?"

"I've told her I want to talk and I'm willing to listen. But she hasn't broached the subject and I haven't forced her."

"Are she and Matt getting along?"

No one in their household seemed to be getting along. But Kristin wouldn't confide that fact. "About the same as before. He's been at work a lot recently. There's some reorganization going on in the recruiting department."

The Colonel came in. "All the more reason for him to get back into Special Forces where he belongs. You need to convince him, Kristin. You know that's what's best for all of you."

Without facing him, she knelt on the soft blue carpet to dust the legs of the chest of drawers. "Matt makes his own decisions."

"But what's holding him back is you and the girls. If he knew you were in favor of his returning, the decision would be simple for him."

Still kneeling, Kristin turned her head to meet his eyes. "Why is it so important to you for him to return to Special Forces?"

For a second, William Brennan just blinked at her. "A man should work to his full potential."

"Why does that necessarily mean Special Forces? Or the Army at all?"

"What else would he do?"

Kristin looked at Matt's mother. "Do you want to see him back in the Special Forces? Possibly missing in action again, or wounded...or dead?"

Elena's hesitation said more than words. "I'm very proud of Matthew's career."

"Why not just be proud of the man he is? Why does he have to be attached to the Army?"

"Now, see here—"

"I beg your pardon?"

Speaking at the same time, both Brennan parents stared at her in outrage.

"He's honorable and gentle and responsible, not because of the Army but because that's just Matt. If he were a truck driver or a...a teacher, his personality wouldn't change. So why push him back into the most dangerous job in the Service?"

She set one foot on the ground and braced her hands on her bent knee, preparing to rise. About halfway to standing, the pain struck again, searing through her hip. With a gasp, Kristin doubled over.

"Kristin?" The Colonel put a hand on her shoulder. "What's wrong, m'dear? Can I help you?"

"I—I'm okay." She drew a deep breath. When she

tried to stand, she crumpled again. "Just let me sit down." Panting, she eased down onto the floor, folded her legs loosely together, tailor-style, and leaned over slightly. "The doctor says it's just a spasm in some of the ligaments that support the baby."

After a long moment, Mrs. Brennan said, "Baby?" Her voice was like ice water dribbled down Kristin's spine.

Kristin looked up, finally. Faced with the situation she'd dreaded, her fear of her mother-in-law's reaction dropped away. "Yes, a baby. I'm pregnant again. Isn't that wonderful?"

Mrs. Brennan narrowed her eyes and gave a cool, sarcastic smile. "Does Matt know?"

CHAPTER THIRTEEN

AFTER A GRUELING DAY with the area C.O., Matt gave his staff permission to leave half an hour earlier than closing time. All of them needed a break from the tension.

So he was alone in the office when a couple came in the front door. The red-haired young man—a boy, really—looked nervous. "Are you still open?"

"Sure. I'm Major Matt Brennan." He shook the boy's hand. "What can I do for you?"

"Uh..." He glanced at the girl. She looked sweet, even younger than he did...and about six months pregnant. "I was thinkin' about joinin' up with the Army."

"Why don't you both sit down?" Matt gestured to some chairs in the waiting area, and took a seat across from them. "Want to tell me your names?"

"Alan and Terry Garth."

"Glad to meet you both. How old are you, Alan?"

"Eighteen." He glanced at his wife, ducked his head and repeated himself. "Eighteen."

Matt doubted it. "Have you finished high school?"

"N-no. Does it matter?"

"Not if you're old enough. We do accept recruits without high-school degrees." He sat back and propped one ankle on the other knee, hoping to put the two young people more at ease. "What are you looking for from the Army? Why do you want to join up?"

Terry stirred and put a hand on her stomach. "You get medical care, right?"

"Right."

"And your pay comes steady," Alan added. "They got housing for Army folks."

"Most of the time. What would you like to do in the Army?"

Alan and Terry looked at each other in question. "Just be a soldier," Alan said finally. "I'm pretty strong and fast. I learned to shoot with my daddy when I was little. I figure I got what the Army needs."

"You could be right." Matt got to his feet. "You'll need to take a couple of tests, and a physical, but for this afternoon you can fill out the preliminary application form and we'll set up an appointment for the rest. Come over to the desk."

As if chained together, both Alan and Terry crossed the office. Matt passed Alan the form and a pen. "Take your time. If there's something you're not sure about, leave it blank and we'll figure it out. I'll be back in a few minutes."

He left them consulting over how to complete the form and went to his own office. Instead of sitting down, though, he stood in front of the bookshelf, staring sightlessly at the spines of Army procedural manuals while thinking about Alan and Terry Garth.

It was his job to run this kid through the application process and give an initial judgment on his fitness for service. Alan looked too young to be signing away years of his life, and too desperate to discourage. Even if he cleared the admission process, Matt doubted they'd get into the system in time to provide a doctor to deliver their baby. What would Terry do for the six weeks Alan went to boot camp?

What would Kris do for the days, weeks, even months *he* would spend on assignment with the Special Forces? Assuming, of course, they were still married at that point.

"Major?" Alan called from the outside office. Matt shook his head and rejoined the couple. The young man pointed to a line on the form. "It says here I have to get my parents' signature on this form."

"If you're under eighteen, you do."

"But I said I'm eighteen."

"Yes, you did." Matt watched color climb up Alan's neck and into his face. "Did you have any other questions?"

Staring at Terry, he shook his head. "I guess not. What happens now?"

Matt set up an appointment for a physical and an aptitude test. He went through what Alan could expect after enlistment. "Once you complete boot camp, you'll be assigned a duty station, depending on what specialty you're selected for and where you're needed. At that point, you'll be eligible for housing on post."

"Where're we supposed to live till then?"

"Where do you live now?"

Alan ducked his head. "With Terry's folks. But they're not real happy about it."

"Would they let her stay with them until you finish boot camp? Until the baby comes?"

Staring at her husband, Terry took a deep breath. "I guess so. It is only a few months, right?"

"Right." Matt gave her a reassuring smile. "We'll process these papers as fast as we can."

Terry's face relaxed. "That would be good. We're pretty tired of sleeping on the pull-out couch."

After seeing the Garths on their way, Matt stopped by his parents' house and found his mother seated in the family room. "Well, this looks promising. You must really be getting better fast." He bent to kiss her cheek, and noticed that she didn't put her hand on his shoulder as she usually did. Matt straightened. "What's wrong?"

Her hands were folded in her lap and her blue eyes were angry. "Kristin was here at lunchtime."

He backed away to a nearby chair. "And?"

"And she revealed, *quite by accident*..." The words were spoken in biting tones. "Quite by accident, that she's expecting a baby."

Matt muttered a curse to himself. "Yes, she is. Isn't that great?"

"Is it?"

"I think so."

"Why weren't the rest of us told?"

"You would have been, Mom. Things have been... complicated. We were waiting to get Erin a little more settled before we broadcast the news."

"Yet another secret being kept from your parents, almost as if you can't trust us. I have no idea why you would be so suspicious—you didn't used to be."

Because his mother had been sick, Matt didn't want to upset her any further. "Let's not worry about it, Mom. I'm glad you know. I hope you celebrated with Kris about the baby. She could use some encouragement."

"She doesn't want this child?"

"Sure she does."

"How long have you known?"

"Since July fourth." He saw the trap only after he stepped into it.

"Kristin says the baby will be born in late December. She was more than three months along before you found out? She kept the secret from you, as well?"

Matt couldn't deny the truth. "Like I said, the situation has been difficult."

"Are you even sure this baby belongs to you?"

He had no right to be so furious—he had asked the same question. But he stood up to his full height and looked down at the woman in the chair. "When you got sick, I decided to ignore a lot of what you'd said before, because you're my mother. But if you take this any further—with me or anyone else—I won't be back. Kristin doesn't deserve that kind of question, and neither do I."

She had the grace to blush. "You must admit that her secrecy is confusing and upsetting."

"Kris tries too hard to make things right for everybody. She rarely does what's best for herself." He realized the truth of the words as he spoke them. "But since so many of the people in her life have opposing viewpoints, she can't hope to please them all. She should get credit for trying."

"I shudder to think what will happen when you go back to Special Forces duty and she's left solely responsible for these children."

"What could possibly happen? Kris is a wonderful mother."

"I think she's unstable."

"Give me a break!"

"Seriously, Matthew. She only seems able to function when there is a man taking care of things—first Luke, and now you. If you're away for weeks or months at a time, what will Kristin do?"

"What she'll do is take care of her children. She might have to ask for help occasionally, and I would have liked her to be able to turn to you and Dad for that help."

"Matthew—"

"But it's really clear that you can't or won't be fair to

Kristin. I give up trying to understand why. Why you think you can sit in judgment is something else I don't understand. You've made your share of mistakes, Mom. You've practiced your own deception. What makes you better than Kristin?''

''I did not choose—''

''And neither did Kristin. She didn't argue with me nine years ago about going to Africa, because she didn't want to interfere with my career.''

''She simply made sure that when you returned, whatever happened, you would be obligated to marry her. And when you couldn't come back, she entrapped your brother, instead.''

''That's it.'' He stared at a woman he didn't recognize as the mother he loved and shook his head. ''I won't listen to another word. Don't call, Mom. Don't drop by. Kristin won't be coming over tomorrow…or any time in the near future. I hope you feel better soon.''

She followed him down the hallway to the front door. ''You can't divorce your parents, Matthew.''

At the front door, he faced her one last time. ''We'll be waiting for an apology…and a change in attitude. Goodbye, Mom.''

She didn't call him back. His father pulled into the driveway as Matt backed out, and put up a hand as if to stop him. Without even a nod, Matt simply drove away.

SINCE MATT'S PARENTS knew about the baby, Kristin told her mother, too, when she returned from the Brennans' house.

''Really, Kristy?'' Her mother's expression was doubtful. ''Are you happy about it?''

''Yes.'' Kristin thought for a second, then put her face in her hands. ''Maybe. I don't know.''

"What does Matt think?"

"He says all the right words, but things aren't going very well right now."

"I'm not surprised, with his mother so sick."

"No, it's not his mom...well, not the fact that she's sick. Matt and I just can't talk to each other."

"Have you told the girls?"

Kristin shook her head.

Her mother clucked her tongue. "That will be hard. Erin is very confused and unhappy now. You're probably wise to wait."

"If so, that'll be the first wise thing I've done in months. Maybe years."

"I'm worried about you, Kristy. You didn't used to be so negative."

Life didn't used to be so difficult. "I know...I guess I'm just tired today," she hedged. "I really am looking forward to a new baby. Erin and Jenny are getting so grown-up, I miss having a toddler."

Reassured, her mother got up to leave. At the door, she put a hand over Kristin's. "Matt's a good man, Kristy."

"Yes, he is."

"If you told him what you're thinking and feeling, I believe he would listen."

"I know. And I'll try," she said in answer to her mother's expectant stare. "Really, I will."

As the afternoon moved toward dinnertime, Kristin gave some more thought to her mother's simple advice. Maybe if she confessed her confusion, her uncertainty, Matt would say...

What? She didn't feel as if she knew him anymore. The quiet, somber man she'd married wasn't the brash officer who'd gone off to Africa nine years ago. His time as a prisoner, the hurt and anger of finding her married to Luke, and their struggles with the girls had made Matt cautious, self-contained.

Kristin knew she had changed as well. She wasn't twenty-two years old, an airhead without much in the way of ambitions or goals. Having a baby, becoming a parent, had changed her into a responsible person in a matter of weeks.

So the woman Matt had come back to wasn't the one he left. Looking back, she realized that they'd scarcely known each other as the people they'd become. Matt had only proposed after Luke moved out—why? Because he loved her? Or because, without Luke in her life, she had become Matt's responsibility?

Kristin had said yes because she loved the man who left.

Now, two years later, she stood alone in her kitchen, terrified to ask herself the most important question of all.

Did she truly love the man who'd come back?

ELENA HAD KNOWN she would have to explain to her husband what had happened with Matt. She hadn't realized William would be quite so angry.

"Dammit, Elena! Why didn't you leave well enough alone? Why couldn't you swallow your hurt feelings and just congratulate Matt on the new baby?"

She lifted her chin. "I consider it my responsibility as a parent to help him see the reality of his marriage. He can't live in a fantasy, pretending everything is hearts and flowers."

From across the room, William stared at her. "Why not?"

"Because…" She surrendered to the need to cough. Her breath rasped in her throat as she drew in air. "Be-

cause he'll only be that much more disillusioned when
he finally has to admit the truth. Blind trust does no one
any good.''

He shook his head. ''Matt's not blind. He loves Kristin. You're putting the worst possible interpretation on
everything she does.''

''At least then he won't be completely disillusioned.
He'll have been warned.''

''Warned about what?''

Elena closed her eyes. If he didn't understand, she
didn't have the strength to make things clear. ''I can't
talk anymore, William. Let's just drop the subject.''

She didn't hear him leave the room, but the quiet lasted
so long she thought he must have. When she opened her
eyes, though, he still stood before her, his arms stiff at
his sides.

''I won't stand by, Elena, and lose my son. That last
heart attack convinced me—time's too precious to waste
on hurt feelings and power plays. I intend to enjoy my
grandchildren and their parents. If that takes apologizing
for you, then that's what I'll have to do.''

''Apologize?'' She sat up straight in her chair. ''Whatever for?''

''You're being mean-spirited and unforgiving, Elena.
I've tried to ignore that fact for the years of our life
together. I can't do that anymore. My sons are too important to me.''

''More so than I?''

William's stare was sad, angry, resigned. ''I never
thought so before. But they're trying, and you aren't.''

He left the room then. She heard him take the stairs
up to the guest room and close the door.

''Very well.'' Elena got to her feet and made her slow
way to the downstairs bedroom. Once under the blanket,

she turned to her side, facing the place where William had always slept. Empty now.

He would relent, given time. They had never indulged in serious marital disagreements—she had prided herself on seeing what her husband needed and providing exactly that, acquiescing to his decisions without arguments, making his career hers. She had no real interests, apart from William and their children.

Matt's wife should have been a woman of the same stamp. Had *she* been widowed, Elena knew she would have honored William's memory for the rest of her life. She would certainly not have married within a matter of weeks.

Reliability. Dependability. Commitment. Persistence. Unwavering dedication. These were the characteristics she had sought to instill in her son, and the characteristics of the woman he deserved as a wife. Why couldn't Matt see that his mother had his best interests at heart?

Why couldn't Kristin just get out of his way?

KRISTIN PLANNED a simple dinner. She put chicken in the oven to broil, turned down the heat under a pot of rice and set a pot of beans to cook. She checked on Jenny, who'd fallen asleep in the big recliner in the family room.

Then she went upstairs to talk with Erin.

Her daughter's door was shut, as was usual these days. "Erin?" Kristin knocked. "Could you open the door?"

Through the door she heard a sound suspiciously like a sigh. The door panel swung back, and Erin faced her across the threshold, looking wary and far older than her eight years. "Did I do somethin' wrong?"

"Um...no. But I think we need to talk."

"What about?"

Kristin just waited. Erin shrugged, finally. "Okay."

"Thanks." Kristin held out her hand. "Let's go where I can keep an eye on Jenny."

Erin stepped forward, but she didn't take Kristin's hand. Swallowing the hurt, Kristin followed her daughter and the ever-present Buster down the stairs.

"Do you want to sit out on the deck? It's pretty cool this afternoon." They'd be able to see Jenny through the glass doors in the family room if she woke up.

Erin chose her favorite candy-striped lawn chair. Kristin sat nearby but not facing her. Sometimes it was easier to talk without looking at each other.

Clearing her throat, she took the first step. "We haven't pressed you to talk about what's happened, Erin. We hoped you would let us know when you were ready. But it's been weeks since you were in the hospital and the situation seems to be getting worse. So…" She drew a deep breath, thinking of the way Dr. Rose had dealt with them all. "So now you know that Matt is your father, and Luke is Jenny's. What do you think about that?"

"Nothin'."

"What do you mean?"

Erin hunched a shoulder. "I don't think about it."

"Everything is just great for you? You're really happy?"

"Sure."

"Well, I'm not." The flat statement earned her a quick, suspicious glance. "I'm not happy with the way you stay in your room all the time. The way you fight with Jenny and try to…to make me mad—like the time you refused to go to Grandma Irene's so I could go help Grandmom Elena. And I don't like it that you won't talk to Matt or to Luke. And since I'm not happy, I want to do something about all these things."

"I'm not talkin' to him."

"Who?"

Erin set her jaw.

"Matt?"

"The other one."

"You won't even say his name?" The harshness of that attitude almost defeated her. "Why not?"

"He lied."

Kristin had thought about that point ahead of time. "What did he say that was a lie?"

Erin obviously did not want to answer.

"What did Luke say that you know is a lie?"

After a tense minute, Erin got out of her chair and went to toy with the leaves of a nearby philodendron plant. "He said he...he...he liked me."

"How do you know that's a lie?"

"He's not my dad. He doesn't have to."

"He rocked you to sleep when you were a baby. He sat up all night with you when you had a fever or a cold or an ear infection. He taught you to play soccer, told you the names of the stars and how to tell a sandpiper from a seagull. Men do things like that for little girls they love."

One of the philodendron's glossy leaves, jerked from its stem, dropped to the deck floor.

After a long silence, Kristin started from a different direction. "So if Luke isn't your dad, and Matt is, why won't you talk to Matt?"

Another leaf fell. "He left."

"He's in the Army, Erin. That was his job."

"He doesn't know me."

"He wants to."

"He just took us to get you back."

Kristin caught her breath. She didn't have an argument

prepared for that point. "I don't think that's true, Erin.
If I went away, Matt would still want to be your dad. He
loves you."

"He has to."

"No, he doesn't. The way you've treated him the last
couple of years, I have to believe that if he didn't love
you, he wouldn't be staying around."

Erin mumbled something Kristin couldn't hear. "Say
that again, love." When Erin didn't reply, Kristin walked
over and knelt down in front of the girl. She put her
hands on Erin's shoulders. "I want to know what you
said."

The blue eyes were wide with unshed tears, the face
pale beneath its tan. "I said you two should just go away
together. That's what you want to do."

"No, it's not. I want a complete family—you and
Jenny and me and…and Matt."

"That's so *stupid!*" Erin twisted out of her hold and
backed away. "Why did you have to change things? We
were already a fam'ly. Then he came and…and you made
Daddy leave and then you m-married Matt and it's all
been awful ever since."

"Erin—"

"I tried! I tried to like him. I tried to be nice. But he
never laughs. You never laugh anymore, either, not like
with Daddy. You sent us away with Daddy and Sarah so
we wouldn't bother him. I thought maybe you'd be hap-
pier when we got back, but everything was just worse.
Nothin's been right since Matt came, since you decided
to like him and not Daddy. It's all your fault!"

Quicker than lightning, Erin ran down the deck steps
and across the yard, taking shelter in the old dogwood
tree she liked to climb. Buster whimpered briefly, then
lay down beside the trunk. Ignoring the stab of pain in

her hip, Kristin got to her feet and started to follow. As she reached the edge of the deck, the door into the kitchen opened. She looked back.

"Mommy! Mommy!" Jenny stumbled out onto the deck, sobbing and rubbing her eyes. "Mommy, somethin' smells funny. An' it's all cloudy inside."

Puffs of gray smoke billowed out the door Jenny had left open. "Oh, God." Kristin rushed to the little girl, grabbed her up and carried her out to Erin's tree. "You stay here with Buster, Jenny. Don't move. Erin, watch your sister. I have to see what's wrong in the kitchen."

What was wrong became obvious immediately. The chicken under the broiler was a flaming mess. Kristin turned off the heat and left the oven door closed to let the fire burn out. Smoke leaked from one of the pots on the stove, too. She shut down the gas and opened the pot. Her rice was a belching, crackling, black disaster.

"But I lowered the flame!" The beans should have been cooking, not the rice. But when she checked, the beans were as cold as the chilled air blowing around them. She must have turned up the rice and turned off the beans.

Kristin muttered a very rude word. Twice. Then she doublechecked to be sure all the appliances were switched off. Leaving the door open, she went outside again and found Jenny underneath the tree, still crying. Erin had retreated so high she was hidden in the dogwood's thick leaves.

"Shh, shh, Jenny. Everything's all right." She cradled the little girl, trying at the same time to make eye contact with Erin. "I let the dinner burn, that's all. We can have pizza, instead. Doesn't that sound good?"

At the mention of pizza, Jenny's sniffles died away. Kristin gave up trying to find Erin and simply sat down in the grass, with Jenny on her lap. She watched smoke drift out of the kitchen and kept her mind a careful blank.

Matt found her like that about an hour later. He appeared at the door to the kitchen, his eyebrows drawn, his mouth tight. "Kris? Are you and the girls okay?"

That depends on your definition, Kristin thought. "We're all fine," she called back. "But I ruined dinner."

His shoulders visibly relaxed. "Sounds like a good excuse for pizza. I'll go make the call."

He joined her on the grass a few minutes later. Jenny had recovered enough to play on the swing set at the other end of the fenced yard. Seated with his back against the dogwood's trunk, Matt spoke without looking Kristin's way.

"I stopped by to see Mom this afternoon."

Kristin kept her eyes on the blades of grass she was weaving. "She seems to be getting better every day. When does she go back to see the doctor?"

"I don't know. It doesn't matter. You're not going back over there again."

She jerked her gaze to his face. "Why? What's wrong?"

"I've had it with her insinuations, her suspicions, her damn hard head and harder heart. I don't want you putting up with her anymore."

"What did she say?"

"She told me that she'd found out—'quite by accident' was her phrase—that you're going to have a baby. She was rude and unkind about the whole situation. I don't intend to give her that opportunity ever again."

Kristin heard the words. She also heard a startled gasp in the leaves above them. And then the scrabble of sneakers against bark as Erin jolted back to the ground.

They met almost eye to eye, Kristin on her knees and

Erin with her feet planted far apart, her hands propped on her hips. The little girl spoke first.

"You're going to have a baby? Another baby?"

Matt put out a hand. "Erin—"

She ignored him. "You and him are having a baby?"

With shivers running up her back, Kristin nodded. "Yes, we are."

The storm in Erin's face defied description. She opened her mouth, but couldn't seem to form words for what she felt.

Matt tried again. "A brother or sister for you and Jenny, Erin. Won't that be fun?"

She turned her head slowly to look at him. Their gazes held for a long time.

"I wish you had never come back," Erin said finally. "I wish...I wish you *did* die."

With that pronouncement, she turned on her heel and walked with a deliberate pace across the grass to the deck, up the steps and into the house.

CHAPTER FOURTEEN

HIS DAUGHTER wished he was dead.

Numbly, Matt watched Erin march into the house. Then he looked back at Kristin, white-faced and kneeling on the ground.

He had to clear his throat to get words out. "I didn't realize she was up there."

Kristin didn't look at him. "I know."

"What can we do?"

She shook her head. "Nothing. It's all been done." Starting to rise, she gasped, and doubled over.

"Kris? What's wrong?" Matt reached for her.

"Nothing." Hands up, she warded him off. "Just a muscle in my hip that's stretching as the baby grows. When I move the wrong way, it hurts." On the second try, she got to her feet. "Was that the doorbell?"

He hadn't heard anything. But she clearly wanted him gone. "I'll check." He made himself leave her there, forced his legs to carry him across the grass and onto the deck, through the house. The pizza delivery-man stood at the front door. "Large pepperoni, large mushroom and sausage, six-pack of drinks?"

Matt swallowed back bile. "That's right." He thumbed two tens out of his wallet. "Keep the change."

"Wow…thanks!"

Matt took the pizza into the kitchen. Kristin and Jenny were there, setting out paper plates and cups. Jenny looked up as he set the boxes on the table. "I love pizza!"

His grin felt stiff. "I know you do." He waited a few seconds. "I'll go tell Erin dinner is here."

For the first time, Kristin looked up. "I don't think…" Her words faded away before whatever she saw in his face.

He nodded. "Back in a couple of minutes."

At Erin's door, he didn't hesitate. "Dinner's here, Erin. Pizza."

She didn't answer, so he knocked. "Come on, Erin. We don't want to start without you."

When she still didn't answer, Matt opened the door.

At first he couldn't find her. He couldn't even comprehend what he saw—the room was blurred, covered with a gray-and-white blanket like some bizarre blizzard had hit.

Then he realized—there was paper everywhere. At his feet were pages from a book about volcanoes. Crouching, he picked up sheets showing the structure of flowers, the skeletons of dinosaurs, the countries of Africa. Matt raised his eyes to Erin's bookshelf.

Empty. She had torn apart every book she owned.

"Erin?" Scanning the room, he finally found her huddled in the corner, concealed from the doorway by the chest of drawers, with her knees drawn up and her face hidden in her arms. Buster had curled himself at her feet.

He sat down on the floor facing that corner. "This is sad, Erin. You love these books."

"Doesn't matter. I didn't want them anymore."

That she spoke at all surprised him. "Why?"

"I just didn't."

"You're really mad, aren't you?"

She flashed him a glare of burning reproach. Eyes buried again, she said, "Yeah."

"I'd be mad, too."

Her shock stilled the anger in the air. But she didn't speak.

"I mean, your whole life has been ripped apart. Nothing you thought was true seems true anymore. And now your mom and I are going to have a baby together."

She sighed.

"Maybe you think we're hoping for a kid who'll be nice to us. That would make me furious, if I were you. Here *we* messed up, ruined everything, and we're making it seem like *your* fault."

No reply.

"I'd want to tear things up, too. I'd probably punch a wall. I did that once, and I forgot about what I was mad at right away. You know why?"

Erin peeked at him with one eye.

"Because I broke three of my knuckles when I hit the wall. That hurt so much I couldn't think about anything but getting to a doctor. I wore a cast for six weeks and missed most of baseball season that year."

The one eye he could see closed.

"If you're mad at somebody—if you're mad at *me,* Erin—don't hurt yourself. Yell at me. Say anything that you're thinking. But don't hurt yourself. I'm not worth that. Nobody is. You're more important than all of us. Maybe it doesn't seem like we think so, but it's true."

Erin didn't move. Matt sat there for quite a while as the sun moved across the windows, spotlighting the ruined books all around them.

Kristin's footsteps on the stairs brought him to his feet. He left Erin's room, closing the door behind him, and met Kris in the hallway.

"Is she okay?"

Matt wanted to reach for her. But even if he held her, they wouldn't really be touching. "She's okay. You don't want to go in there right now."

"What's she done? Are you sure she didn't hurt herself?"

"I'm sure." He told her about the books.

"Oh, God." Kristin put her hands over her eyes. "I'll talk to her."

"No, you should leave her alone." She looked at him, and he heard the clash of their wills in the silence. "I'm right about this, Kris. She needs to be left with her feelings out in the open. Let her see them, touch them, sort them out. Then she'll figure out what to do with them."

Behind Kristin, Jenny appeared at the top of the stairs. "Mommy? Where's Erin?"

"She's in her room, love." With a sigh, Kristin turned and went to sit down on the top step. "She doesn't want to see anybody right now."

"She never wants to see anybody. Why is she always mad?"

"Erin's figuring some things out, Jenny. Sometimes that makes you feel mad at everybody."

"Figurin' what?"

Matt waited for the answer.

"Well...she's figuring out how she feels about Matt being her daddy, for one thing. And how she feels about getting a new brother or sister."

Jenny tilted her head to look up at her mother. "Sarah's havin' a baby."

"Yes, she is. I am, too."

After a long pause, the little girl said, "Why?"

"Because Matt and I love you and your sister. We

think it would be fun to have another little boy or girl, to make even more love. What do you think?''

''I think there's too many peoples already.'' With her pronouncement, Jenny thumped up that last step to the hallway. She passed Matt without a glance, went into her room and quietly shut the door.

There should be comfort in marriage, Matt thought, gazing at Kristin's straight back. He should be able to sit beside her and put his arms around her and promise they would make things right. That her daughters would come to love him, and the new baby. That his mother would recognize and admit her prejudices. That he would always be here, to hold Kristin and take care of her and love her.

But he didn't believe in making promises he couldn't keep. He doubted she'd believe him, anyway—not since his broken promise to get back from Africa in plenty of time for their wedding. Not since his promise to ''love, honor and cherish'' had fallen victim to a flash of anger: ''I *am* the father, right?''

Why should she trust him? He didn't trust himself.

They might have stayed as they were all night, imprisoned in the hallway outside the girls' rooms, but the phone rang. Matt stepped into the bedroom to answer.

''Hi, Matt. It's Sarah. What's going on?''

My life is falling apart. ''Not much. How do you feel these days?''

''I'm great. I was thinking about doing some baby shopping tomorrow and wondered if Kristin would like to come. Is she around?''

''Sure. Just a minute.'' He took the phone out to where Kristin still sat at the top of the steps. ''I'll clean up dinner. You talk.''

There wasn't much to cleaning up a mostly uneaten

pizza. With the leftovers stowed and the charred dinner in the trash, he scrubbed the burned pans clean, then sat in the family room with the newspaper, trying to read. At eleven, when Kristin hadn't come back down, he turned off the lights, locked the doors and climbed the stairs.

In the hallway once again, he saw that three of the four bedroom doors were shut. Erin's and Jenny's he'd expected.

But even if they hadn't been sleeping together, the door to the room he shared with Kristin had always been open...until tonight. Tonight she had closed him out completely.

The scariest part, though, was the relief he felt when he decided not to try breaking that door down.

Monday
Dear Diary
    Youre one book I didnt tear up.
    Mommys havin a baby with Matt. He talked to me about it but I dont beleeve him. Seems like they want to start over with new kids.
    What am I gonna do? Jenny can go live with her dad. I dont have anywhere else to be. Seems like Busters the only person who cares about me the same as he used to.
    I wish I could no what I did that caused all this.
                                        Your friend
                                        Erin Elena Brennan

KRISTIN CALLED her mother early on the morning after Erin and Jenny found out about the baby.

"So now everyone knows. Isn't that wonderful?"

Her mother clucked her tongue. "Have you talked with Erin this morning?"

"She's still asleep. I eased her door open to check. And her room is still a total disaster. All those wonderful books, Mom…"

"It's very sad, Kristy. But most of them are replaceable, I'd bet. It may be more important that Erin had the chance to act out on her feelings. She might have needed that kind of physical expression."

"That's what Matt said."

"I'm not surprised. I think perhaps you don't give him enough credit for having ideas about how to handle the children."

Something very much like fear bolted through Kristin's chest. "What do you mean?"

"Well, I've sometimes felt that since he got back from Africa, everyone—including Matt, himself—presumes that he can't possibly know what to do with the children because he wasn't here when they were born."

"There's a certain amount of experience that you gain being a parent, Mom."

"Of course. There's also a certain amount of experience you gain in being a leader of men. Matt has undergone training in…in personnel management, and he's learned to control his troops in very difficult, maybe even life-threatening situations. Why shouldn't he be able to apply that experience to dealing with the girls?"

Kristin couldn't understand the criticism. First Matt, and now her mother—telling her she wasn't helping, she wasn't solving problems but *creating* them.

She'd tried so hard to make life with Matt work, she'd tried to make things easy for him as he became a father and a husband. Had she demeaned him, instead?

"I—I guess I see what you mean. Maybe I haven't given him enough credit."

"That can always be changed, Kristy. You don't have to keep repeating the mistake. Just make an effort to consider Matt's ideas before you decide he couldn't possibly know what he's talking about. That's part of the compromise of marriage."

"Sure, Mom. Thanks."

"Take care, sweetheart."

Kristin clicked off the phone and put her head in her hands. Mistake piled on top of mistake. The weight of her misjudgments bowed her shoulders. She wondered if the pressure would crush her.

She wasn't sure she cared.

Later in the morning, she called her mother again. "Mom, I need help."

"What's wrong?"

"Erin and Jenny are at each other's throats. They've been fighting for two hours now, ever since they got up. I can't deal with it. Erin won't listen to me, and every time I get Jenny settled, Erin initiates another argument. I'm afraid…afraid I'll lose my temper and just make everything a thousand times worse."

Her mother was silent for a moment. "Losing your temper might not be a mistake, Kristy."

Kristin swallowed a protest at yet another piece of maternal advice, another motherly pointer on how she was messing up her life. "Mom—"

"Why don't you bring Erin over here?"

Kristin sank against the wall in relief. "That would be great, Mom. All I need is a little break to help me get things settled with Jenny."

"In fact, I don't have anything planned this week. Erin

can stay for a few days if she'd like. We'd love to have her.''

Ashamed of her impatience, Kristin straightened. ''Thanks Mom, I'll ask her.''

''Tell her she can bring Buster, too.'' Her mother chuckled. ''Your father enjoys playing with him.''

''That would be great. I don't think I can separate them right now.''

''Of course not. I'll be home all afternoon. Just come when you're ready.''

''Thanks so much.''

''Anything I can do, Kristy. Always.''

Erin, of course, was ecstatic at the thought of getting away. But Jenny wasn't happy at being left behind. ''I wanna go!'' Big tears rolled down her cheeks.

Kristin knelt to hold her. ''You can stay with Grand-mom next time, okay?''

Jenny shook her head, and put her thumb in her mouth. Kristin's heart broke over the little girl's forlorn expression.

She made her next call to Luke. ''Is there any chance that Jenny could take a trip to your house for a few days? She's so very sad.''

''Let me check with Sarah. I'll call you back.'' In ten minutes the phone rang. ''Sounds great. How soon can you get here?''

They left the house at one, dropped Erin at her grand-mother's first, and then established Jenny at Luke and Sarah's. By three, Kristin was home again. Exhausted, true. But home.

She walked into her quiet house and stood for a mo-ment, appreciating the peace. Pouring herself a glass of water, she went into the family room, put her feet up in the reclining chair and tuned the television to an old movie. The adult voices made a welcome change from the high-energy children's programs she usually heard at this time of day.

At first she thought she might take a nap. But she couldn't seem to loosen up quite that much. Concentrating on the movie didn't work, either. She found herself listening for the girls.

"Relax, for heaven's sake!" She put her head back and closed her eyes again. Surely the low voices on the TV would lull her to sleep.

When the movie ended, she was still wide-awake.

So if rest wouldn't work, she'd get some work done, without the interruption of children's fights and demands. She couldn't make herself face the devastation in Erin's room, but she got Jenny's bedroom tidier than it had been all summer. She took down the curtains, washed and ironed them and put them back up. She cleaned the carpet and organized the closet.

Standing in the doorway admiring her work, she felt the ache of weariness in her knees, her back and her hands. The baby had begun to fill out her tummy, changing her center of gravity, and all the bending was a strain. But she did like the results.

Downstairs again, she got out her gloves and prepared to wipe out the oven. She felt almost successful—maybe she couldn't manage the rest of her life, but she surely was competent at cleaning house.

MATT MET with Alan and Terry Garth the afternoon after Erin's attack on her books.

"You've got a lot of potential," he told the young man, surveying the test results. "You scored high in science and technology and math. The Army would be glad to get someone with your abilities."

Alan grinned. "Does that mean I'm in?"

"When we get your parents' signature."

His face fell. "I told you—"

"You also gave me your Social Security number. The records say that you're seventeen. You don't think your parents will give you permission to enlist?"

"There's just my dad. My mom left when I was little. I haven't seen him since I told him Terry was pregnant. He threw me out."

"Have you tried to get in touch?"

Alan nodded. The pain in his face made further explanation unnecessary.

Matt sat back in his chair. "Why don't I give him a call? Doesn't sound as if that could make things any worse."

After the Garths left, Matt sat staring at the number he was supposed to call. Why was he putting out such effort for someone he barely knew? What stake did he have in whether or not Alan Garth joined the Army?

He got part of his answer when he talked to Alan's dad.

"The boy's lost. Bewitched. He couldn't keep away from that girl, no matter what I said. She had a reputation for being, well, easy. I told him to stay clear, he'd only get into trouble with one like that. Don't I know how that goes? I doubt the kid's even his—I think she found an easy way to get herself taken care of. She's playing the boy for a fool."

Disgust cramped Matt's gut. He forced himself to focus. "That may or may not be, Mr. Garth. But Alan wants to enlist in the Army to support this family he's taken responsibility for. He needs your permission to do so because he's under eighteen. Will you sign the papers?"

"I guess so. Why not? He's already ruined his life. Serve them both right if he goes to some godforsaken place and gets himself killed."

"I'll bring the papers by this afternoon, Mr. Garth." He spoke through clenched teeth. "Five minutes will take care of everything."

"Whatever you say."

Matt hung up with a sick feeling that only worsened when he met the older Garth face-to-face. The boy bore no resemblance to his black-haired, swarthy father, which hinted at family secrets best left undisturbed. Not that Matt was given a chance—Mr. Garth didn't invite him into the house, but stood on the doorstep to sign the papers.

"The boy'll get what's coming to him." He backed inside and began to shut the door. "Just tell him to stay away from me."

"Don't worry," Matt muttered on his way back to the car. "I'll make sure he knows how lucky he is to make his escape!"

Instead of driving straight home, Matt parked in one of the public lots and walked across the dunes to watch the ocean. He got a couple of puzzled glances—he probably did look strange standing there in his uniform, polished shoes and cap. Not standard beachwear.

He let the waves and the wind and the sun fill his brain for a few minutes, let the beat of water against sand clear his mind. He was so tired of thinking. So damn tired.

Alan Garth had what he wanted—a chance to join the Army. Given his talents, he'd be eligible for specialized training. If his self-discipline was good enough, he could even get promoted to a Special Operations unit. He could be one of the Army's best.

But was that the best plan for Alan Garth?

Was it the best plan for Matt Brennan?

His unofficial deadline for returning to his unit got closer every day. He and Kris got farther apart. But he couldn't blame his hesitation on the state of his marriage. Running Alan Garth through the process of enlistment had brought one fact clearly in focus.

Matt wanted out of Special Forces. Out of the Army completely.

In the long nights he'd spent trying to sleep in the guest room, he'd decided that he had nothing to offer the Army now. He wasn't afraid of going back. He just didn't want to. Nothing excited him about the prospect, or challenged him. The only compelling reason to return to his unit was a desire to make his parents happy.

And his parents' happiness wasn't a priority with Matt anymore.

So, if he didn't stay with the Army, what would he do? He wasn't sure about that, either. He would have talked it over with Kris, except that there were so many other problems to resolve first. His future employment looked like a pretty minor detail, compared to the dissolution of his family and the breakup of his marriage. If he didn't get those issues settled first, there wouldn't be much point to having a future at all.

WHEN MATT WALKED into the kitchen, he met the sight of Kristin's cute, round bottom filling in the open door to the oven. He grinned and leaned against the door frame.

"Great view," he said finally.

Kristin gasped and jerked her head out of the oven. "Matt! You scared me!"

He couldn't seem to stop smiling. "I'm sorry. I didn't mean to. What are you doing?"

''Cleaning the oven.'' She eased around to sit on the floor.

''Why?''

''Because it was dirty.''

''Isn't that something somebody else could do for you?''

She lifted a skeptical eyebrow. ''Who, exactly?''

''Well...me, for instance.''

''You weren't here when the oven needed to be cleaned.''

Or when I needed a husband and a father for my child. She didn't say the words, but Matt felt them in the air. The grin dropped off his face.

He straightened up. ''Is there a reason this particular task needed to be done this afternoon? Couldn't it have waited until tonight? Or the weekend?''

Kristin shrugged. ''I wanted a clean oven when I broiled our steaks for dinner. That's all.'' She got to her knees and started to get up...and gave that same gasp of pain he'd heard before.

''Damn.'' Matt stooped down and put his hands under her elbows. ''I don't believe this is normal. I think we should see a doctor about that pain.'' Taking most of her weight in his hands, he lifted her up. ''Right now.''

She stepped back from him, slightly swaying her hips as if to loosen up. ''I saw the doctor just last week. There's nothing wrong. It doesn't hurt even as much as it used to, because the muscles and—and whatever are stretching. I just react the same because I think it will hurt.'' Pulling off her yellow work gloves, she turned away. ''Don't worry about it.''

''I want to worry about it.'' He thought for a second. ''And I want to know when you're going to the doctor. I'd like to come along.''

"Why?" She faced him again, her eyebrows lifted in question. "Nothing happens, really. It's just a checkup."

"I missed all this the first time around. I'd like to ask questions."

"Such as?"

"What does the baby look like right now? When does it start moving? When do we start taking childbirth classes?"

"I can tell you all those things."

"You could if we ever actually talked."

Her cheeks flushed. She held out a hand. "Well, here we are. Talking."

"Where are the girls?" He suddenly realized the house seemed too quiet.

"Erin's at my mother's. Jenny is with Luke and Sarah."

"What happened?"

"I couldn't take the fighting anymore. I needed a break."

"So you could clean the oven?"

"So I could clean the oven in peace, yes!" She moved past him to the refrigerator. "Dinner will be about thirty minutes, if you want to change."

"There are many things I'd like to change." He took hold of her arm and drew her back in front of him. "My clothes aren't on the list right now."

He hadn't touched her in weeks, literally. The softness of her bare skin against his palm streaked through him like wildfire. Kristin's eyes widened, and Matt saw an answering spark of desire in her gaze...along with a good measure of fear.

"You're afraid of me?" His voice sounded brittle to his own ears. He opened his hand to let her go. "Why?"

"N-no. I'm not afraid of you." But she backed away

again, until the oven door pressed against her calves. She turned to shut the panel. "But we aren't...doing very well...and I'm not sure how to react."

And that was the problem. "A reaction isn't something you think about, Kris. It happens automatically. And you looked at me as if you thought I would hurt you."

"But I don't think that!" She slapped her hands against the top of the stove. "So let's drop it, okay? Do you want baked potatoes or rice with your steak?"

"I want some honesty between us, dammit!"

Kristin turned back as she heard the frustration in Matt's raised voice.

She tried to keep her own words calm. "I'm being honest. It would never occur to me that you would hurt me. I might be...uncomfortable...with...with responding to you when there's so much wrong between us. S-sex doesn't solve problems."

"No, I'd say sex makes more problems than anything else."

Despite her efforts, she bristled at his comment. "Do you mean children?"

"Among other things—like using sex to hide your thoughts and emotions."

"I haven't ever—"

"Really? You never used our lovemaking to get away from how you were feeling?"

She remembered the night in Sadie Chisholm's lovely bedroom. The night she discovered she was pregnant, she'd used sex to forget all the problems that would cause.

"I can see by your face that I'm on target, Kris. So, I'm not going to touch you." He held his hands up in the air, palms facing her. "Now, tell me what you think.

About me. About us. About what's gone wrong in this
family and how we're going to make things work.''

A day of struggle…a whole summer of pain and effort
and heartbreak…years of thinking and worrying and hoping and trying…tumbled like a rockslide onto Kristin's
shoulders. She felt each separate boulder strike. And she
broke under the onslaught.

"What's gone wrong is simple.'' She put her hands
on her hips and stared Matt in the eye. "Me. I'm what's
wrong.''

He opened his mouth, but she held up a hand. "You
asked for this. Be quiet and listen. I've spent the last year
trying to conciliate, mediate, tolerate. I spent the two
years before that in hell, not knowing what was right, not
knowing who deserved my loyalty, like wandering in…in
a cave without a light. I made what I thought was a good
decision…and the situation got worse. I've been pulled
one way by the girls, and another by Luke, and your
parents and mine…and *you* until I don't know where or
even who I am anymore.''

Her voice was scratchy, too loud. She stopped trying
to control it. "I did everything I could to make you a
good wife. I wanted to be what you wanted. I wanted to
be the mother the girls needed, the daughter my parents
expected. I owe this new baby the chance to be welcome,
to be expected, to be loved. I've tried as hard as I know
how to do everything right.''

She took a deep breath. "I can't do this anymore. I…I
just can't.''

Blindly she reached for her purse and keys on the
counter. Matt grabbed her arm as she headed for the door.
"Kristin, hold on. Let's talk about this. It's important.''

"I have to think. By myself.'' She stared at his hand
on her arm until he let go. "I'm sorry about dinner.''

Before he could stop her, she'd shut the door to the kitchen at her back. She started the engine of the van with hands that shook. As Matt strode through the open garage, she backed into the street.

And then she took the nearest road out of town.

CHAPTER FIFTEEN

KRISTIN HADN'T INTENDED to drive so far. But her mind just seemed to stop working. She tuned the radio to the country music she usually enjoyed, then turned it off again. Silence was as much distraction as she could handle. The highway mileposts flashed and were gone, without making an impression. Before she knew it, she'd crossed the state line into North Carolina.

She started getting dangerously sleepy about 1 a.m., as she reached southern Virginia. She found a motel room in Emporia and fell on the bed, asleep within seconds.

When she woke up, the clock by the bed read nine-thirty. She hadn't slept so late since...since Erin was born. Matt would be sick with worry. She hadn't even called to say where she was.

But the receptionist at the recruiting office surprised her. "Major Brennan took a personal-leave day, Mrs. Brennan." Curiosity edged her tone. "Can I give him a message if he calls in?"

"Um...no, thanks." If he wasn't at work, he must be at home.

But her own voice on the answering machine replied to that call. Kristin had no choice but to leave a message. "Matt...I'm okay. I spent the night in Virginia." She hesitated, wondering what else to say. "I'll be home...soon. Take care." Weak. But she couldn't do better right now.

Luke answered his phone with an edge to his voice. "Kristin? Where the hell are you?"

"Don't swear at me. I'm in Virginia."

"Matt's a wreck. This wasn't a good idea. What am I supposed to tell Jenny?"

Her stomach twisted with guilt. "I...I went on a short trip and I'll be back soon. Get her to make me a present for when I come home. That will distract her, don't you think?"

He muttered a curse. "I've never seen you run out on your responsibilities like this!"

"I know." She fingered her keys, thinking with dread about the drive back. "I needed some time...some space..."

There was a moment of silence. Then Luke sighed. "I guess I can see that. You've had a tough summer. It's just—"

Kristin waited.

"Never mind." His voice softened to the familiar drawl. "Look, why don't you take a couple of days? Get some rest, a chance to catch your breath?"

The sudden surge of relief almost choked her. "But—"

"No, really, it's okay. We'll keep Jen too busy to mope."

The tears spilled over. "Thank you. Give Sarah my love."

"I will. Be safe."

Her mother's initial reaction was much the same as Luke's. "Erin's unsettled as it is. She won't be comfortable knowing you're so far away."

Kristin took a deep breath. "Maybe I should talk to her."

"Maybe. Or...no." Her mother paused. "On second

thought, Kristy, I think Erin will do just fine here for a few days. She already looks more relaxed. And you sound...so terribly tired.''

More tears.

"Take a day or two for yourself, honey. Your girls will be safe right where they are. Matt can manage. You get yourself together.''

"Thanks, Mom,'' Kristin whispered.

"I love you.''

KRISTIN'S FIRST MESSAGE told Matt nothing. Well, maybe that she was safe. She still sounded stressed. Tired. Her voice made him think of trees bent double by the winds of a hurricane.

She'd sounded like that for some time now, he realized. The thought made him wince.

He took a personal-leave day because he couldn't face being out of the house if she called. After a mostly sleepless night, he forced himself into the shower at about ten o'clock. And that, of course, was when Kristin phoned. He waited around all day, sure that she'd get tired and stop early. The garage got straightened up, all the tools put back in their proper places, the bikes and skates and helmets stored straight, the garbage cans washed out with soap.

Still no call. So he washed and waxed his truck.

At five, sick with worry and hunger, he decided he had to get something to eat. But staring into the refrigerator, Matt realized he couldn't cook in Kristin's kitchen. She kept everything so clean, so organized, he'd worry about messing things up.

Not that he hadn't already messed up the most important stuff.

So he dashed out for a fast-food burger and dashed

home…to find her second message. "I'm in Washington, Matt. I'll let you know when I start home. It won't be long."

Hell. It had already been too long!

But she sounded a little better than she had this morning. What was she learning about herself, traveling alone three states away? Matt couldn't fault her instincts, really. Being together hadn't solved anything. Maybe with a little distance they could both see more clearly.

Wednesday
Dear Diary

I'm stayin with Grandmom Irene. Jenny is at Luke and Sarahs house. Matts at home and Mommy went on a trip. Our whole family is breaked apart.

Me and Buster are still together. He scared me last night when he got out of the backyard and started runnin down the street. I caught him and brought him back and Granddaddy Frank put a board in the hole Buster dug under the fence.

Today I talked a little with Grandmom about Mommys new baby. She said babies sometimes come before you expect them. Mommy didnt mean to make me feel bad. She just got surprised.

So many things are difrent now. Im kinda glad Im here at Grandmom's house. I can think when Im all by myself. I dont no any ansers yet, but I dont feel so mad.

Maybe Mommy needed to be alone to. Maybe thats why she went away. Grandmom says she will come back soon. I hope thats true.

Your friend
Erin Elena Brennan

THIS TIME, Matt was home when Kristin called. "I'm at the Chisholms'."

Just hearing her voice weakened his knees. He sat down at the kitchen table. "Are you okay?"

"I'm fine. Really."

He couldn't let her go this fast. "The girls are doing well. I went to see them both this morning."

"You're not working?"

"Uh…no. I took some leave time I had saved up." Did she understand what that meant…that he couldn't function normally without her?

Matt didn't know what to read into her silence. "I'm glad to know you're at Sadie's. She'll take care of you."

"I can take care of myself." The words were quiet, yet filled with strength.

"I know you can, Kris. I just…" He heard Sadie's voice in the background.

"Lunch is ready, Matt. I'm going to go for now. Take care of yourself."

"You, too." He let her disconnect without a protest. But he sat for a long, long time with his face buried in his hands.

That night, he sat down at the kitchen table to eat yet another cold hamburger. Halfway through the first bite, the doorbell rang.

His father stood on the front step. "Hello, Matt. How are you?"

If it hadn't been impossible, Matt would have thought his dad looked nervous. "I've been better. Is something wrong?"

"No. Oh, no. I just wanted to talk to you for a few minutes."

"Come on in."

The Colonel looked around as they sat down in the

family room. "Seems awfully quiet. Where's the family?"

"Kristin and the girls are…away."

His dad's eyebrows drew together. "Away where? What's going on?"

Matt cast a glance at the ceiling and stopped trying to evade the issue. "Jenny's with Luke. Erin's with Kris's mom. Kris has gone to Washington."

"She's left you?"

Good question. "I don't think so. But she needed some time away."

He braced himself for an inquisition. After a moment, though, his dad relaxed into the couch. "I understand. I guess I'm too late, then."

"For what?"

The Colonel sat up again and clasped his hands between his knees. "I wanted to apologize. I can't actually make amends for your mother, because she's her own person. But I'm sorry for my contribution to the whole situation. I'm not willing to stand on hurt feelings when it could cost me my grandchildren."

Matt blinked. "Well, thanks, Dad. I appreciate your effort. God knows Mom's attitude hasn't made anything easier this summer."

"I realize that. I've tried to caution her. I don't know if she'll ever change. I'll just have to hope so."

"Yeah." In the pause that followed, Matt realized he had his own message to deliver. And he didn't relish the reaction.

But his dad had a right to know. "I've made a decision about going back to my unit, Dad."

"Good man!"

"That's not what I meant. I'm separating from the Army. Resigning my commission and getting out."

"What?" The Colonel surged to his feet. "What in the hell do you think you're doing? What kind of crazy decision is that?"

Matt stood and faced his father on level ground. "The best one for me, and for my family, and for the Army. A man can't serve his country with...with only half of his heart committed. And that's the most I'd be giving. I think the job should go to someone who's totally involved."

His father's cheeks were red. "Is this Kristin's responsibility?"

"Oh, for God's sake!" Matt pressed the heels of his hands against his temples, trying to keep his temper contained. "You came over here to get that stupid idea behind us, didn't you? No, this is not Kristin's responsibility. She doesn't even know about my plans. Bottom line—I don't want to stay in the service, Dad. I want to earn my living some other way. Is that clear enough for you?"

"Four generations of our family have served in the U.S. Army."

"And before that they did something else. I'm going back to *that* tradition."

"I don't appreciate your sense of humor." Standing rigidly straight, his father looked him over. "You're an adult. You make your choices as you see fit. But I want to register my complete and sincere disapproval."

"Okay. It's registered. I'm sorry it's such a blow for you. But it's my life—mine and Kristin's. I intend to be here to share it with her. If she'll let me."

"I guess we'll just have to see about that, won't we?" The Colonel executed an about-face and went to the front door. "The two of you seem as confused and purposeless as high-school dropouts to me. I can't imagine what kind of disaster this will create for Erin and Jenny.'' The door closed on those words.

Matt blew out a deep breath. ''Their mother's in one place, I'm here, and they're somewhere else. How much more of a disaster could we get?''

''THIS IS ONE of them reenactment weekends.'' Sadie poured them both a glass of lemonade and set a plate of sandwiches in front of Kristin. ''George got himself all excited and decided to join in. He's up in Pennsylvania, campin' in a tent all weekend. I expect he'll be stiff as a board when he gets home Sunday night.''

For the first time, Kristin had a moment of doubt. ''Are your rooms full, then?''

But Sadie smiled. ''No, honey. This is just a little show. The big ones happened earlier in the month. Have another sandwich.''

Kristin did as she was told. She couldn't remember the last time food had tasted this good.

''So I'll put you up in the same room you and Matt stayed in last time, if that's okay.'' Sadie's eyes asked a question, but she didn't pry.

''That's wonderful. I think I might take a nap before dinner.''

''Good for you, missy! I'll call you when it's ready.''

Kristin had picked up a few clothes at the mall in Washington. Now, though it was just a nap, she changed into a soft white nightgown and brushed out her hair. She started to turn from the old-fashioned oval mirror, but the sight of her reflection brought her back.

For the first time she took the chance to appreciate— to celebrate—the changes the baby had brought to her body. Alone in this room, she didn't have to hide the pregnancy or apologize for it or defend it. Here, she could be overjoyed at the prospect of a new little person to hold, to help, to watch grow. Cupping her hands around the soft swell of her belly, she smiled. Matt's child.

She went to sleep with that smile on her face and awakened only when Sadie tapped on the door.

There were two places set at the table when Kristin went downstairs. "Just us?"

Sadie nodded as she set out a plate of sliced tomatoes. "I had one other couple for the weekend, but they're up at the battlefield. They'll be back Sunday night."

By Sunday night, Kristin figured, she should be headed home. She had two days to figure things out.

"So, where's that husband of yours?" Sadie asked after dinner. "Too busy workin' to come with you?"

Kristin shook her head. "I, um, took off by myself. Kind of on the spur of the moment."

"Looks to me like you've been pushed 'bout to the end of your rope. I'm not surprised you needed to get away."

"My daughters didn't like the idea of a new baby."

"Mmmhmm."

"Erin found out that Matt is her dad, but Jenny's dad is Matt's brother." She explained the circumstances. "She lost her father twice in one year."

"Hard on the girl, wasn't it?"

"Oh, yes." Kristin turned her lemonade glass between her fingers. "Matt and I aren't...well, anything, really. We barely talk. When we try to talk, we end up arguing."

Sadie nodded.

"I'm not sure anymore why we got married. We're such different people from the ones we were before he went away. Do we still love each other? Or are we just pretending?"

"Does it matter?"

Kristin looked up. "What do you mean?"

The older woman sat down across the table. "You made choices, then you made promises. Now you live up to the promises."

"You're saying we should stay together no matter what we feel? For the children?"

"Not for the children. For yourselves."

"I don't understand."

Sadie reached for her hand and cradled it between her palms. "Kristin, honey, marriage is work. Hard work. The people who don't understand that simple fact are most of the people who push the divorce rate sky high."

"But a husband and wife should care about each other."

"True. Don't you care about Matt? Not the man you knew, but the one you're married to?"

She didn't hesitate. "Of course I do."

"And I'm pretty sure he cares about you, just the way you are today."

"But—"

"Now what you do is build on that foundation. Maybe it's not the head-over-heels love you had years ago. How long would that have lasted, anyway? Me an' George, you never saw two people crazier in love afore the weddin'. A year later, we had a colicky baby, a pile of debts and nothin' to say to each other."

"What did you do?"

"It's what we didn't do that matters. We didn't quit."

"And things got right again?"

"Up and down, missy, for forty years. Mostly up, mostly good. Sometimes I thought about walkin' out— when he worked graveyard shift at the railroad, so he slept all day and was gone all night and I had four children to look after by myself. No relatives to help out, neither.''

"But you stayed."

"I did. And so did he—when I was miserable and pregnant, miserable goin' through the change of life, miserable mournin' my only son. We didn't always talk about what we thought, what we felt. We just kept keepin' on, as they say.''

Kristin took those words to bed with her, and woke with them on her pillow. She and Sadie didn't talk so personally again. Rain on Friday afternoon and all day Saturday drove many of the reenactors to shelter, including George and the couple who were supposed to be back Sunday night.

Keeping to herself except at meals, Kristin watched the rain from her window, and from the front-porch rocker. She walked down to the pool where Matt and George had fished, to study raindrops spattering the smooth surface into a million interlocked circles. Then she walked into town. Even with the rain, the streets of Boonesboro were packed with shoppers and tourists. Moving easily through the crowds, she savored antiques, browsed in the bookshop, checked out the different types of hammers in the old-fashioned hardware store.

Sunday morning she went to church with George and Sadie, and ate pot roast with homegrown onions and carrots for lunch, topped off with blueberry pie. When the other guests left the table, she looked at her hosts. ''I think it's time for me to start home again.''

George nodded. ''That's good. We'll miss you, but I imagine that man of yours is missin' you more.''

They didn't let her pay for her stay. ''We don't charge friends,'' Sadie insisted. ''Just come back sometime and bring all your little ones. We want to meet them.''

Sunday evening, she called Matt from a hotel in Richmond. "I'll be home tomorrow afternoon."

"Thank God." His voice was rough, tired. "I've been crazy. Whatever it takes, Kris…please just give me the chance to make things right."

"Oh, Matt." Tears dripped onto her fingers as she held the phone. "We'll talk tomorrow night. I promise."

"I'll be here waiting." The intensity of his words stirred up waves of longing deep inside her. "Drive carefully."

"I will."

Surely, with such strong intentions, they could find a way to make their marriage work!

MATT HAD BARELY gotten his breath back from talking with Kristin when the phone rang again. "Matt, it's Irene."

"I just heard from Kris. She'll be home tomorrow afternoon."

He heard her deep sigh. "That's good. But right now we have another serious problem on our hands. Buster is missing."

"Damn. What happened?"

"He dug out under the fence a few days ago. Erin caught him and Frank repaired the hole. We let him out of the house when we came home from church a little while ago. Now we can't find him."

"How's Erin?"

"Not good. If she loses this dog—"

"It's not gonna happen. I'll be right there."

He called Luke with the cell phone on his way to Irene's house. "We need to mount a full-scale dog hunt. Buster has to be found."

"I don't think I can get there."

"Excuse me?"

"Sarah's photographing a wedding tonight. And Jenny's been under the weather all day long. Cranky, a little feverish, just miserable. I don't want to take her out."

"I guess not. Kristin will be home tomorrow—that'll make her feel better."

"No doubt about it."

"But you'll call the doctor if she's not better tomorrow morning, right?"

"You don't need to explain my job, bro. Go use those Special Forces skills to find Buster."

ASHEN-FACED and speechless, Erin sat completely still on the couch in the Jennings' den. Matt crouched in front of her.

"I'm going to find him, Erin. Chances are good he's gotten himself into somebody's backyard and can't get out. All we have to do is find which one."

She simply looked at him, her eyes brimming with tears.

Rising, he pressed a kiss onto her hair. Frank Jennings came into the room with two heavy-duty flashlights. "We'll be back as soon as we can," Matt promised. Erin didn't move.

The sun set as they combed the neighborhood. Surrounded on three sides by water and marsh, the subdivision was a nightmare to search. Hundreds of huge azalea bushes could easily hide a dog Buster's size. Most of the houses had fenced yards—often stockade-type fencing, impossible to see over or through. Those required a knock on the front door and a request to search inside the fence. By full dark, they hadn't found a single person who'd seen Buster. And no trace of him anywhere they'd searched.

Matt stood with his father-in-law at the end of the Jennings' street. "Where could the crazy dog have gone?"

Frank considered. "You suppose he headed home?"

"I don't even want to think about that." Matt and Kristin's house was on the other side of heavily traveled Highway 17. "A dog would have to be magic to get across those six lanes uninjured."

"They sometimes do, though."

"Yeah. I know." He sighed. "Let's go back to the house and I'll head out in the car. You can tell Erin I'm still looking."

And he did, until exhaustion drove him home at 3:00 a.m. He fell into the recliner and slept until six, when he grabbed a banana and started searching again. With no success.

At noon he went back to see Erin. She stood in front of the living-room window, staring at the street. "You didn't find him, did you?" There was no hope in her voice.

"Not yet. I called the animal shelter, but nobody's brought him in. I came up with an idea, though, and you could help me with it."

"What?"

"I made some flyers about Buster—his name and description and our phone number. And I offered a reward. I thought we could put them up around the nearby neighborhoods. If somebody sees him, they can give us a call and we'll come running."

His daughter gazed at him, assessing the idea's potential. "Okay," she said finally. "Let's go."

They posted signs in the Jennings' neighborhood first, and in the subdivisions on either side, across the marsh.

Driving with the windows down, they called Buster's name at frequent intervals, and stopped often to investigate a rustle in the bushes or a random bark.

Across the highway, he and Erin papered their own neighborhood with signs. Matt got out to post the notice on telephone poles at major intersections. He felt they'd covered all the bases. And he'd put his cell-phone number as well as the home number on the sheet, to be instantly available, no matter where he was.

No one called.

Driving back to the Jennings' house, Matt decided he'd better prepare Erin for bad news. Or no news. "Sometimes a dog will just follow his nose, you know, when he gets a good scent. He doesn't watch where he's going, and he gets kinda turned around and…and can't find his way back home."

"I know." She was very composed, reminding Matt all too much of her mother.

"Then again, dogs sometimes stay gone for quite a while, and end up coming home again when you don't expect them."

"I watched *The Incredible Journey*. They got home. Lassie gets home. I think Buster will come home."

"I hope you're right." He glanced at the clock and remembered Kristin. "Your mom's coming home this afternoon. Do you want to be there to meet her?"

Again the careful consideration. "Okay. Let me say goodbye to Grandma."

While Erin packed up her clothes, Matt waited with Irene.

Kristin's mom was close to tears herself. "I hate that this happened while she was here."

Matt put his arm around her shoulders. "He could have gotten lost from our house just as easily. I think Frank's right and he tried to get home. If we're lucky, he'll make it.''

He started to move away, but she held him with a hand on his arm. "What are you and Kristy going to do?''

She wasn't referring to the dog. Or even the girls. "I'm not sure. I don't know what she's decided while she's been gone. But I know I'm not willing to let her go. I'll do whatever it takes to keep her here, with me."

"Have you ever thought of…of…'' She was obviously hesitant to finish the question.

"Go on, Irene. Ask.''

"Have you ever considered leaving the Army? Kristy doesn't expect it,'' she added in a rush. "I just can't help thinking it would be best for the girls and her. And you.''

For the first time in twelve hours, Matt could grin. "That one's already taken care of. I sent in my resignation Friday. It'll take a few months, but eventually I will be unemployed!''

THE HOUSE was completely empty when Kristin got home. She walked through the silent rooms, fighting disappointment. Okay, so she hadn't expected a brass band. But Matt had sounded anxious to see her. Would he have gone out when he knew she would be arriving soon?

She smiled slightly as she noticed dust on the tabletops and a cobweb high in the corner. Housekeeping hadn't been on Matt's mind. On the other hand, nothing in the house had been disturbed. The beds in the master bedroom and guest room were smooth and untouched. Jenny's room was just as she'd left it. Gathering all of her courage, Kristin turned the knob on Erin's door and pushed it open.

"Oh, Matt,'' she said into the empty room.

He must have worked most of the weekend. All the

torn pages had been gathered up. A stack of large manila envelopes sat on the bookshelf in place of the ruined books. Kristin crossed the room to look at them. Each envelope was labeled with a title, an author, or a subject and, in many cases, all three. Inside the envelope were the pages for that book, tears taped, wrinkles smoothed, arranged in the original order. Hours of work lay on that bookshelf. Hours of work and an immeasurable love.

Kristin was still mopping tears off her cheeks when she went downstairs again. Just as she poured herself a glass of water, the phone rang. She hurried to answer before the machine could pick up. "Matt? Is that you?"

"Sorry, Kristin, it's Luke. Welcome back."

"Thanks. It's good to be here. How's Jenny? Can I talk to her?"

"Uh, that's why I'm calling. See—"

A commotion at the front door distracted her. "Just a minute, Luke. Somebody's here." Still carrying the phone, she rounded the corner of the hall to the front door.

Erin shot through the open door and barreled straight into her arms. "Mommy!" Then she burst into tears. "Buster's lost, Mommy. He ran away and I couldn't find him and Matt couldn't find him and we put up signs everywhere but we still don't know if he'll come home." She collapsed against Kristin's breast, sobbing.

Matt came close and knelt down on one knee. He put a hand on Erin's head and the other along the line of Kristin's jaw. "Sorry to greet you with such bad news," he said in a low voice. "But welcome home."

As if she hadn't seen him in years, Kristin stared into his face, relearning the features she'd come to take for granted. His blue eyes were gentle, his eyebrows drawn together in worry. His mouth was a beautiful curve, even when he didn't smile. His fingers shook a little at the tip of her earlobe.

Gradually, she became aware of a squawk somewhere nearby and realized she still carried the phone as she held Erin close.

"Luke!" she gasped and was aware of Matt pulling back.

She juggled the phone to her ear. "Luke, I'm sorry. Matt and Erin came in just as you called, and Buster is lost. What were you saying?"

His words were drowned by the sound of Erin sobbing. "Wait one more second, Luke." Pressing her lips to Erin's hair, she rocked back and forth. "Hush, love, hush. It'll be okay. We'll keep looking for Buster, I promise. Just let me hear what Luke has to say."

Erin hiccuped and settled. Kristin put the phone to her ear again. "Now. Tell me about Jenny."

"Sorry to do this to you, Kristin." He paused just long enough to stop her heart. "Jenny has chicken pox."

CHAPTER SIXTEEN

THE MATT BRENNAN FAMILY was back together. Sort of.

Jenny came home from Luke and Sarah's house with a raging case of chicken pox. Covered with itchy little blisters and running a fever, she was as miserable a child as Matt had ever seen.

She sat in Kristin's lap for most of the first six hours she was home.

"Jenny, love, let me up," Kristin said about midnight Sunday night. "I need to go to the bathroom."

"Uh-uh." Panting, the little girl leaned harder against her mother's breastbone. Beside Kristin on the couch, Erin had sprawled into sleep. Matt, watching from the recliner, didn't know whether to laugh or cry.

"I'm sorry, Jenny," Kristin said finally, easing forward. "I know how bad you feel. I had chicken pox when I was a little girl. But I really do have to get up."

"Mommy!"

Matt slid out of his chair. "Com'ere, Miss Jenny." Ignoring the protest on Kristin's face and Jenny's frustrated cry, he took the child firmly into his arms. "Let's go for a walk."

Kristin hesitated, then quickly left the room. Holding Jenny close, with her head on his shoulder, Matt strolled through the darker rooms of the house, where the air was cool and moved slightly around them. Jenny sobbed, then cried, then sniffed and, finally, was quiet. When they met

Kristin in the hall, she opened her mouth to say something—then stopped, as if the words had been stolen away.

"Why don't you lie down with Erin," Matt suggested. "You've got to be tired after driving all day. Jenny and I will be okay for a while." He drew his head back to look at the little girl's face. "Won't we, Miss Jenny?"

He heard the smack of a thumb being sucked and felt a small nod. With a grin he couldn't help, he looked at Kristin. "See?"

Her brown eyes smiled back. "I see. I'll be in the family room if you need me. I put the oatmeal bath Luke brought upstairs by the tub."

"Great. Take a break."

Lifting her hand in a brief wave, she left him alone with their sick little girl.

He'd had harder nights, Matt thought, but not outside of an African prison. Jenny slept on his shoulder for about an hour, until her fever medicine began to wear off. For the next hour she whimpered and wriggled while he held her, but refused to move out of his arms. A new dose of medicine at 2:00 a.m. took a miserable half an hour to reduce her temperature. Matt climbed the stairs, desperate enough to try a bath. Jenny had never liked his version of bathtime.

He poured a packet of brown powder under flowing lukewarm water, then set about easing Jenny out of her clothes. She protested with every stroke of cloth across her skin. Matt blinked his eyes against tears when he saw her poor little chest and back and bottom, all covered with harsh red spots.

"Boy, Jenny. You've got enough pox for a whole henhouse of chickens. Want to see if the water makes them feel better?"

She drew up in his arms as he bent over the tub. "No-nononononononono...."

"Aw, Jen." He sat down on the side and settled her in his lap, where she kept her knees pulled in close to avoid touching the sandy water. "The doctor said this would help the itches. You could try, couldn't you?"

She shook her head.

He dipped a finger into the coolish water. "It feels like the ocean to me. The ocean on a summer day when you've been out on the beach making a sand castle and you're all hot and sandy." Wetting his finger again, he let a drop fall on the top of her knee. Jenny sqawked, but didn't draw up any farther. "You know how it feels—you've got sand all in your bathing suit and all over your legs and it's itchy and you're hot. So you run as fast as you can into the cool, foamy waves. You wash off your legs and arms and jiggle your suit to get the sand out. And then you just play in the water because it feels so good. Remember that?"

Another drop trickled down her leg.

Jenny looked up at him and nodded. That thumb was still stuck firmly in her mouth.

"I think this bath would feel just like that. Sure you won't try?"

She wasn't panting as much, and she seemed calmer. The fever would be coming down. After a minute, she lowered one leg and stuck her toes into the tub.

"Good girl! How's that feel?"

For an answer, she put the other foot in. And kicked a little.

Eventually Matt got her all the way into the tub. He scooped water over her shoulders and even over her head. She blinked and protested when the slick bath ran down over her face. But the time for hysterics had passed. At least temporarily.

When the water got too cold he pulled her out and dried her as gently as he could with a fluffy towel. ''Want to pick out a nightgown?''

Jenny trotted buck-naked down the hallway to her room. Matt followed, figuring there wasn't anybody awake to see. She chose the perfect gown, light, thin, soft. He pulled it over her head. ''Should we read a story while we're here? Or play a game?''

Four fairy tales later, the flush was returning to her skin. ''Time for some more medicine, Jen. Let's go back downstairs.''

On the way through the family room, he checked on Kristin. She'd curled up behind Erin and slept with her arms around the girl. That had to make them both feel good. He turned off the last lamp to give them better rest.

In the kitchen, he poured a dose of antihistamine and added some water. ''Drink up. Then you can have a popsicle.''

Jenny took a sip…and spat it out onto Matt's chest and her own clean gown.

Matt frowned at her. ''It's supposed to go inside you, not outside me.''

She giggled.

He grinned. ''Can we try again?''

''Tastes yucky.''

''You won't itch as much if you swallow it.''

''I hate it.''

''You'll get a popsicle to make it taste better.''

She stuck her tongue out in distaste.

Matt sighed. ''I bet Erin takes her medicine when she has to. Without sticking her tongue out or spraying other people.''

Jenny thought that over. Then she sighed. And opened her mouth, though a shudder went through her as she swallowed. The promised popsicle was a big success. Then they went back upstairs for a new gown.

As the antihistamine took hold, the fever medicine started to wear off. They walked the house again, with Jenny sleepy and yet cranky on his shoulder. Finally, he could give her another dose for the fever. And sit down.

As he settled into the recliner in the dark den, he realized that he'd had about three hours of sleep in the last forty-eight. His eyes burned, and every muscle in his body ached as if he'd led a twenty-mile forced march through the mud. He would never have guessed fatherhood could be such a physical challenge.

Jenny snuggled a little closer into the curve of his neck.

Matt smiled. He'd never realized fatherhood could make him feel so good.

Thursday
Dear Diary

I lost Buster. He ran away from Grandma Irene's house an hasnt come home yet. Im afrade he wont anymore. I'm afrade hes hurt an needs me but I cant find him. Thinkin about that makes me feel sick.

I dont no who I can talk to now. Buster didnt talk back but he lissened real good. I need him.

Jenny has the chikenpoks. Shes been grumpy for four days coz she itches. I already had the chikenpoks in first grade. I liked bein out of school an home with Mommy. I didnt like itchin all the time.

Mommy came home the night Jenny got sick. She an Matt are takin turns takin care of Jenny. Matt stays awake an Mommy sleeps, then he sleeps an

Mommy stays awake. 2 times when he an Mommy were both awake Matt and me drove around lookin for Buster. We didnt find him. But that was a nice thing for Matt to do.

He put my books in envelops. I was so mad when I did that an he fixd it as good as it can be fixd. I dont know what to say to him. Im still thinkin.

Our house is a messed up place this week. Not neat like Mommy makes it an lots of stuff goin wrong.

I just wish Buster would come back.

Your friend
Erin Elena Brennan

ELENA KNEW where the album was. William had hidden it from her thirty-two years ago. But in all the moves since, she'd kept track of where that photograph album was stored. She'd never looked at it. Not until today.

William kept the key to his desk in his jewelry box with his medals and ribbons. With the desk unlocked, all she had to do was open the bottom right drawer and take out the book.

Opening the album, she looked at the pictures. Matt, a chubby eighteen-month-old. She, of course, so much younger. Halloween, Thanksgiving, Christmas all came and went in the record. And then, in January, the first picture of Melody Ann Brennan.

Such a beautiful little girl. Elena traced the tiny face with the tip of her finger. An easy birth, a delightful baby. Life had seemed so perfect that cold, snowy winter in Kentucky, even with William out of the country. A wonderful little boy and a precious little girl to take care of. Elena had never felt so richly blessed.

The pictures in Melody's album ended with Valen-

tine's Day. One night—a mere eight hours—had altered
life irrevocably. Elena had slept dreamlessly herself, waking to an unusual silence. In the eight weeks of Melody's
life, her mother had become accustomed to the morning
warbles the little girl liked to practice. This day, there
was only quiet.

Eyes still dry, Elena closed the album cover and folded
her shaking hands on top. She had not relived the morning she'd found her daughter dead in her crib in decades.
She'd stopped trying to discover what she had done
wrong, what possible action she could have taken that
would have saved Melody's precious life. Doctors and
psychiatrists had told her nobody could have prevented
it. Nobody was to blame. Elena had never believed them.
Even today, she bore the responsibility for Melody's
death like the proverbial millstone. The burden had become almost a friend.

"Elena? Elena, where are you?" William's voice approached.

"In your office." She didn't try to hide the album.

"What are you doing in—? Oh." He stopped in the
doorway.

She smiled up at him. "I was thinking about Erin and
Jenny. And it seemed important, somehow, to
visit…Melody." Opening the drawer, she replaced the
album.

"You miss them, I know." He sat in the armchair
across the desk.

Elena nodded. "All three of them, actually. But, yes.
We haven't seen Erin and Jenny for nearly a month. I
miss them very much."

"There's only one remedy. We have to make peace
with Matt and Kristin."

She'd already come to that conclusion. "Yes."

"I frankly don't know how. I thought I knew Matt. Now I feel like I don't know him at all."

"I suppose…we should reacquaint ourselves with both of them. If we hope to see our granddaughters." Now her eyes burned with tears. "I really need to see Erin and Jenny."

William came around the desk and bent to put his arms around her shoulders. He pressed a kiss against her hair. "Well, then, m'dear, we will have to prepare ourselves a meal we've never tasted before and learn to like it."

Elena drew back to see his face. "What are you talking about? What meal?"

He grinned—the same cocky expression she'd fallen in love with forty years ago. "Humble pie, Elena. Humble pie."

By FRIDAY, Jenny had finally started to improve. Fewer new blisters were appearing. More of the old ones were scabbing over. Her fever was manageable for six to eight hours at a time. She looked horrible, but she felt better.

The rest of them were exhausted. Kristin fell asleep every time she sat down. She had plenty of work to keep her busy, of course. The house had fallen into chaos over the days she and Matt had shared nursing duties. Moving slowly, she attempted to reconstruct order.

They'd hardly spoken since she'd come home, especially about anything personal. There hasn't been time. Yet that first night, they'd somehow become partners… parents.

Erin wandered into the kitchen as Kristin unloaded the dishwasher so she could fill it up again with the dishes in the sink. "Jenny's asleep on the couch."

"That's good. When she wakes up we'll give her another bath. What are you doing?"

"Nothin'." She slid onto the stool at the counter. "I wish Buster was home."

"I know you do, love."

"It's too hot to play outside, so I looked at some books." Kristin caught Erin's sideways glance. "Did you know he'd fixed my books?"

"I saw that he'd put the pages together in envelopes."

"That was a lot of work."

"Yes, I think it was."

"Luke would have done it, if he'd been here." Her tone was defensive.

"I'm sure he would have. Why is that, do you think?" Kristin wanted Erin to make the connection herself.

But Erin wasn't ready. She shrugged. "I don't know." After a moment, she sighed. "Buster's not gonna come home, is he?"

Kristin dried her hands and went to put her arms around Erin. "I just don't know. We can keeping hoping. And looking. I'm sure he knows we want him back."

"Yeah." Erin sighed and let her head fall against Kristin's shoulder. Kristin held her breath, afraid to push for any further sign of affection. She ached to hold her daughter tight. It had been so long since Erin had taken comfort.

After a few seconds, Erin straightened. "I guess I'll go pick up the games in Jenny's room. I had to let her win Chutes and Ladders. She's sick."

Carefully, Kristin stepped away. "That's a big help, Erin. When she's well again, you can let Jenny lose or win."

The girl slipped down from the stool. "She does beat me sometimes." At the door to the family room, she turned. There was a slight twinkle in her blue eyes. "But mostly I beat her."

Kristin laughed. "I know."

She was still smiling when Matt came in a few minutes later. "Sorry," he said on a yawn. "I couldn't seem to keep my eyes open after the alarm sounded. How's Jenny?"

"She's asleep on the couch. Do you want some coffee?"

"Um...yeah, thanks. Maybe it'll wake me up. Where's Erin?" Eyes shut, he sat at the table and leaned his head on his hand. Kristin poured a full mug of coffee, then stopped a moment just to look at him.

The shadows she'd seen under his eyes at the beginning of the week were darker, wider. He hadn't shaved today, or yesterday, and a rough stubble covered his lean cheeks and chin. He still wore the wrinkled clothes he'd slept in. She thought he'd lost weight. She'd never seen him look less like himself. She'd never loved him more.

His eyes opened when she set the mug on the table. "Hope this helps."

"Probably the best help would be twenty-four hours of uninterrupted rest." She started to go back to the dishes...and realized there were more important issues than a clean kitchen. After pouring herself a glass of lemonade, Kristin sat down across the table from her husband. "Maybe you could sleep most of tomorrow. Especially if you're going back to work Monday."

He rubbed a hand across his face. "I should. I've got a truckload of paperwork to shuffle through. Getting out of the Army is more complicated than getting in."

Matt heard Kristin's sharp gasp, and thought over what he'd just said. "Hell. I haven't had a chance to tell you that, have I?"

Eyes wary, she stared at him. "Tell me what?"

"I submitted my resignation."

"Why would you do that?"

"Pretty simple, as a matter of fact. I realized I don't have the commitment serving in the military requires. I thought for a while I was just bored with recruiting. But I can't go back to Special Forces, or anywhere else. I don't want to be there."

"I...see." She wrapped her hands around her glass. "Where do you want to be?"

"I'm still trying to figure that out. Any suggestions are welcome."

Kristin didn't smile. Didn't look up or say anything.

Matt cleared his throat. "Kris, I'm sorry I didn't talk it over with you first. We haven't exactly been on speaking terms. And then you were gone, and then Jenny was sick. There just hasn't been time."

"I—I know." She ran a fingertip around the rim of the glass. "I just hoped...we were working...together. Partners."

"When I...when I decided to resign, I wasn't sure we were partners anymore. I didn't know how to talk it over with you, if you'd even be interested. I didn't mean to exclude you. Or hurt you. Please know that."

"I think I do." She loosened her hands around the glass and gazed at the moisture on her palms, then got to her feet. Drying her hands on a towel at the sink, she said, "It's just such a big decision to make for all of us. By yourself."

Matt stood as she turned to leave the kitchen, still without looking at him. He reached for her as she passed, thinking about an apology, a promise...something.

Kristin put a warm hand on his arm. The touch itself stopped him from coming any closer. "I...I'll be okay. Just give me time to think about it." She removed her hand and left the room.

Matt dropped into his chair at the kitchen table. *Way to go, Brennan. You blew it again!*

IRENE AND FRANK JENNINGS came visiting on Saturday afternoon, with a baked ham dinner and presents for the girls in hand.

"We thought you all needed a break," Kristin's mom said as they unpacked the food in the kitchen. "You've had such a difficult week. Are things getting better?"

Kristin sighed. "Yes and no. Jenny's better. Erin's more approachable. Matt and I worked like a team all week long, and then..."

"And then?"

Kristin reached to get a handful of plates. "And then he told me yesterday that he's handed in his resignation to the Army. Your wish comes true, Mom. He's getting out."

"He mentioned that to me Monday, when he brought Erin home. You're not happy about it?"

"It's a decision that affects the whole family. When we were in Virginia, I asked him not to make any big changes in our lives."

Her mother filled glasses with ice. "Do you want him to stay in the Army?"

"I don't want him to go away again." Kristin sighed. "But I don't want to be the reason he's quitting."

"Maybe you should tell him that. See where it takes you."

She stared at her mom as the idea hit home. "Maybe I should."

The surprise dinner proved a respite for them all. Grandma and Granddaddy took the brunt of the girls' attention. Jenny was practically her happy self again, working on a puzzle with her grandfather. Erin reverently examined the book on oceans she'd received—not a replacement, Kristin noticed, but a brand-new addition to the collection.

It seemed strange, in fact, to be sitting in the family room doing nothing. Matt in his recliner looked a bit bewildered, too, as if he'd forgotten something really important. Occasionally Kristin caught his eye, or he caught her watching him. They would smile, uneasily, and look away again.

Then her father glanced up. "You two look like you haven't left the house all week long."

Matt chuckled. "We haven't, much."

"So why don't you take a walk?"

Kristin gazed at him. "A walk?"

"Oh, yes, Kristy." Her mother nodded. "It's cool tonight, and clear. You would feel so much better for just a short walk around the neighborhood. Go ahead. We'll be just fine with the girls."

Her heart pounded at the idea of taking a walk alone with Matt. "Maybe Erin should come, too. She hasn't been out much, either."

Erin glanced up from her book. "Do I have to?"

"No, dear, of course not. You stay right here with us." Irene patted her granddaughter's knee.

"Well...okay." Without glancing at Matt, Kristin crossed to the kitchen, preparing to go out the garage door. With him standing tall and somehow formidable behind her, she looked back into the family room. "We, um, won't be long."

Her father waved them out. "Take your time."

As they stepped out of the shelter of the garage, Kristin gasped with pleasure. "This *is* lovely! I didn't realize how cool it had gotten."

Matt followed her to the end of the driveway. "Seems

like there are usually a few days in August when the humidity clears away and the temperature drops, reminding you that autumn will come…though probably not for a while yet.''

They turned away from the setting sun. "It's great to be outside and not sweltering."

"You bet."

That exhausted the possibilities of the weather as a topic of conversation.

"It was nice of your folks to bring over a meal."

"They're pretty sweet that way, aren't they?"

She heard Matt blow out a breath. "I haven't talked to my dad in almost two weeks. I hope he…they're okay."

"Surely they'd let you know if something was seriously wrong. Luke would, at least."

"I guess."

A long block passed by in silence.

"Matt, I—"

"Kris—" They looked at each other and smiled with embarrassment. "You go ahead," Matt said.

Kristin took a deep breath. "I just wanted to say I'm sorry I reacted badly to your decision about the Army. We weren't exactly talking and there wasn't any way you could have brought it up. If you're sure you don't want to stay in the service, then…then we'll go from there."

He stopped and turned to face her. The anxious expression in his eyes had her blinking back tears. "Kris. Thank you. I probably don't deserve that much consideration from you. I've been such a—"

She reached up to put a hand on his chest. "Hush. I've made mistakes, probably more than you have. I was just surprised… But I love the idea of your coming home every night."

Matt's warm palm covered her fingers. His smile was sweet and amazingly sexy, his blue eyes shining with an intense light. A current of awareness jumped between them suddenly. Kristin's knees trembled.

And then his attention shifted. He turned his head to the side. "Did you hear that?"

She listened. "I don't hear anything."

"I heard—" Matt shook his head. "Wishful thinking, I guess."

Hands still joined, they turned to walk farther. Kristin couldn't feel the street beneath her feet—the wildness running through her was like the night Matt had kissed her for the very first time. Maybe they weren't quite back to that point again. But his palm against hers was the promise of miracles.

Somewhere, a dog yipped. "There it is again," Matt said. "Where did that come from?" He stopped and listened.

Kristin waited, watching him. The sound repeated. "That way." He pointed and pulled her with him toward a side street.

"Matt, what are we doing? What do you think…? Matt!" She stopped and made him stop, too. "You think that's Buster? Could it be Buster?"

"I don't know." He started walking again. "But something about that bark sounds like him. We have to check it out, anyway." Halfway down the street he picked up speed.

Kris pulled her hand free. "You go on," she said when he looked back. "I can't keep up."

With a nod, Matt turned and broke into a jog. He began calling the dog. "Buster! Buster?"

Unbelievably, the barks responded, getting louder and more frequent. Kristin added her voice. "Buster?"

The three houses at the end of the cul-de-sac all had stockade fencing around their backyards. Matt stopped, listening again. "Buster? C'mon, Buster. Where are you?"

Kristin caught up with him, breathing hard. "Sounds like it's coming from the left."

"Yeah." The driveway of the yellow-shuttered house on the left side was empty. Matt went to the front door and knocked, without result. He came back to the street. "Nobody's home. Let's see if maybe the gate's unlatched."

No such luck. The only lock resisted their attempts to pry it open.

"Damn." He stared at the fence, as if he could bore a hole straight through with his eyes. Kristin followed him from one side of the house to the other, clueless as to what he was looking for.

"That might do it," he said finally. On this side, two stockade-fence sections met at the metal endpost of a chain-link fence. "If I could get a toehold, I could go over."

Kristin looked at him in horror. "You could not!"

"Sure I could." Buster barked again. "Hold on, Buster!"

With Kristin standing speechless, Matt approached the fence. Standing high on the toes of his right foot, he put the toe of his left shoe on the widest part of the chain-link post, groaning as his leg stretched.

"Matt…" Her protest went unheeded. He grabbed the points of two boards in the stockade fence, dragged in a deep breath…and jumped.

The thrust took him high enough to balance his right foot on a point of the stockade. Pushing off the chain-link post with his left foot, Matt whooped and hopped over the six-foot fence into the yard on the other side.

Kristin heard the sound of his landing in a succession of thuds. And then she didn't hear anything at all.

CHAPTER SEVENTEEN

"MATT? Matt Brennan, answer me!"

Matt heard Kristin's panicked call. He would have liked to reply. But first he had to get the air back in his lungs.

After a short forever, he managed to move an arm, to lift his head. With an effort greater than it had taken to jump the fence, he pushed himself onto his side. There, he could cough.

"Oh, God, Matt, are you okay?"

"I'm okay," he croaked. "Calm down, Kris. I'm all right."

In another minute he fumbled to his feet. "Go to the gate on the other side. I'll let you in."

As soon as he lifted the latch, she pulled back the gate and stumbled into his arms. "Are you sure you're okay?" Her hands were on his cheeks, his head, the back of his neck, his shoulders. Her full, rounded body pressed close to his. "I can't believe you did something so stupid!"

Matt grinned and let his arms settle across her back. "If I'd known you would react like this, I'd have done it sooner."

She stopped fussing and stared up at him. In response to his wink, her smile softened, her eyes warmed. "Oh, really? You think I'm swayed by this macho display of heroics?"

"Aren't you?" He lowered his head.

"Definitely," she murmured just as his mouth brushed hers.

Everything inside him wanted that kiss, wanted it hard and deep and long until there wasn't anything *outside* the kiss. He ached with need, with joy, with lust, with a desperate desire to possess.

But this was a time to give.

And so he made the kiss thorough but gentle. He satisfied himself with relearning the curve of his wife's lips, the taste of her smile. The sigh she gave, the response she offered, nearly pushed him past his self-imposed limits, but he held firm. Everything in its own good time.

The dog's barks drew him out from under Kristin's spell. Matt pulled back. "I guess, as long as we're here, we oughta at least look at the dog."

Kristin opened her eyes slowly. Her mouth curved in a sultry smile. "Right."

He tightened his hold for a second, then released her to turn toward the back of the yard. Behind a jumble of azaleas and camelias and weeds stood a length of chain-link fence. And behind the fence danced a dog. A white-and-black splotched dog.

"Buster?"

An excited bark accelerated Matt's already racing heartbeat. He hustled to the bushes and eased his way through to the fence. The dog waited for him on the other side, front paws on the highest link he could reach, tongue lolling, black-and-white plumed tail fanning wildly.

"Kris, it's Buster!" Matt reached over the fence to ruffle Buster's ears, his head, his snout. "Hey, buddy, where ya' been? Bad planning, leaving without a map to get you home."

Kristin pushed through the branches to stand beside him. "Oh, Buster, thank God! You're such a mess—what in the world have you been doing?"

On Buster's side of the fence, a palmetto grove stretched for half a mile or more before giving way to pines. "Looks like he came all the way across to get here."

"From where?" Kristin reached over to rub Buster's head. "What's over there?"

"Marsh, judging from how filthy he is. You're lucky you didn't meet any bad-tempered copperheads, Buster."

Kristin shuddered. "I don't want to think about snakes. Let's get him home."

"Good idea." Belly braced on the fence, Matt leaned over. "Give me a little help here, buddy." He braced his hands around the dog's ribs. "Here…we…go!"

Buster's helpful push brought him up into Matt's arms. And the extra momentum sent both of them backward into the middle of an azalea bush.

Matt lay there getting his face licked. "Thanks, guy. Yeah, I love you, too." A tongue swooped across his mouth. "Oh, yuck. Get off of me, mutt. Come on, move!" Kristin laughed.

He'd just gotten back to his feet when a new voice joined the chaos. "What the hell are you doin' in my backyard?"

Holding Kris's hand, Matt eased them both in front of the bushes. "Sorry, sir." The man observing them from the center of the yard was taller than Matt, heavier, and mad. "We came back to rescue our dog. He was trapped on the other side of the fence."

"How'd you get in?"

"I jumped."

The man made a rude comment. ''Did you break my lock? You're gonna pay for it.''

''No, sir, not the lock. The azalea back here's in pretty bad shape, though. I'll be glad to pay you for that.''

After ten minutes of negotiating, they escaped with Buster to the street. ''That was close,'' Kristin said. ''I thought I was going to have to leave you as a hostage while I went to get the checkbook.''

''Me, too. Lucky I've been trained for the job.'' Matt grinned. ''Let's get this guy home. I believe he's expected for dinner.''

Buster led them at a fast pace straight to the house. Matt opened the front door and managed to block the dog's entrance. ''Erin? Erin, there's somebody out here who wants to see you!''

Irene came around the corner first. ''Matt? What in the world?''

Erin slipped by her. ''Who wants to see me? What— *Buster!*''

Matt let the dog by. Animal and girl met in the center of the hall, Erin on her knees with her arms around Buster's filthy coat, Buster's yips clear signals of delight. Kristin was wiping tears off her cheeks with the heels of her hands. Grinning like a fool, Matt closed the front door and leaned back against it, blinking a few times to clear his vision. A minute later, Jenny came in to hug Buster, giving Erin a chance to ask questions.

''Where was he? How did you find him?''

''Matt heard him barking while we were walking.'' Kristin explained the whole episode, with too much detail and an exaggerated estimate on the height of both fences. ''The back fence stretched as far as we could see in either direction. If Matt hadn't lifted him over, I don't know how we would have gotten Buster home.''

Matt felt his cheeks heat up as Erin stared at him. "Hey, there he was on the other side. I just gave him a boost over."

She gazed at him a few seconds longer. Then she rushed across the floor and into his arms, her own tight around his neck.

"Oh, *thank you!* Thank you." Her sobs shook them both. "Thank you so much." She sniffed and, after another moment, added in a nearly soundless whisper, "Daddy."

SUNDAY MORNING, Kristin decided it was time to reestablish their normal routine. While Matt and Jenny dozed in the family room alongside a bathed and fed Buster, she and Erin got ready for church.

Brighter and more agreeable than she'd been in months, Erin chose her own dress and stood quietly to get her hair braided. "Do they have kids' church today, Mommy?"

"I think so. You like that, don't you?"

"It's easier than sittin' while the preacher talks forever."

"I bet it is."

Fortunately for Erin, the children's service was scheduled to take place. But the time had been moved back thirty minutes to the regular fall schedule. Since they were early, Kristin and Erin waited out on the live oak–shaded playground.

Instead of rushing off to the swings or the climbing bars, though, Erin sat down on the bench next to Kristin. "I don't want to run around in this dress," she confided. "It might get messed up."

"That's true." A butterfly danced past. Kristin watched her daughter as Erin followed the bright creature with her eyes. "What are you thinking about today, love?"

The butterfly landed on a nearby weed, keeping Erin's attention. "Just…stuff."

Kristin waited.

"He worked hard to bring Buster home, didn't he?"

"Very hard."

"An' he put my books back together."

"Yes."

"An'…an'…he's still here. You went away. But he didn't."

"That's right. I really needed some time by myself. But I couldn't have gone if Matt hadn't been here. I knew I could trust him if…if you needed him."

"Grandma Irene said your new baby was a surprise."

"Pretty much. We'd planned to wait for a while so you and Jenny could feel good about this family."

"I guess maybe you'd have told me and Jenny sooner if you thought we'd be happy about it."

"You're very wise today, Erin."

"So…" Turning, she put her hand lightly on Kristin's belly. "Is it a boy or a girl?"

"We don't know yet. Which would you like?"

"A boy would be different."

"Definitely."

"But we have a lot of girl clothes and toys already. We wouldn't have to get more."

Kristin swallowed a smile. "A girl might be more efficient."

Erin's blue gaze lifted to her face. "I guess we'll just have to wait and see."

"Sometimes that's the best thing to do."

As the church bells rang to announce the start of services, Kristin settled Erin with her friends in kids' church and stopped to chat for a moment with the leader of the children's service, then left the room for the short walk to the chapel.

"Kristin?"

The refined Southern voice coming from behind her was unmistakable. With her breath caught in her throat, Kristin turned back to face the woman beside the door. "Hello, Mrs. Brennan. Are you feeling better?"

"Much better, thank you. You're…looking well."

"Thank you." Smoothing down her loose-fitting dress, Kristin moved out of the way of a family bringing their children to the service. "Is Colonel Brennan with you?"

"He's gone ahead into the chapel."

There weren't too many alternatives to walking with Elena into church. Kristin fell into step beside her mother-in-law, trying to invent innocuous conversation.

"Jenny came down with chicken pox last Monday. She's had a pretty hard time of it, though she's getting better now."

"I spoke with Luke and he mentioned she was sick. He also said your dog had gotten lost. I imagine that upsets Erin very much."

"It did. But Matt found him and brought him home yesterday afternoon. Erin's thrilled, of course."

"Of course." They reached the door to the chapel and stepped into the aisle. The Colonel sat a few pews ahead on the left.

Kristin hesitated, thinking she'd really rather sit alone. But Mrs. Brennan extended her arm. "Will you sit with us? There's plenty of room."

And so she shared the service with her in-laws…for the first time ever without Matt. Each elder Brennan possessed a good voice, and singing beside them was a pleasure. The chance to sit in the cool peace of the chapel did much to restore Kristin's spirit and to prepare her for the encounter sure to come.

After the service, they passed one of the church parlors on their way to Erin's classroom. Mrs. Brennan put a hand on Kristin's arm. "Could we step in here a moment?"

Swallowing hard, Kristin did as she was asked.

The Colonel glanced at his wife. "Kristin, we've been quite harsh with you and with Matt in the last few months. While we may have thought we were right at the time, the end result has been to alienate us from our children and grandchildren. We're not comfortable with this state of affairs."

"Neither are the girls. They've missed you."

Mrs. Brennan closed her eyes briefly. "I doubt an apology could be sufficient to expunge the accusations and criticisms I've made. I—I am sorry. I am sure that you have always tried to do what you thought best for your children." She straightened the hem of her lavender suit jacket. "I miss the girls. A-and you and Matt, of course. I hoped that, perhaps…"

Kristin took a breath. "I think it would be great to start fresh."

Elena's austere face relaxed slightly. "How do you think Matt will feel? We know he's very angry." She looked at her husband. "His father didn't take the news that Matt is leaving the Army at all well."

"Neither did I." Kristin smiled. "We all probably need to discuss the issue further." She took a risk, putting one hand on the Colonel's arm and one on Mrs. Brennan's. "Meanwhile Luke and Sarah are coming for dinner tonight. Why don't you come, too?"

The Colonel cleared his throat. "Maybe you should ask Matt, first."

Kristin shook her head. "I don't think that's necessary." She smiled to take the sting out of her next words. "Maybe he'll understand what it feels like for somebody else to make decisions without consulting him!"

She didn't let it go that far, of course. During a lull after lunch, when Jenny and Erin were stretched out on the family-room carpet, immersed in Candyland, Kristin stopped Matt in the upstairs hallway.

"I saw your parents at church this morning."

His face hardened. "I'm sorry about that."

"Don't be. They apologized."

"It's not enough."

"Now you're being just like them."

"They don't change, Kris. Give them another opportunity and they'll try to run our lives again, just as they always have."

"That's because they're parents. They feel responsible for your happiness and well-being."

He stared at her for a long moment, his eyes half-angry, half-amused. "You want this to happen, don't you?" His hand came up and his fingers caught a strand of her hair, brushing lightly over her ear as he curled the tendril around his thumb.

Her breathing got a little faster. "I think it would be best for everybody if we settled things and then forgot them."

"Mmm." He stepped closer and brought his other hand to her shoulder. "Do we have to forget everything?"

Kristin let her palms rest at his slim waist. "Like what?"

Without words, he gave her a taste of what he meant…hot kisses that stole her breath, the slow stroke of his hand on the bare skin of her arm, the welcome weight and size of him as he pressed her against the wall, molding their bodies into one. The Sunday silence filled with soft, desperate sounds of desire.

"Mommy?" Erin called from the bottom of the steps.

Matt froze. Kristin moaned and let her head rest against his shoulder.

"Mommy, Jenny scratched one of her poxes and it's bleeding!"

"I'll be right there, Erin. Would you get her a tissue?"

"Sure."

With a smothered laugh, Kristin slipped away from Matt's hold. "Um…I guess I'd better get downstairs."

When she looked at him, he was smiling. "Dogs. Kids. Always an interruption."

Kristin put her hand on the baby under her shirt. "Not always," she teased before heading down the steps.

LUKE AND SARAH arrived about five o'clock. "Look what we have," she cried, holding up several copies of a thick, glossy magazine. "Pictures!"

"The Southern beaches article," Luke added. "With Sarah's pictures of two little girls I know. What do you think?"

"Oh, wow, let me see!" Erin claimed her own copy.

Jenny jumped up and down. "Lemme see, too!"

Luke picked her up and sat down on the living-room couch. "You look a trillion times better than the last time I saw you, Jenny Penny. Sure, let's find your pictures."

Matt flipped through his own copy as Kristin hurried in from the kitchen. Just as she reached his side, he found the article.

"Oh, my," Kristin sighed. "Isn't that just gorgeous?"

The lead picture was a double-page shot of Erin and Jenny as they danced barefoot by the ocean. Rich with color and light and emotion, the photograph drew the reader immediately into the scene.

A year ago, Sarah had taken pictures of Luke and the girls on the beach, dressed in the fancy clothes they'd worn for Matt and Kristin's wedding. They'd all been strangers then, but the photographs had brought Luke and Sarah together to fall in love. During that summer, Sarah had received an offer to publish her shots in an upscale travel magazine. After waiting a year, the results were everything they'd hoped for.

Matt looked at his sister-in-law and grinned. "Wow, Sarah. What more could you ask? Your name is in nice big letters, too. Are you ready to field all the phone calls from potential clients?"

"I'm ready when they are. The shots did turn out well, didn't they?"

Kristin turned the page to another picture—Erin and Jenny crouched on the sand, their blond heads close together as they examined a seashell. "They're beautiful. This should tempt even more people to vacation in Myrtle Beach. The tourism board will be after you, too."

The doorbell rang. Matt looked at Kristin. "And who would this be?"

She frowned at him. "I'll get it." In another minute, his parents joined the crowd in the living room.

Erin reacted first. "The magazines are here, Grandmom! Come see the pictures of Jenny and me."

Elena Brennan's smile was unusually bright. "I'd love to, Erin, dear." She stepped by Matt. "Hello, son."

Matt forced the image of their last meeting from his mind. "Mom. How are you feeling?"

"Very well, thank you. Now, Erin, let's see these pictures." She knelt by the coffee table, an arm around her granddaughter.

Matt heard a familiar cough to his right. He turned to face his dad, standing by the far wall. "Come on over, Dad. You should see these, too."

"Er, thanks. Be glad to." He leaned over the arm of the couch where Luke sat with Jenny. "You've quite a talent, Sarah. Yours are easily the best photographs in the article."

The air of conciliation was almost too much for Matt. He laid the magazine on a table. "I think I'll go get the grill started."

Out on the deck, he took his time cleaning up the rack and wiping off the case of the grill, adding fresh hickory chips to the coals before actually igniting the fire. Then he stood for a moment, watching flames lick at those chips.

"Matthew?"

"Hi, Mom." Now that he saw her alone, he thought she looked even thinner than usual. And a little tired.

She closed the door to the kitchen behind her and crossed the deck. "I wanted to speak with you privately, if you don't mind."

He set down the spatula he'd been fidgeting with. "Sure."

"I do want to apologize." His mother faced him with her chin up, her eyes steady. "I've already told Kristin that I realize an apology can't erase the accusations and criticisms I've made. I know I haven't given her enough credit in the past. I hope to amend that behavior from here on."

Matt managed a smile. "I'm sure Kris will be glad about that."

"I...I haven't been fair. But I have always cared about you and your well-being."

"I care about you and Dad, too. But, Mom...I'm

grown-up. I don't need my decisions and choices second-guessed anymore."

"You rarely did. You always had good judgment, even as a child."

"Well, then. You're going to have to work at remembering that." He grinned. "I can remind you if you forget."

She recognized the olive branch. "Please do. I'm getting older and my memory doesn't serve as well as it used to."

"I don't believe that for a minute." Matt crossed the deck and put his arms gently around his mother's shoulders. "Thanks for taking the first step."

"You're welcome, son." Her voice was husky with tears.

He placed a kiss on her smooth cheek and stepped back. "I think I'd better see about getting the chicken on the coals. It looks like it might rain."

A few minutes before the chicken was ready, Luke poked his head outside. "Kristin wants to know if you need anything."

"A platter."

Luke brought the plate outside and held it as Matt transferred chicken pieces off the fire. "Smells good. I'm glad to be hungry."

"You're always hungry."

"Well, yeah. Erin's looking pretty happy this afternoon."

"Getting Buster back has been a big relief."

"How's it goin' between you two?"

Matt thought back to that whispered "Daddy." "Better. I think."

"I wondered if maybe we should sit down and talk—you and Erin and myself. What do you think? Is it time?"

Matt looked at his brother and saw the bleakness of the last month in his serious gray gaze. "I think that's the best idea I've heard from you in a long time!"

THE EXCITEMENT of so much company sent Jenny's temperature spiking up. Eyelids heavy, face flushed, she became increasingly cranky as the evening wore on. Finally, Kristin excused them both to take the little girl upstairs for a bath, some medicine and bed.

Matt and Erin said goodbye to Luke and Sarah and the grandparents, then shut the door together.

"Whew. What a night."

Erin nodded. "It's nice to have things quiet again."

"Do you want a snack?"

Hand on Buster's head, she thought it over. "I think I'm about as tired as Jenny. Maybe I'll just go read."

He walked her to the stairs. "I'll check on you in a little while."

She climbed a couple of steps and looked at him eye to eye. "I might fall asleep. Good night." Leaning forward, she pressed a kiss on his cheek. Then, face flushed, she scurried up to her room.

Matt stood at the foot of the stairs for quite a while. He had a lot to be thankful for.

When he finally went up, he found Erin's prediction was correct. She'd fallen asleep with the light still on, a book on her chest. He set the book aside, turned off the light...and returned her kiss.

Jenny had settled into a peaceful sleep, her cheek pillowed on her hands. He watched her for a few minutes, then realized that he was bone tired and would need to be up early to get to work.

The door to Kris's room wasn't completely closed, but inside was dark and quiet. Staring at that door, Matt fought a battle with himself, with his need to return to their bed, to return to his wife. He thought she would welcome him. Her response this afternoon had shown him a yearning as desperate as his own.

But welcome wasn't enough. Their marriage had started with good intentions but no real communication. This time, they should have the issues resolved, the problems—like his resignation from the Army—settled, before they got lost in each other's arms. So he left Kris's doorway and went down the hall to the guest room.

The door was locked from the inside.

Too tired to be irritated, Matt reached up to the molding above the doorway. The key that popped the lock open stayed on the top of that molding, just in case this happened. He ran his fingers along the ledge formed by the door frame, from one corner to the other. The key was not there.

"Okay." Every other door had exactly the same key. He checked above the bathroom door. Jenny's and Erin's doors. Finally, carefully, the door to Kris's room. All the keys were missing. He'd been locked out of the guest room.

His heart pounded as he considered the possibilities. The missing keys could be just…coincidence. The girls could have been playing tricks. He could no doubt find a key above one of the doors downstairs. Hell, he probably had a screwdriver that would do the trick. Or…

Silently, he pushed open the door to Kris's bedroom and stepped just inside. The darkness had been lessened by the light of a small bedside lamp. Kristin lay on her side, her head propped on her hand, watching him.

Matt couldn't form a thought, let alone a word. The dim light gleamed in her golden hair, left loose around her shoulders, which were mostly bare. Her eyes were dark, but she smiled. Then she reached out and turned back the covers on the empty side of the bed.

"You belong here," she said, her voice low, inviting. "Come to bed."

Kristin held her breath, half-afraid Matt would refuse. He stood still for so long, she nearly panicked. And then he moved, back two steps, to close the bedroom door. She heard the lock click, and closed her eyes in relief.

When she opened them, he stood by the bed. His shirt and shorts were gone. Wearing only his briefs, he set a knee to the mattress, then a hand, and slid easily between the sheets.

She knew how *she* felt, knew how much she wanted this man, needed him, desired him. But she didn't know quite what to expect now. Having arranged the situation, Kristin suddenly wasn't sure what to do.

Matt's hand came to rest along the curve of her cheek. "I'm sorry, Kris."

"Sorry?" Her pulse was going so fast, she couldn't get her mind to work.

"Sorry I didn't tell you about the resignation. Sorry I've been such a bastard this summer. Sorry you didn't think you could trust me with the news about the baby."

"Oh." Her breath shook as she drew it in. "I haven't done such a good job, myself. I thought I could keep everybody from suffering for my…mistakes. I didn't say things I should have at the right times. Maybe I just didn't want to face what had to be done for us to move on. And so everybody ended up hurt. Erin and Jenny and Luke and…" she put her palm over the back of his hand "…and you."

He brushed the pad of his thumb over her mouth. "I'm okay."

"And the girls will be fine. You knew better than I

did what Erin needed to heal." She risked a joke. "You must be related."

Matt's teeth flashed in a grin. "Must be."

His thumb stroked her lips again. And again. Tension hummed inside her, making her tremble. "I guess we still have things to talk about."

He nodded. "I'd say so. We haven't really had a chance to settle much of the important stuff."

"Sadie talked to me about working at marriage. About not quitting. I don't want to quit. I want us to stay married. Until death us do part."

Matt squeezed his eyes shut. "Dear God, Kris. So do I."

"But..." His eyes opened again. "But...I...don't want to do the work right now."

"No?"

Her patience broke. "Please, Matt." She pressed against him, put her arms around his ribs and across his back, feeling every inch of his smooth, warm skin with every inch of hers. "Make love to me. Please, love me."

His answer was a low, tortured groan as he closed her in his arms.

She was demanding that night, more demanding than she would have believed possible. With words and with her own hands she told him what she wanted, where she wanted, and how. He laughed, again and again, as she demanded his attention, his caress. Then he gave exactly what she wanted. And more.

In the peace afterward, Kris curled under his arm as their breathing slowed. "I love you," she said almost conversationally.

Matt chuckled. "I'm glad to hear that." Somehow, tonight, he'd known it without being told. "I love you. Now. Always." He let his free hand come to rest on the small swell of her stomach. "And I love this baby. Our baby."

"Our children," Kris whispered, smiling through tears.

Leaning close, Matt sealed the present and the future with a kiss. "Our *family*."

Sunday night

Dear Diary

I was so exsited last night I couldnt write you. Buster is home. Matt and Mommy found him and brought him back. We gave him a bath an a big bowl of food. An he slept on my bed just like before. I waked up a couple of times while it was still dark to check on him. He was there evry time.

Luke came outside tonight while I was throwin a ball for Buster. Then Matt came out and we started talkin. I dont feel so bad anymore. Maybe things happen to grownups that they dont expekt—like Mommys baby. Matt didnt expekt to stay in Africa. Luke and Mommy got married coz they didnt expekt him to come back. I know how bad it feels to lose somebody you love. Even if I would have had another dog, and then Buster came back, I still would love Buster just as much. I would love the new dog to. Things would get really messed up.

Luke said he wants to be my frend and see me if Id like to come over with Jenny. I told him I think he is more than my friend, even more than my uncle. I said I didnt know if I could call him Daddy Luke an he said thats okay. Hay you would work fine, he said. Hes always so funny.

I dont know if I can call Matt Daddy all the time. But he is my dad. I think he cares about me the way dads are sposed to. I think I care about him at least

like a frend. Maybe more. Mommy says sumtimes
you have to wait and see.

So things are better now than in a long time.
Jenny looks really ugly but I wont tell her that. I
think if I can be happy with things the way they are
that she will be to. An I think we will both like havin
a baby brother.

Im glad I have you to help figger things out.
Mommy really does have good ideas.

Your happy friend
Erin Elena Brennan

EPILOGUE

Christmas

"MOMMY, look what Sarah and Daddy Luke gave me! A chemistry set!"

Kristin craned around Jenny's new dollhouse to get a view. "Wow, Erin, that's fantastic. Just promise you won't blow up the house."

"See, Mommy." Jenny tugged on her robe. "The daddy doll works in here 'cause this is his office. The boy and girl study in the kitchen with their mommy."

"I see that, love."

"Don't worry." Luke toasted Kristin with a cup of coffee from across the room. "The worst that'll happen is some white smoke and an indelible stain on your kitchen counter."

"And little plastic dishes of crystals all over your house, with signs threatening death and dismemberment to anyone who moves them. I remember that phase." Matt stepped into the paper-strewn living room. "Sarah, there's a bundle of blankets in the crib who'd like to see you."

Eagerly, Sarah left the chair by the Christmas tree. "Time for breakfast."

"Meanwhile…" Matt knelt beside Kristin. "This little guy is dry and clean and wants to know what Santa brought him."

She took Calhoun Jennings Brennan from his father. "Cal *is* what Santa brought." Dark eyes wide, tiny lips pursed, her week-old son stared up at her. She stared back at him in equal fascination.

Jenny turned around to look. "He's pretty."

Kristin smiled. "Yes, he is. You and Erin were pretty, too."

"Are all babies pretty?"

Matt sat down beside them on the floor. "Absolutely every single one. Show me this fancy dollhouse of yours, Miss Jenny."

"Well, see…" She turned immediately to the task.

Nearby, Erin unwrapped yet another gift. "A bone for Buster! See that, buddy?" Buster accepted his present with a wag of his tail and a deliberate crunch.

Sarah came back as Luke was gathering discarded wrapping paper into a garbage bag. "Here's another little boy ready to celebrate Christmas."

Grinning, Luke took the baby into the crook of his arm. "What's under the tree for you, Daniel, my son? Baseball glove? Racing bike? Keys to the car?" He sat down in the armchair again. "Or maybe this state-of-the-art stuffed duckling?"

Kristin smiled drowsily, watching Cal's eyelids begin to droop into sleep. She would love a nap, but there wasn't time now. In a little while they would need to get dressed for dinner at the Brennans' beach house. Elena had invited Kristin's parents to join them, and Matt had invited a young couple he'd met at work—the Garths. Alan Garth had recently completed boot camp and was headed for communications training. He and his wife Terry had just had their own baby—a little girl. It was going to be a very lively meal!

At least there would only be one huge meal to feel

guilty about. Losing the pounds she'd gained during pregnancy was at the top of Kristin's New Year's resolutions list.

Second on that list was her intention to enroll in a basic sciences class at the community college. A nursing certificate would take quite a while to achieve, one course at a time. But as Matt pointed out, if she didn't get started, she'd never get finished.

With their marriage on solid ground, Matt had recovered his enthusiasm for the profession he'd pursued for so much of his life. He'd rescinded his resignation, to his father's delight and with Kristin's full approval. If he stayed in the Army for his full twenty years, he could retire with benefits, which would give them a cushion when he pursued his new career interest—teaching. History, of course. Starting in January, he would be spending the weekdays at Fort Bragg, two hours north in Fayetteville, North Carolina, but would get most weekends at home. At the end of the school year, she and the children could move to Fayetteville, too. And he'd arranged to be primarily involved with the training aspects of Special Forces, so the chances of an overseas assignment were considerably reduced.

"What are you thinking about?" Her husband sat beside her, slipped an arm around her shoulders and placed a gentle hand on his son.

"The new year." Kristin leaned into him. "More changes."

"That's okay. We can handle change. Look how good we are with diapers after only a week."

She chuckled. "We've had a lot of practice in only a week."

Erin dropped to her knees in front of them, holding

out a gift wrapped in red and gold. "Mommy, this is yours."

Shifting the baby back to his dad, Kristin took the present. "Who is it from?"

"Me."

"Ah." She unwrapped carefully, slowly, giving Erin the full benefit of expectation.

The open paper revealed a photograph in a clear acrylic frame, hand-decorated with spirals and squiggles of colorful paint. "We made it in Brownies," Erin explained.

"It's wonderful." Kristin blinked back tears. "I love the bright colors."

"Sarah took the picture for me. I wanted to take it, but then I wouldn't be in it. So I guess it's a present from Sarah and me."

They had posed on the front step of the house that first day home from the hospital with Cal—Kristin held the baby, while Matt balanced Jenny on one arm. Erin stood in front of them, Matt's free hand on her shoulder, Buster at her side, and a grin as wide as the sky on her face.

Across the bottom of the frame, she had written, *My family.*

"It's perfect, Erin." Kristin looked up at Matt, seeing in his face the joy flooding her own heart. "Absolutely perfect."

HARLEQUIN
SUPERROMANCE

You are now entering

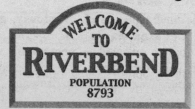

WELCOME TO RIVERBEND
POPULATION 8793

Riverbend...the kind of place where everyone knows your name—and your business. Riverbend...home of the River Rats—a group of small-town sons and daughters who've been friends since high school.

The Rats are all grown up now. Living their lives and learning that some days are good and some days aren't—and that you can get through anything as long as you have your friends.

Starting in July 2000, Harlequin Superromance brings you Riverbend—six books about the River Rats and the Midwest town they live in.

BIRTHRIGHT by **Judith Arnold** (July 2000)
THAT SUMMER THING by **Pamela Bauer** (August 2000)
HOMECOMING by **Laura Abbot** (September 2000)
LAST-MINUTE MARRIAGE by **Marisa Carroll** (October 2000)
A CHRISTMAS LEGACY by **Kathryn Shay** (November 2000)

Available wherever Harlequin books are sold.

HARLEQUIN®
Makes any time special ™

Visit us at www.eHarlequin.com

HSRIVER

**Don't miss
an exciting opportunity
to save on the purchase of
Harlequin and Silhouette books!**

Buy any two Harlequin or
Silhouette books and save
$10.00 off future Harlequin
and Silhouette purchases

OR

buy any three
Harlequin or Silhouette books
and save **$20.00 off** future
Harlequin and Silhouette purchases.

**Watch for details
coming in October 2000!**

PHQ400

HARLEQUIN®
Makes any time special ™

Silhouette®
Where love comes alive ™